ALL OUR YESTERDAYS

PETER RIMMER

ABOUT PETER RIMMER

~

Peter Rimmer was born in London, England, and grew up in the south of the city where he went to school. After the Second World War, and aged eighteen, he joined the Royal Air Force, reaching the rank of Pilot Officer before he was nineteen. At the end of his National Service, he sailed for Africa to grow tobacco in what was then Rhodesia, now Zimbabwe.

The years went by and Peter found himself in Johannesburg where he established an insurance brokering company. Over 2% of the companies listed on the Johannesburg Stock Exchange were clients of Rimmer Associates. He opened branches in the United States of America, Australia and Hong Kong and travelled extensively between them.

Having lived a reclusive life on his beloved smallholding in Knysna, South Africa, for over 25 years, Peter passed away in July 2018. He has left an enormous legacy of unpublished work for his family to release over the coming years, and not only them but also his readers from around the world will sorely miss him. Peter Rimmer was 81 years old.

ALSO BY PETER RIMMER

≈

FOREWORD

PETER RIMMER WAS twenty-four years old when he began writing *All Our Yesterdays* in January 1961 in Salisbury, Rhodesia (now Harare, Zimbabwe) and he completed it in Melbourne, Australia in June 1962. In the following years he sent the manuscript to many agents and publishers in the United Kingdom with the hope of having his first novel published. Sadly it was not to be, but Peter never gave up and he continued to write, producing many more books until, in 1994, *Cry of the Fish Eagle* was published by HarperCollins, Zimbabwe. Peter felt he had finally arrived and was recognised as a bona fide author.

If you have read any of Peter's later books, you will find *All Our Yesterdays* to be a very different experience, and it was interesting for us, his publishers and family, to see his writing develop through his subsequent work. But what strikes us most in the story you are about to read is his perception, and the almost prophetic vision he had of what was to become of Britain's last African colony.

We hope you enjoy reading what is perhaps Peter's earliest novel.

Kamba Publishing
   March 2020

INTRODUCTION

This is not a true story; I hope it never becomes one.

She should have died hereafter;
There would have been a time for such a word.
To-morrow, and to-morrow, and to-morrow,
Creeps in this petty pace from day to day
To the last syllable of recorded time,
And all our yesterdays have lighted fools
The way to dusty death.

Macbeth, Act V, Scene V
William Shakespeare

PART I

England, 1939 to 1960

1

DANCING LEDGE, 1939

*E*ric Stearle crouched over the bicycle as it freewheeled down the hill towards the village. The cold wind cut into his overcoat and gnawed at his flesh. It had been dark for two hours past and the silence of winter hung coldly on the English countryside. Across a bridge buttressed with Purbeck stone; the torment of being unable to go any faster up a steep hill; the never-ending darkness of hedgerows and trees. He turned onto the main road and, labouring to move the pedals faster, he forged on towards the small nest of lights he had seen from the hillcrest.

He reached the pub and hurriedly lent his bicycle against the wall. His legs were heavy. He tried to regain his breath as he went inside.

"May I have your phone, George?" he called to the publican.

He took the telephone which his friend handed to him from behind the bar, lifted the receiver and waited for the operator to answer.

"Can you get me the doctor at Corfe Castle in a hurry?" His left hand ran nervously along the bar counter as he listened to the buzzing. A male voice answered and he recognised the doctor.

"Eric Stearle here, doctor. Could you come up to the farm right away? I think the wife has started and I don't want to take any chances."

"I'll be there in half an hour," replied the doctor. The farmer felt light-headed as he put back the receiver. He'd got through; now the doctor would do the rest.

"She'll be all right," said the publican with a warm smile.

"Thanks," Eric replied. "I must start back again as Harriet's alone in the house."

He couldn't maintain the same energy for the return journey and only arrived at the farm a few minutes ahead of the doctor's car.

He was told to go and sit in the lounge while the doctor busied himself in the kitchen with kettles of water.

Eric heard him go back into his wife's bedroom and when she moaned, his stomach wrenched and the pain reached out to him. Her birth pangs echoed through the still farmhouse; in his mental suffering he forgot the fire. Slowly the cold reached back into the room. The flames had shrunk to a red glow and were finally submerged in a layer of cold white ash.

He sat hunched at one end of the high-back sofa, prey to a tortured imagination. His mind roamed over the many horrors he had heard of childbirth. His frustration surged and yet he knew he could do nothing but wait and hope. And wait he did, while the hours went by, punctuated by the groans of his wife.

Horrid shouts echoed through the house and he rose, then gripped the mantelpiece to hold back the fear which cut into him. The cries rose in pitch then suddenly, as if a door had closed, peace descended and he sank back onto the sofa and waited with the stillness.

A moment later a newborn's cry splintered the silence.

He heard the bedroom door open and footsteps drew closer. The doctor came into the lounge, and there on his face was a broad, benevolent smile.

"She's all right, Eric," he said. "In fact they're both all right."

"Is it a... What is it?"

"You have a healthy baby girl."

The farmer took the doctor's hand, unbelieving at first and then, as the words sank in, he gripped with his large, coarse hand and shook with a force made stronger by relief, thankfulness and sheer excitement.

"Thanks, doctor," he said. "Thanks, thanks," repeating himself again and again. "Could I see her, doctor?" he asked hopefully, not expecting to be allowed.

"Of course you can."

He wanted more than anything to go, yet he hesitated. "You think it will be all right?"

The doctor made a gesture of encouragement. The farmer turned uncertainly, moved across the room and out into the corridor. When he reached the bedroom he stopped and listened for any sound, but all was quiet. Slowly, he pushed open the door and went inside.

His wife lay deep in the double bed, her long black hair curled amongst the pillows and blankets, her face still flushed and burning hot, yet beneath it all was a calmness born of pure contentment. The child was cradled in her right arm and lay silent. Her father came forward and took her mother's hand and the two were joined in a new-found bond of perfect happiness.

THE WAR HAD BEEN six weeks old when Marguerite was born and the world seethed in hatred. Asleep, the child provided some consolation against the pervading air of gloom and anxiety but when she was awake and ready for a feed, the house resounded to her crying and her tiny hands beat the air in fury.

Harriet had watched her husband brood as the days passed and finally she rallied her courage and asked, "Eric, what's the matter?" though she already knew the answer.

"I don't know which is the right thing to do. One half of me wants desperately to go and fight while the other hates the thought of leaving you and the baby. Most of my friends have gone already," he finished unhappily.

"I'll be all right," she said. "In times like these we can't be selfish."

"It will probably be over in a few months, or a year at the most," he said to reassure her. He saw the small tears form, sliding down her face, and held her close.

"When are you going?"

"Monday. There's no point waiting any longer."

"My God," she said. "That's only two days from now."

He lifted up her chin and looked down into the tear-soaked eyes. "It won't be for long, and when we're together again it will be even more wonderful."

And so it was that throughout the first six years of her life, Marguerite barely knew her father. She grew strong and by the time the Germans had been thrown back in North Africa, she could speak.

"Where's my daddy?" she asked her mother yet again.

"I think he's in Egypt."

"Where's that?"

"A long way away where the sun is very hot. And now you must go to bed; and not so many of your questions as mummy has a lot of work to do."

"When will he come back on leave again?"

"I don't know, my little one. Now be a good girl and run along to bed."

At the beginning of 1944 Eric spent three wonderful weeks with his family and was astonished to see how much his daughter had changed. He spoilt her and romped round the house and farm with her riding piggyback, and their laughter mingled loud and clear. He did not worry about the farm and promised himself he would get it back in order when the war was won.

In no time the reunion was over, and he had to think of returning to his regiment. He left with a cheery smile and a breezy, "I'll be back for good in six months," but it was not soon enough for Marguerite, who cried and cried till at last her mother shouted at her to be quiet.

Harriet was making pastry in the kitchen with a limited quantity of butter as she listened to the wireless. She knew the end must be close. The news had been growing progressively better and the Allies were closing in on Berlin. Her daughter was playing with paints and brush at the other end of the long kitchen table when the announcement came through, clear and brilliant, that Germany had capitulated. She was so overjoyed that without washing the pastry from her hands she ran round the table and hugged Marguerite.

"It's all over, darling, all over and now your daddy will be home forever."

"Oh goody goody," the girl said, hugging her back.

A little later, and with a deep frown furrowing her brow, Marguerite looked up at her mother.

"What will they say on the news now the war is over? Will they stop having news?"

"No I don't expect so, my pet," Harriet said, laughing. "They'll find something to say."

He drove up to the farm in a taxi, still wearing his uniform, with the beret tucked into his epaulette. Marguerite ran down the path to the four-bar gate which her father had opened and threw herself into his outstretched arms. He lifted her high above his head and she cried out in her excitement.

Eric kissed his wife, and they clung to each other without speaking. Six years of uncertainty was at an end and from now on they could return to their life together and no one would be able to separate them.

HE WORKED hard on the farm and raised a heavy mortgage to buy new fruit trees and machinery. Many of the outbuildings needed repairs and the house was missing a multitude of tiles. But one by one he set about the tasks and as the months went by, a semblance of order returned.

The following summer was warm in that part of Dorset; the

range of hills, which dominated everything, held back the rain clouds and let the sun shine long through the days.

Harriet was not inclined to leave the farm as she had a routine of work which she hated to have interrupted. On weekends, throughout the summer holidays, she would watch the pair of them set out for the sea.

A basket of food, a flask of tea and their bathing costumes were all they took. They wound their way up through the Purbeck Hills, where the lanes were narrow and thickly hedged; hawthorn, grass, and the tangles of Old Man's Beard crowded in on the winding tarmac and left little room for passers-by. At last they would burst into the open to see the rolling fields which curved down on either side of the hills to the sea: a gentle backcloth to the cows and flocks of sheep that browsed in the warmth of a summer's day.

Their favourite haunt was the stretch of rock called Dancing Ledge. The cliff dropped steeply and sheltered the ledge which looked out over the sea. In summer the waves gurgled through the rocks and the long fingers of seaweed curled and uncurled with the leisured rise and fall of the water.

She grew more and more to love such days with her father. One Sunday, towards the end of the summer, Marguerite told him she wanted to stay with him at the ledge forever and ever.

The years after the war were full of such happy days for Marguerite and she lost her silent moods, substituting them for spontaneous gaiety. When she went to bed she longed for the night to be over so she could run out into another day. Even when her father became ill, life never lost its happiness: she only had to go into the bedroom and he would make her laugh. "Oh, and what's this we have today? Methinks 'tis a fawn just fresh from the woods who's come to bring the morning dew." And then he'd lean on one elbow to get a better look and add with a merry chuckle, "And by the looks of things, most of the mud as well."

She was certain, anyhow, that he would soon be up and well, even though he seemed so tired. She argued when her mother would not allow her to go into the bedroom. As the days went by she continually questioned her mother, but to no avail.

Eric Stearle was very tired and for a while he sank into a fevered sleep which took away the agonies of mind and cancer. Time was short and the pain would have it all, bringing him back to consciousness. With a twisted irony, his mind cleared and for a while let him dwell on the future, not of himself but of his family. He saw the small child, lost in the vast uncertainty of life and calling to her mother who had little time to spare: the farm would have to be run, the washing done and the cooking too, the dressmaking, the darning and, when she remembered, she would need to find a moment for her daughter too. Then the dog would whine and she'd realise she hadn't fed the animals. Poor Harriet, poor, dear, darling Harriet, he thought, and wondered if the past eleven years of happiness would make up for the future toil. And then again his mind recalled a picture of Marguerite at Dancing Ledge. For him, he knew, the pain would soon be over, but for his eleven-year-old Marguerite it was only just beginning, and he bitterly regretted the times he'd welcomed her deep affection...or did he?

His thoughts roamed back over his past and he was not unduly ashamed to recognise that he had achieved little of material value. For him it had been enough to love a wife so deeply and see a small child grow up in an atmosphere of perfect happiness. Only one persistent disappointment gnawed at his conscience: he had been unable to build up the farm and the mortgage still cast a long shadow over the property. Money would be very short and yet, for all that, he knew the worst for Harriet would be having to play the double role of mother and father to Marguerite.

Eric would never see his daughter as a woman; how pretty she would be in a printed dress. He wondered who she would marry and hoped she would find someone to give her the kind of love she could return in such abundance. His mind weighed heavy with a multitude of helpless thoughts and for a moment the pain overcame him. He lay bathed in its agony till the sweat flooded from his face and for a time he lost consciousness. He came round to the reality of the cold flannel with which Harriet was cooling his brow. He would have liked to take the hand and tell her with firm conviction how much she meant to him, but he no longer had the strength. He waited till he had gathered what little remained and spoke with a voice so low and cracked that she had to bend forward to catch his words.

"I love you, Harriet," he said.

She found it impossible to speak so she leaned across the bed and kissed his lips.

The pain returned and he was unable to fight any more. Instead, he let it take him down the long deep path at the end of which he knew he would find oblivion.

She watched him for hour after hour but consciousness did not return. Late in the evening his breathing stopped and she knew his time was over.

She turned away from the corpse that was her husband and sobs rose from within her breast. She let them course the length of her body in the hope that in some way they might relieve her pain. She wanted to hit the table, kick the wall, do anything to mitigate the torture in her soul.

"The life we knew is over," she said quietly. "Your daddy's in heaven now and there's nothing left for us but to go on alone."

Marguerite heard her mother's words and as a child, accepted them at face value. She wanted to be by herself, out in the fields and hills and by the sea, where she could look up into the sky at the moon, casting its watery light on the floating clouds, and maybe see where they had taken her father. She took her coat from the hall and without a word, not knowing where she was going, went out into the Dorset night and felt nothing of the cold.

The path cut across wet fields and the trees spoke to each other; the tall birches swayed with the wind and changed the pattern of their shadows, which were deep black and moulded by the moon. A powerful gust of wind fought with the tops of the trees and split them like a well-parted head of hair, but only for a moment as the trees fought back. With a crack, a bough broke loose and crashed to the path ahead of Marguerite. So troubled was her mind that she walked round the fallen, crushed, dead branch, stepping over the clumps of wet tufted grass, and thought nothing of the danger.

The trees and hedgerows gave way to the low stone walls of the Purbeck Hills, the expanse of fields; there was nothing to deflect the wind from its path. She leant into the gusts and went on towards the moon-bathed sea. Broken clouds scurried across the night sky and patterned themselves on the angry water where the moon shone deep into the troughs of the waves.

She had not consciously decided on a path but found she was drawing close to Dancing Ledge. She reached the cliff and slid from one wet rock to another, stumbling to the bottom, then striking out towards the neck of rock which cut furthest out into the boiling sea. Alone, she stood and let the cold spray hurl itself into her face. For a moment she felt the pleasure of its pain; salt water sank deep into her clothes and hung heavy on her hair. Numbed, she watched by moonlight the angry rollers mount and dash themselves on the ledge. From behind, the caves boomed their response and flung the waves back into the sea. Noise, spray and wind saturated the small figure cast up on the ledge.

She strained to catch the meaning of the waves and thought she heard them call her name, and at last she was sure, she was sure she heard her father's voice. Why yes, it was speaking to her.

"Marguerite, be brave, be brave, my little one."

Gently, and for the first time, warm tears ran down her cheeks and mingled with the steel-cold of the spray. The wind caught at her scarf and blew it out behind; slowly she returned to her child's mind, drew back the scarf and turned away from the sea. She was going to be brave, because her daddy wanted it that way. Her heart was stronger. She climbed up the cliff and with a firmer tread headed back to the farm. A secret glow had been kindled; she thought with that glow she could live without her father. She knew he was really close at hand and when she wanted to speak to him, she could go again to the sea and listen to the waves where, deep out amongst them, she could hear her father's voice.

The farm became too much for Harriet and when Marguerite was twelve, she was forced to sell up in order to keep herself and her child. Consequently, she took on a job as housekeeper at a big house. She had withdrawn into herself and wished only to be alone with her memories. As housekeeper she could live a solitary life and at the same time be sure that Marguerite was properly clothed and fed.

With the small amount of money which had been left over from the sale of the farm she sent Marguerite to a convent. The school helped her with the fees and it was mainly clothes and books which ran away with the money. But at least it was what Eric would have liked her to do. The child seized her education with both hands and benefited by it. Much of her spirit had been lost at her father's death and, like her mother, she preferred her own company. The villagers often talked of the pretty Stearle girl who was never seen with anyone save her dog. Many of them blamed the mother for her shyness. People rarely understand.

She grew quickly and, by the time she was fifteen, had reached over five and a half feet, with long, well-formed legs. She loved to roam the hills in shorts and a sweater which had grown too small, and now clung to her newly formed figure. Her auburn hair was cut short and swept back over two elfin ears. Her skin was firm and dark, with all the freshness of a country life. She left school and began the difficult transition from schoolgirl to woman.

MARGUERITE, SUMMER 1956

*M*irelton was set high on the cliff and held court over the surrounding hills. Few who passed along the beach below looked up at the white house without feeling curious as to the kind of people who might be living inside. From the foot of the cliff, a veranda could be seen running the full length of the top storey. The house looked clean and fresh, and indeed it was; Guy Featherstone looked after his home.

Guy Featherstone OBE had spent his working life in the Sudan as a District Commissioner of the Colonial service. He had retired at fifty-five to his native county of Dorset with a worthwhile pension and a fortune left to him by his father. The Featherstones had lived in these parts for centuries; his father had been the squire of Mirelton before him and now it was his turn and he loved it all.

He had never married so there was no heir to carry on the family tradition. Such was his luck, he would say; he could hardly have expected a white woman to live in the oppressive heat of Anglo-Egyptian Sudan. He had never seriously pursued the possibility anyway, and the opportunity had soon passed him by. Africa, up till now, had been his whole life and there had been little time for anything else.

Nevertheless, the influence of thirty-five years in Africa was scarcely apparent within the house. There was a tribal helmet made out of a shell case from the Sudan wars, still showing a stilted red feather – a farewell present from the chief whose territory he had administered. There were a few other small pieces as well, but nothing of any size or importance.

He often thought of the past with happiness, and sometimes, mainly in the winter months, wished he were back there again. But whenever he caught himself slipping into such a mood he would look around Mirelton and once more fall in love with the grace and spaciousness of the house.

Today was warm. His white hair shone in the morning sun as he looked out past the Purbeck stone terrace, past the trellised lawns to the cliff and the sea beyond while he drew contentedly at his pipe. He loved the view.

The coast cut back on his right to show where the sea left a white line of breakers on the distant sands. The hills rolled away, in perfect ranks, to the main range; the dominating hills ran the length of the Isle of Purbeck.

Guy swung his eyes away from the sea and inland, to what the family had always called their own range of hills, the hills that finished at the edge of the Island itself. And there it stood on its man-made mound: a ruin, yes, but a castle for all that, astride a neck of land, demanding the allegiance of all before any were allowed to pass. It was the castle that they had always felt gave them the right to call their pear-shaped piece of land an island. He walked down the steps which led from the terrace to the well-kept lawns, across to the flower bed, then on through the garden to the cliff edge where he looked down to the point at which the rock shore joined with the blue-green water of the sea far below.

The morning sun was hot on Guy's back. It ate into the distant morning mist, and the blue sky was filmed with a gentle haze. He recognised the beginnings of a hot day, the very best of an English summer.

And today he was even happier than usual as his young nephew, Myles, was due for lunch.

Myles was in his first year at Brasenose, Oxford, studying law and playing cricket; mainly playing cricket. In the summer he liked to spend a weekend or two with his uncle at Mirelton. Myles had spent many happy days in the house, firstly with his grandfather and latterly with his uncle. He liked the old boy, said so to his face.

Uncle Guy never fussed over him, but let him lead his own life when he came to the house. There was much to do at Mirelton: sailing, swimming, and sometimes, when he could get down early on the Saturday, he would play cricket for the village side.

The white-haired old man, looking at the sea, was hoping his nephew would be down early as the local side were banking on him playing. This was hardly surprising as Myles was good, very good, and may even get his Blue. He was a charming member of any team; all liked him and often spoke of him.

When he returned to the house his breakfast had been laid out for him on a white table under the terrace awning. Coffee and toast were his custom. Guy enjoyed the hot Kenyan coffee as he watched a small red sailing boat making lazy progress a little way off the shore.

Then after a while, "Good morning, sir, have you had enough?" asked his housekeeper, Mrs Stearle.

Standing behind him, having come through the French window, Harriet had decided that his mind was not on his breakfast. The coffee cup, aimlessly poised in an uninterested hand, well away from his lips, gave the game away.

"Not quite, Harriet, not quite," he replied, quickly pulling himself together. Then he changed the subject to where his thoughts had been. "My nephew will be down from Oxford today. He's playing for the village in an all-day match; you'll need to prepare his room... No meals, though, no need for them." And then as an afterthought, "He won't be here, you see. Playing cricket. Can't be in two places at once, if you see what I mean."

No one in his entire career had ever questioned his last remark to them, so he returned to his toast without waiting for a reply.

"It will be nice to have him with us," the housekeeper said. "It must be over a month since he was here last."

"Yes," he replied, drowning the toast with some more coffee, "and the cricket captain has been getting impatient." He waved his free hand. "Just as well to placate him at least once a month." The other hand was then brought back into action.

"They do appreciate him playing," she said. "I believe he made thirty-eight last month. I hope he can do it again."

"Thirty-nine," he corrected her, choking on a piece of toast in his hurry. "Yes, I hope so."

He half leant forward and drained what was left of his coffee, wiping off what had slopped onto his chin with the back of his other hand.

"Well, that's that," he said, surveying the empty cup and plate. The saucer, however, still had something in it. She took the tray and went round the side of the house to the kitchen. Harriet was smiling to herself about that extra run.

Marguerite saw her mother coming and opened the door.

"Myles is coming for the weekend," said her mother casually.

Marguerite turned away to hide the sparkle of excitement which sprang to her face.

"Will he be playing cricket?" she asked, trying to keep her tone neutral.

Her mother, emptying the breakfast tray, failed to notice the difference that had suddenly come over her sixteen-year-old daughter.

"Yes," she said. "There's an all-day match today."

Marguerite was alive, excited, though if anyone asked she would have been unable to explain her feelings. She had only ever seen this Myles...caught his eye, yes, but never spoken to him.

It had happened seven weeks before. He was alone in the high-ceilinged lounge when she had ventured into the main part of the house in search of her mother. He had put down the paper and turned as she came through the door. Their eyes met and held. He was about to get up when she turned, unable to face him, and went quickly out of the room.

For many mornings afterwards she woke excitedly, then remembered why: a clean, urgent face, soft eyes speaking kindness. She could see his face clearly – the square-cut chin, the strong nose and the dark, well-kept hair. She loved dreaming of him.

Her thoughts squirrelled away, she turned to her mother.

"May I go out this afternoon?"

"Where to?"

"For a swim. It will be very warm in the water."

Marguerite would have liked to go before lunch but wished to guard her secret and not arouse her mother's suspicions. She hoped the village side would field first, then she could watch him bat after lunch. He usually went in on the second wicket down and, if the village batted in the morning, he might be out before lunch, before she got there. This last thought made her unhappy – so she refused to dwell on it. Her luck could surely never be that bad.

Taking up a cloth, she dried the dishes for her mother with renewed energy.

Guy Featherstone was pruning his prize roses when the old Riley ground its way up the drive and parked on the level below the terrace. Myles Featherstone got out and made his way across the lawn to meet his uncle.

"Good morning, Myles. How nice to see you again."

"Hello there, Uncle. How are you?"

"Very well. Just cutting the roses. Not really the time of year, but they seem to grow. Shall we go inside?" he said, taking his nephew by the arm. "You can bring your case with you. How's that damn car of yours going by the way?"

"Going is all one can say about it, Uncle Guy. I think one of the cylinders packed up on the way down, but she still runs."

"I don't understand your confounded mechanical terms. We'll have a drink. A bit early; ten-thirty in fact... I expect you could do with one after your drive."

They went up the terrace steps and through into the lounge.

The morning sun shone back from the polished floors and picked out the deep blue of the Chinese carpet which covered the centre of the room. Set back out of the sun's reach was a large, extremely good portrait of Myles's grandfather, which looked down on a grand piano.

"What would you like?" asked his uncle, going over to the drinks cabinet.

"A glass of beer if you have one," Myles replied, putting down his case.

"It won't be very cold, but you can try it."

They walked out onto the terrace with their drinks.

"Who are we playing today, Uncle?"

"Worth Matravers. I said you'd be ready to start at eleven-thirty. It only takes ten minutes to drive to the ground, so you've plenty of time." He took a sip of his drink and went on. "Had a letter from your mother last week. She says your father's overworked and underpaid. I always told him he was a fool to go into the Foreign Office... Didn't do any good."

"He loves it really," Myles said lightly.

"I know he does, and anyway a little hard work never hurt anyone. I heard rumour that he may get a new job in Buenos Aires. Do you know if it's true?"

"We're all hoping," Myles replied. "But these things are very difficult to predict."

They stood in companionable silence for a while, taking in the beautiful view and enjoying the warmth of the morning sun on their faces.

"What are you going to do when you leave Oxford?" Guy asked eventually. "Can't play cricket forever you know, though I can see why you might want to."

"Go into the army for two years. National Service, and then I hope to think of a career. Father wants me to continue with law and study for the bar, but it will be a long time before I have to make a decision."

"You're wise," replied his uncle. "Many things can change your mind in four years. Mark you, barrister would make a sound profession."

Myles finished his beer and put the glass on the white table.

"Thank you for the drink. Just what I needed."

Guy looked at his watch and stood up.

"Time's getting on," he said. "You'd better be off. Is your cricket bag in the car?"

"Yes, I've got everything I want and will change in the pavilion. If it isn't too late I'll hope to see you when I get back from the match."

"Hope you make some runs," said Guy from the top of the steps as Myles climbed into his car.

"Thanks."

He let the clutch engage the reverse gear and turned the car to face down the hill. He waved as the car rolled forward again and then turned his attention to the road.

For the first time Myles was looking forward to the game for a reason other than the cricket. Normally the excitement of hoping to score runs would create nervousness, but as he drove the car onto the Langton road it wasn't cricket which churned inside of him.

He laughed at himself. In all probability she wouldn't be watching the game today. It was surely chance that she had been there before and this time his luck would run out.

It was difficult to understand his joy when previously he had managed to find her amongst the spectators. Ever since that brief encounter in the lounge he had picked her out twice in the same deckchair, near the tea stand. The first time that same afternoon, he had seen her by chance when he was fielding; then last month he had looked for her and found her in the same place.

He had wanted to go over and speak to her but could think of nothing to say, and even when he had found himself in her vicinity at the tea interval, he had been unable to start a conversation. He had thought of many approaches, all hackneyed, and then the game had started again and he moved away. He could feel the tension of some powerful emotion building up inside of him.

After their first meeting he had learnt from his uncle that she was Mrs Stearle's daughter, which made it much more difficult. Why this elfin girl had such a power of attraction over him he was unable to say, but she did, and it was strong and alarming. She was only sixteen, he estimated; an oval face picked out by a pageboy hairstyle; soft auburn hair; clear skin, too, with a rich, healthy bloom; her walk was graceful. She was a girl untouched by the ways of the modern world. When he looked at this small girl he was certain he saw how truly beautiful a human being could be. At nineteen, he'd never seen anything like it before.

The car accelerated through the twisting lanes as his thoughts ran on. He managed fifty on the stretch leading to the cricket ground and applied the brakes in time to turn into the car park. Collecting his cricket bag from the back seat, he walked over to the pavilion. He scanned the people waiting for the game to start, but was unable to see her. There was no one on the other side of the field, so she couldn't have arrived. It was early, he tried to convince himself, so she may be along later.

Myles opened the low white gate of the enclosure and made his way up the wooden steps into the pavilion. The captain came across and shook his hand.

"Hello, Myles," he said, "I hope you're on form. Worth Matravers have brought a strong side." Doug Green was a much-liked man of middle-height in his early forties. His life was cricket, particularly that played by Langton. He was a leg-spin bowler of considerable accuracy who, in the previous season, had taken seven of a touring side's wickets.

"We're fielding first," he said. "Can you change straight away? We're only waiting for Clive Austrell and he'll probably arrive in his whites."

"Thanks," said Myles, "I won't be more than a couple of minutes."

He waved to some friends as he passed and went into the changing room.

"Hello, Myles," said Keith Cambourne, a one-time beer-drinking companion. "How's Oxford?"

"Very good," replied Myles, as he began to change. "How's life with you?"

"Not so bad, I suppose. My girlfriend ran off with another bloke at the club dance last week, so I'm figuring on giving that a rest for a bit. Pity you couldn't get down as apart from that, the dance was quite good by all accounts."

"I'd have liked to, but I just had too much to do. It cuts into your reading if you keep taking too much time away."

"I guess you're right."

"We're going out," called a voice through the door.

Myles quickly pulled on his boots, laced them firmly and followed Keith out of the pavilion. The wicket was brown and, to start with, a batsman's paradise. He thought it would crack towards the end of the afternoon when the spin bowlers would make it turn.

He still couldn't see Marguerite so settled down in the outfield to a hot, Saturday morning's fielding. There was little wind and the yellow and green flag of the Langton Cricket Club hung heavily from its masthead. The spectators were clustered under the elm trees to the left of the tea pavilion. He walked in with the bowler but when the ball was played he looked for his elf-like girl.

By lunchtime the visitors had scored sixty-two for two wickets and with the clock showing a little past one o'clock, the field went in. Myles was glad of the shandy Doug Green handed to him and looked hungrily at the cold lunch set out on a long wooden table in the centre of the room.

He was feeling considerably overfed when they went out again. He looked for her once more without any success and as the first ball was played, his concentration returned to the cricket. A little later he saw her walk through the gate and he forgot to walk in with the bowler. Unaware that he was holding his breath, he watched her find a deckchair near the tea pavilion, thinking she was looking at him though he couldn't be sure.

The visitors declared at three-thirty with 132 on the board, which left his side three hours to make the runs. Certainly worth a try, thought Myles, as he tried to concentrate on the game and not on a girl called Marguerite.

She had watched him turn round and look in her direction and thought he did it again on other occasions when the field changed over. Relieved to see that the visitors would be fielding, Marguerite knew she would see him bat. She loved to watch; he made the strokes so easily and there was great power when he hit the ball.

The game restarted and fifteen minutes later, Keith Cambourne was out for twelve and Myles came to the wicket. He took guard, looked round the fielders, and then faced the medium-fast bowler from the pavilion end. He played the first ball straight back down the wicket and Marguerite surged with happiness.

As the runs mounted he began to play the ball with more confidence. She watched the score go to twenty-five and joined the small burst of clapping which followed. The home side was three wickets down when they came in for tea, with fifty-seven on the board and Myles still batting.

The game was going well, Myles thought, and his confidence was high. He had made up his mind while batting that he would ask Marguerite to join him for tea. He had convinced himself there was nothing to lose. She could only say no, and if she did, that would be that and nothing would be gained or lost.

With the feeling of power left by his unfinished innings still running warm through his veins, he made his way across to the pavilion. Without stopping he walked straight past it and on towards Marguerite. She pretended not to see him and he lost some of his confidence, but by then it was too late.

Stopping in front of her he asked, very simply, "Will you join me for tea, Marguerite?"

She looked up and met his eyes, and they both smiled so that the embarrassment was lost.

"Are you allowed to?" she asked, in a voice unusually low for a girl of her age.

"Anyone can get tea if they ask," he said, "but if you're not playing you have to pay for it, which makes it a little difficult."

"Where do we go?"

"You stay there and I'll be right back with a tray."

He left her and made quickly for the teas set out on a counter, ready to be taken by the players. He was both relieved and excited that she had accepted his invitation without question. Ordering two teas, and paying for the extra one, Myles rejoined Marguerite. It was so simple after all, he thought to himself. He seemed to be walking a little above the grass, with the heavy tray as light as a feather in his hands.

Watching him return, it was as though she knew him so well there was no reason to feel any embarrassment. She had never dared hope that her afternoon would end by having tea with him.

They talked together easily, and she told him about the convent school near Swanage she had just left where she had passed four subjects in the General Certificate. She was now helping her mother at Mirelton while trying to decide what to do next.

"I think I may take a secretarial course in Swanage. I can catch a bus into town from Mirelton. It only takes half an hour. Unless a girl can do shorthand and typing, it's difficult to earn very much money."

He agreed with her. "Then you can go and live where you like and be able to support yourself."

They talked on and he told her of his studies at Oxford without trying to impress her and she teased him about it and they both laughed. Before tea was over she had agreed to go for a drive with him after the game.

They parted for the moment and he joined his partner to walk to the crease. His mind ran back to Marguerite and he wanted to run to the wicket. Halfway out he turned and waved his bat to her.

The game began and Myles's partner faced the first ball. They had one hour to get seventy-six runs, a tall, but not impossible, order.

From the start he hit the ball strongly and was soon placing it exactly where he wanted. This was going to be his best innings for Langton; he was happy and Marguerite was watching him, and he was going to score a lot of runs. He drove a ball off his back foot straight past the bowler for four, and he was pleased to hear the spectators clap.

The score moved on and he lost three partners. By six o'clock they had reached the hundred and with the same stroke, Myles reached his fifty. They wanted thirty-two runs in thirty minutes with four wickets to go. Doug Green came to the other end and Myles asked him what to do.

"Have a go," said the captain. "Hit anything that's loose."

Myles smiled and went back to his end. The first ball of the over was a slow one and he hit it hard through the covers and they ran two. Ten minutes later, with eighteen runs to go, Myles skied a ball and was caught at mid-on. He returned to the pavilion amidst loud applause. The board showed his score of sixty-two runs.

The eighteen runs came quickly once the last batsman-but-one came in. He was a big hitter, either scoring quick runs or blocking firmly. He played with spirit and at one point hit the ball in the middle of a beautiful cross bat for two successive fours. With five minutes to spare, Doug Green scored the winning shot and the game was over.

It took Myles ten minutes to extricate himself from the pavilion and with his cricket bag gripped in his right hand, he walked briskly across the field. Marguerite was waiting by his car and he waved as he drew near.

"Where are we going?" she asked.

"Where do you want to go?" he countered. It was as if they'd known each other for years.

"Anywhere you say."

"Let's run round to Poole. It'll only take fifty minutes and we can have dinner there. In fact, I know a waterside restaurant where you can get fried prawns. I hope you like them." He frowned roguishly, daring her to protest.

She laughed at his expression. "I've never had them, but I'm sure I will."

"Let's go then," Myles said, opening the door for her. He returned to his side of the car, threw his bag into the back seat, and they drove out through the gate.

Once away from Langton he quickened his pace and the hedgerows sped past. They came to Corfe Castle and Myles drew up at the Greyhound pub.

"I don't think they'll serve me," she said.

He briefly put an arm round her, smiling, and said that she looked at least twenty.

"We'll sit outside," he went on. "If you grab a table over there, I'll go and get the drinks. What would you like?"

"Just a lemonade please."

"Why not try a shandy?"

"I don't even know what that tastes like."

"I'll get one and you can see if you like it," he called back over his shoulder, pleased to be able to introduce her to so many new things. Marguerite went over to the stone table set back in an alcove, and sat on the wrought-iron and stone chair. It was very warm and the summer heat hung heavily over the village. He was away longer than she expected, and she started looking for him.

The whole thing was incredible, she thought; it had all been so easy and happened so quickly. Yesterday she had only dreamt of talking to him and now here she was, and inside he was buying them drinks.

Her heart tripped as she saw him coming.

"Sorry I've been so long," he said, putting down her half pint of shandy, a pint of bitter in his other hand. "I thought I'd better phone your mother. I told her we'd met at the cricket and were off for a drive."

"Oh dear," she said, "I told Mother I was going to the beach." She blushed deeply when he looked at her sideways with a sharp twinkle in his eye.

"Why did you tell her that?" he said, teasing.

"Because I only watch the cricket when you're playing, and I didn't want Mother to guess. She knew you were playing; in fact it was she who told me."

"You're very sweet," Myles said, sitting down next to her, "and shall I tell you something? I watched everyone come through that gate till I saw you, so that makes us square."

They looked at each other and laughed.

"Cheers," he said, raising his glass.

"Cheers," she replied and took a sip as she watched him lift the pint and slowly drink.

"It's not bad," she said in surprise.

"Of course it isn't, though it's a lot better without the lemonade. You must try that before long."

"I don't think I will," she said seriously. "It may take a number of weeks to get completely used to this one."

They drank whilst eating packets of potato crisps Myles had fished out from his pockets. The evening shadows began to lengthen and they bet each other on the number of swallows there were catching flies in the air above the village well. She finished her drink first but wouldn't have another, so he finished his and they went back to the car.

The evening road was empty and they sped on through Wareham with the sunroof open, and the cool air was fresh and exciting. They entered Poole and drove slowly along the twisting road close to the sea. Opposite a narrow fishing jetty Myles found his restaurant and parked the car.

Marguerite found the fried prawns particularly to her liking and enjoyed the French salad which he ordered specially. She thought a little less oil might have made it taste better but said nothing and let him talk. It was nearly dusk when they finished their meal. They thanked the proprietor and went out onto the street, crossed to the other side and walked out onto the wooden jetty. The air was full of salt and the sea swirled heavily round the barnacled pillars. They were alone at the end of the jetty; they lent over the rail and watched the water in silence. He bent across and kissed her on the cheek and she blushed. Walking slowly back to the car she took his hand. It was warm and she could not remember when she had felt happier.

On the following morning at Mirelton, Myles and Marguerite were the first to rise. They had arranged to meet on the upstairs veranda at seven o'clock, have a quick breakfast, pack a lunch and then sail Myles's fourteen-foot dinghy to Lulworth Cove.

The early morning sun held little warmth and the cold orange juice was a challenge to the stomach. Marguerite had cooked them both a large plate of bacon and eggs. The bacon was thick and salty, and mingled well with the soft yolks of the eggs. After liberal hot coffee and toast they were ready to go but before leaving, Myles took a pot of tea to his uncle's bedroom and told him his plans for the day.

They talked over the tea while Myles poured. When the door had closed behind him, the shrewd ex-civil servant wondered if it was quite right for the future heir to Mirelton to take the housekeeper's daughter sailing at eight o'clock on a Sunday morning. He leant across the tall bed and, propped on one elbow, poured himself a second cup of tea, making sure that the milk was added last. He felt a little old and refreshed himself by thinking how pleasant it was to have Myles in the house again and completely dismissed the girl from his mind.

They reached the boat shed and dragged the dinghy across the shingle to the sand, where Myles set up the mast and ran up the sails. It took them some time and after he had shown her what to do as crew, where to sit and how to change sides when they altered course, they put the boat into the light surf and with the white sails flapping hungrily, floated the dinghy and brought the sails under control.

It was cold and she was glad of the heavy sweater he had made her bring. Myles warned her he was changing course, shouting, and even then she only just managed to duck under the boom and grab the rope so as to catch the wind in the one small sail that was hers. He caught her eye as she struggled to master the rope and shouted that she made a fine sailor and she felt better as at that moment she hadn't been sure if she would make a sailor at all.

Once on course, and with the wind behind them, it was easier, and she relaxed. She was reassured when she looked across at Myles, calmly seated in the stern, with the mainsail rope in one hand and the tiller in the other. The wind was light and only occasionally did they have to lean back to counteract the angled sail. The sun warmed and she grew to love the graceful movement: the sea lapping away in their wake, the rigid sail high above her taking the wind's force and using it to its own advantage.

It took them two hours to reach Lulworth Cove. They beached the dinghy and lowered the sails. After leaving the boat they walked up under the tall cliff, spread out an old blue rug, stripped to their bathing costumes, and sunbathed till their flesh was hot and the cool sea seemed inviting enough to make them swim.

Marguerite loved the water and they swam out to a group of bobbing corks which marked the local fisherman's lobster pots. The English Channel was cold, even in the summer, so they swam briskly. When they returned to their rug she lay exhausted and once more let the sun warm her flesh. She was at home, no longer self-conscious, and she had been here before with her father.

Myles watched her where she lay, her skin kissed with salt, looking fresh and cool. Only youth, and the uncertainty of inexperience, prevented him from touching her face...and more. She opened her eyes briefly and smiled up at him but he was embarrassed that she had caught him looking at her. Lying down on the rug beside her, he closed his eyes and let the imprint of her features remain as long as he could make it stay.

Marguerite had longed for him to touch her but was afraid that the emotions he aroused were wrong and if she showed them he would think less of her. It was enough that he was there and she did not wish to mar their day.

They lunched, he mixing a small shandy for her, and they laughed at her preference for the mix. Soon afterwards they took everything back to the boat, raised the sails and pushed the dinghy out into the surf. The run back to Mirelton took them longer than their outward trip as the wind was less favourable. Myles tacked the boat and she realised that sailing needed a deal of strength. After two hours he put into the shore to give her arms a chance to rest from holding onto the rope.

They reached the shore below Mirelton at teatime, happy but very tired.

When they drew near to the house he knew they must part, and however much he wanted to stay with Marguerite it was right for him to spend the evening with his uncle.

They stowed the boat in the shed and as they reached the path which led up the cliff face, he took both her hands in his and thanked her for a wonderful day. Very gently he kissed her on the forehead. She slowly raised her face till his breath was on her lips and when they came together her head swam. After a while they turned and he led her up to the top. After softly saying goodbye, they went their separate ways.

The Riley made the journey down to Dorset on another three weekends that summer. They were each as perfect as the first. It was a rare summer, the kind you only seemed to get once every ten years, and the hot sun persisted into September. Marguerite grew from a girl into a woman and found true happiness for the first time since her father had died six years before. Everything was new and exciting, as it so often was at the start of life. The sailing she grew to love, especially when she became confident. Myles took her out when the breeze was strong and the dinghy would heel over, cutting strongly through the water, and it was all they could do, by leaning back, to hold the straining sail from dipping into the waves. They were long days, days when she was always content and had no wish for anything other than what she had.

Uncle Guy and Myles had finished dinner. It was his last weekend of the summer vacation at Mirelton and he had resigned himself to a period of intense study for his second year examinations, with the certainty of not being able to visit Dorset for several months. His uncle asked him a direct, but not unexpected question.

"Your parents would never approve of Marguerite, would they, Myles?"

He said nothing. His throat was choked and his mind numb. It couldn't form a reply.

His uncle went on. "I'm very fond of both her and her mother. I don't want you to upset them. Youth can override many things, but not this one, and I hope you will appreciate the fact. You will understand that Mrs Stearle is being placed in an extremely awkward position, which must reflect on everyone in this house. I am sure that your intentions are of the best quality, but I would ask you to think hard, and put yourself in my, and Mrs Stearle's position, before you next come to Mirelton."

"If only her background wasn't what it is," replied Myles miserably.

"It is certain that you cannot have everything you wish for in this life," his uncle said firmly. "It's one of the hardships we must endure in a class-conscious community. Society does not tolerate such a breach. If you wish to maintain yourself in that society then you must adhere to its principles, live by its code. Life is rarely simple, often very hard." And that was that. The subject was closed.

That night, as he drove home, Myles felt sick; so hurt and helpless in his own inability to answer the paramount question that his uncle had forced upon him. If he stood by Marguerite, and was lost to his family, then he would have little to offer her, without any training or means to earn a solid living. His very soul would not let Myles think of the alternative, and when he reached home he could not sleep. He was glad not to have told Marguerite his uncle's words, and was determined to say nothing until his examinations were complete and he could once more leave his studies for a weekend at Mirelton.

But as the weeks went by, and the situation took on a harsher perspective, Myles realised the weight of his uncle's warning. With his mind centred on law, he found the picture of his Marguerite drawing further and further away; her letters no longer produced the yearning they had at first. He came to realise that last summer's happiness was a wonderful memory which had no definite end, but yet it would vanish in the mists of time.

He tried to write down everything he felt in a letter to her, but due to his youth and lack of confidence he fumbled it and couldn't express himself the way he wanted to. Over the next twenty years he would find out how wrong he had been to let convention overrule his heart, but by then it was too late. At nineteen we often take the wrong path or make the wrong decision. We can blame life, or ourselves, but in the end it makes no difference where the fault lies – the outcome is still the same.

Marguerite only grew to understand the true meaning of Myles's letter when she herself had gained some experience of life, but at the time her misery was complete, as complete as her happiness had once been. Her world had collapsed again, and she fled to Swanage to embark on a secretarial diploma.

As the months went by, Myles still consumed her unguarded thoughts but the ache never went away.

The following year, she decided to leave Mirelton for London. Her mother agreed and Mr Featherstone found her a job in the City. She took her courage in both hands and launched herself into a new life, a new adventure. She left the house with a sad heart but with great determination to fight for what she wanted. She would need all the strength of character she could muster in the years to come.

3

TIM, 1959

*M*arguerite settled quietly into the teeming life of London, a small soul in a vast expanse of people. She had waited two and a half years before taking the plunge, having spent that time working in Swanage and catching the bus back to Mirelton each day. She knew no one when she arrived and having never had to mix with others in the slow domestic life of rural Dorset she found that London, with all its size, could be lonely and very cold to an outsider. But since she had always relied upon her own company, it didn't matter so much.

Having found a comfortable bedsit in Holland Park, she settled down and discovered the enjoyable parts of the capital. She loved to walk in the park and along the avenues, coloured by the green of many sycamore trees. She painted her room, made a heavy counterpane for the bed and scattered around the many coloured cushions which she had sewn. She fell in love with a tall, creeping plant which she saw at a florist's by the station and gave it pride of place on a low table in one corner of the room.

She had use of the downstairs kitchen and often cooked for her landlady, a frail, elegant old lady in her early seventies who never murmured a word of disapproval and only spoke kindness.

Mrs Fenton had always been a staunch supporter of the local

Conservative Association, but as the years passed by she found it more and more difficult to take an active part. A crucial general election was two months away and she was hopeful that for the first time in twenty years, the Tory constituency would oust the Socialist member. In the previous election, the Labour majority had been cut to three thousand two hundred and the coming fight would be close, needing maximum effort.

The Young Conservatives maintained an energetic and progressive branch in the area, and Mrs Fenton suggested that Marguerite might find it interesting to go to their next meeting. Marguerite knew nothing of politics but had little to lose so followed her landlady's suggestion. It was the Association's first pre-election campaign get-together and she was assured of meeting a large number of young, interesting people. It appeared that at such times of crisis the politically-minded came forward to offer their assistance and enthused the socially-minded with political purpose.

Having followed Mrs Fenton's directions the next Wednesday, she found the hall and went inside along with a group of others. There were only a few seats left on one side and as there was no organisation in the seating, she took one of these, settling down to await events. The hall, she thought, must have been a small theatre, capable of holding two hundred people. The speaker's platform held the centre of the stage and was fronted by a large Union Jack. At the back, about three feet above the floor, stood the Young Conservative shield emblazoned with its rampant lion. There were three chairs behind the table; once these were filled, the meeting began.

The chairman, a man of perhaps thirty-five, was congenial and efficient. He spoke clearly and with confidence of the necessity for a hundred per cent canvass. A large number of volunteers would be needed to go from door to door to find the Conservative voters and make absolutely certain they reached the polling booths. He was confident they could win but only with a great deal of hard work, from now right up until the last booth closed on polling day. He went on to give details of the following month's programme.

The prospective Tory candidate made a brief appearance and thanked them in advance for their expected help. Marguerite was pleased to see that he was a working man of strong opinions, speaking his mind in straight, forthright words. She learnt later that he had caused more than one stir at Conservative party meetings with his solid, down-to-earth approach.

The meeting closed on a request for the names of as many canvassers as possible. Newcomers were assured that the older hands would show them the ropes before they did a door-to-door canvass on their own. Coffee was being served for the vast sum of 3d. Self-consciously Marguerite made her way across the hall to buy herself a cup but was stopped by a young man asking her if this was her first meeting. On learning that it was, he introduced her to a number of people. Many voices encouraged her to join and help them with the canvassing. The group she had been introduced to were going on to a local coffee bar and, without being given the option to refuse, she was taken along. She reached home a little before twelve o'clock, having agreed to meet at the hall the following Wednesday, to listen to a debate on Colonial Affairs in which a young Rhodesian would speak on the racial problems in the Central African Federation. At least Marguerite had enjoyed her evening, and anyway, she hadn't anything else to do – better to do something than nothing at all.

THE THIRD SPEAKER SAT DOWN, having advocated yet again the words of the left-wing press. The motion under discussion was whether the Rhodesian Federation should be given Dominion status in 1960; it was then that their constitution was due for reappraisal.

The British people, he had said, could not be held responsible for relinquishing their right of government to a small, white settler minority, who he was certain would not respect the rights of the African; their new-won power would be used to maintain European supremacy and nothing else. He could not see why a universal franchise could not be introduced and the people of the Federation, both black and white, asked to choose their constitution. "Surely it is against all the principles of our modern civilisations to allow a small minority to dominate the destinies of millions of black Africans. It is essential for the people of Britain to vote, in the 1959 October elections, for a party that is bound to consider the rights of the African people in her colonies and to return to them the country which is rightfully theirs in the quickest and most peaceful way."

Marguerite watched the fourth member of the panel, whom she imagined to be the Rhodesian. During the barrage he remained calm and immovable with his arms folded. Twice she thought she saw a shadow of sadness cross his face, but it was gone quickly and she could not be sure from where she sat.

He rose to speak for the motion that the Federation should be allowed to attain Dominion and consequent self-government. He was a slender, healthy-looking man of twenty-five, just a little short of six feet. His voice was well educated, with a slightest guttural quality presumably derived from his Afrikaner roots. He spoke slowly with a measured tone that reflected his firm belief in everything he said.

It would be difficult to disbelieve a man of such sincerity, she thought.

"The last speaker finished with three words, 'most peaceful way', which I would ask you to consider again, to properly realise their implication, while I briefly sketch the history of my country." He paused and there was silence in the hall.

"Seventy years ago a small column of South Africans, mainly of English origin, made their way from what is now the Union of South Africa into the hinterland under the auspices of Cecil John Rhodes and his British South Africa Charter.

"They followed the old missionary route along the border of the Transvaal Republic and eventually made their final camp at Fort Salisbury, named after the then British Prime Minister, Lord Salisbury. Their new home was in the land of the Mashona, who had for many years owed allegiance to, and been under the domination of, Lobengula, King of the Matabele.

"The impis of the Matabele, a small Zulu tribe not indigenous to the country, made continual war on the Mashonas, leaving them in continual fear for their lives, their cattle and their kraals. They had few possessions and, to avoid the Matabele warriors, they led a nomadic life; anything to keep away from the pangas of their black cousins.

"At this time the total population of the Southern Rhodesian tribes amounted to two hundred and thirty thousand. To ensure peace and enable a country to be built, King Lobengula was subdued by the white pioneers. Six years later, with rinderpest devastating their cattle, the Matabele rose up and slew many of the Europeans. After the white man's armed reprisals had failed, due to the Matabele withdrawing into the Matopos Hills, and to prevent further bloodshed, Cecil Rhodes, with the courage of a man who was known even in his lifetime as 'the Colossus', went in person, unarmed and with only a few friends, into the camp of the Matabele and made peace with them. It was the finest act of his life. Tribal warfare ceased and it became possible for all the tribes to live in harmony without fear and to build the kind of wealth which had never been seen before in southern Africa.

"Over the next seventy years the country grew and the African was shown the ways of the twentieth century. Mistakes were made, of course, but roads were built along with schools and hospitals, food was grown, and the African began to see the benefits of modern husbandry: soil conservation, to prevent the land being washed away; running fewer but healthier cattle on the same land. This was all gained with European knowledge and capital so that today we are proud to say that any African, if he is prepared to do a normal European working week, can have all the benefits of sufficient food, housing, clothing, free hospitals and, if he requires it – though this is unfortunately not always the case – free education. Just recently a multi-racial university has been built with half the students being African.

"The African has gained peace and, with it, prosperity. The European minority pays nine-tenths of the national tax. From two hundred and thirty thousand in 1889, the African population in Southern Rhodesia has risen to three million whilst the European population has reached two hundred and fifty thousand.

"However, I do not believe that South African Apartheid is a workable proposition; it goes against the very instincts of human nature. Two societies living side by side and bound to the same government can only live in harmony if they respect and trust each other. I do not believe that this will ever be the case in Apartheid South Africa and it is therefore necessary for us in Rhodesia to look around for a practical alternative.

"We sincerely believe that this is exactly what we have found.

"We wish to build a multi-racial society where we are all Rhodesians, with common problems, aims and ambitions, where, with the best sides of both communities, we can blend a country into one spirit and do what has never been done in the world before: create a healthy, Afro-European country.

"I believe it is possible. I see the vast problems which weigh on the minds of black and white: the mistrust, the ignorance of the African masses, the arrogance of the die-hard Europeans who consider themselves the embodiment of almighty power, the lack of money, the many languages, and above all this antipathy in the heart of man when it comes to mixing the African and European races in every form.

"But I am convinced that with calm, unbiased logic on both sides it can be achieved. The first step along the path of sanity lies in giving the African his dignity. Remove the useless and harmful artificial barriers of the colour bar and produce a mutual respect which will grow into trust. It is the people of both races who can make such a society work and it is up to the leaders of both factions to ensure that the legislation and finance is available. The seven-year-old Federation has been a fantastic financial success and with the Kariba Dam on the verge of unleashing limitless power for industry, with the minerals and agriculture catalysed by modern science, the potential of my country is as great as anything the world has seen since the founding of America, if not greater.

"But to achieve such progress it is essential we continue to reap the benefits of the Federation and, in 1960, go ahead with the next stage in forming a powerful country. Rhodesia faces the greatest challenge of any in the twentieth century. With the help, support and faith of the British people, we will do all in our power to meet that challenge.

"We hope to face a Conservative government in the 1960 talks and because of this, and because I believe that Socialism is workable only in theory, I hope to join you in canvassing this district and provide one more small cog in what I sincerely hope will be a victorious campaign."

Marguerite saw the Rhodesian had made a deep impression. Here was no fanatic but a man who saw a problem and wanted to tackle it in practical terms to produce a tangible outcome.

There was a pause after he sat down, followed by loud clapping.

The chairman called for a division by a show of hands; Marguerite was happy to see the large majority give the Rhodesian the benefit of their support.

Afterwards, Andy Carly, a committee member, asked her to join a group at his flat for coffee. She was pleased to find the Rhodesian already there when she arrived. He sat next to her and they fell into conversation.

Tim Carter's family, she learnt, grew tobacco at a place called Macheke which was near the town of Marandellas. He had started his working life as an assistant on a farm and spent three seasons growing tobacco before moving to Salisbury, the capital, to take a job with a public relations firm. His father had died but the farm was well run by the manager. It was through his company that he came to London and was employed, with a number of others, in selling the Federation to the British public. He expected to be in England for another year. He was enjoying his stay in London but talked longingly of the sun and warmth of his own country. She liked him and they talked easily together. He drove her home that night and promised to pick her up the following Friday for the first of the door-to-door canvassing.

They grew more and more to like each other's company and their meetings were not only confined to politics. Tim was forced to vacate his flat and found one close to Marguerite's so that she could cook for both of them at the weekends. They shopped in the Portobello Road market and spent many hours wandering hand in hand round the antique stalls. The nights were closing in by the end of September and they would often stay in the market until after it was dark, going from one lantern-lit stall to the other, into the shops, whose doors were never shut, on again into the individual markets, with the rickety stairs which led up to more and still more tables laden with every imaginable article; much was junk though not all.

They went to the theatre on Saturday evenings and always seemed to leave the market at the last moment so that they just had time to cook a meal and drive Tim's Morris Minor into the West End; and then there was the parking with all its multitude frustrations, meaning they often ended up parking the car well away from the theatre and had to catch the Tube.

Marguerite had not seen Myles for over a year, and only then for a brief moment when he had paid a short visit to his uncle, and now she found that his memory was being replaced by the thought of Tim and she was very happy.

The election drew closer and they canvassed each evening after work. In the final week, an intense programme of public meetings was held and they and their friends attended to give the Tory speakers support. The Gallup polls were forecasting a small Conservative majority but it was anyone's guess. Their own constituency became tense as the margin narrowed. They had certainly detected a small swing to the Conservatives from the numerous cards they had compiled on the possible political leanings of the occupants of the houses they visited. It was encouraging to see the majority of young people, voting for the first time, saying they were going to give their vote to the Conservatives.

It may have been that they realised the necessity for Socialism was dying with the country's continued prosperity.

On polling day they checked each voter against the cards as they voted, and as the day drew on, whenever it became apparent a potential Tory voter had not cast their vote, a car was sent out to collect them. Marguerite and Tim were exhausted by the time the polling booths closed and they went back to Tim's flat for a meal before joining the Young Conservatives at the chairman's flat where they would watch the results on television.

That evening, they crowded into the large flat and, sitting mainly on the floor, awaited the first result. When it came in, a stunned silence hung in the room – the Socialists had retained a seat in Lancashire with a large, increased majority. For half an hour their hopes were strained. The first gain was a Tory victory from the Socialists and a cheer broke out in the room which helped relieve the tension. Shortly after, there were two more Conservative gains and their smiles were becoming a little less forced. There was a lapse in the results and apprehension returned. The tension mounted again but slowly, as the night went on, it seemed certain that the Conservative government would be returned. In the midst of their jubilation, reality hit with a cold hand – their own constituency had been retained by the Socialist candidate with an eight hundred majority. They had cut it by two thousand four hundred, but it wasn't enough, and even as the results continued to mount, ensuring an overall Tory victory, their spirits could not be raised. And at three o'clock in the morning, when the Socialist leader conceded victory to the Tories, they went home, tired and with heavy hearts.

Tim's flat was part of the result of splitting up an old Victorian house into self-contained units. Flat number nine consisted of a small bedroom and a not much larger lounge, with a kitchen and bathroom made from a third room. The result was haphazard and obviously improvised but he had made it pleasant enough and enjoyed coming back in the evenings to something that was his.

He had bought a small radiogram, which had two speakers, and the stereo reproduction was particularly good. Tim's only wish was for a large enough sum of money to buy all the concertos and symphonies that he couldn't afford. The furniture was out of date and very heavy for the small lounge, and the carpet needed a damn good clean to brighten it up but it was all that could be expected from a rented, furnished flat. Marguerite had made some curtains for him which were neat and new, and served to counteract the lack of paint on the window sill.

The radiator finally began to warm the room. Tim removed his overcoat and hung it on the back of the door. He had just got home from the office. He hadn't been cold on the Tube – hardly surprising with so many people in such a confined space, all generating their own heat – but when he got out of the station and started the half-mile walk to his flat, he realised that all the tales of cold misery in an English winter were true. He stood with his back to the radiator and closed his mind to the fact that this was only the middle of October and it was sure to get worse.

He quickly answered a knock on the door and let Marguerite in, but soon had the door closed behind her to keep in the slowly accumulating heat. He took her coat and put it on the peg next to his.

"Anybody would think it was winter, the way you act," she said, after he'd kissed her gently on the cheek.

"I expect I'll get used to it," he replied, "but at the moment I find it most unpleasant."

She walked across to the mantelpiece, collecting the waste paper basket on the way, and with calculated force began to thrust dead chrysanthemums from the vase into the basket.

"What are you doing?" he cried in astonishment. "They're good for at least a couple more days and they do give the place a bit of colour..." His objections died away as he saw it was no use protesting.

"The only colour left in them is brown," she said teasingly, "and anyway, they're dropping dirty curled-up petals all over the place."

"Okay, you win," he said, grinning at her. "Are you hungry? We won't be eating dinner before nine and I'm starving. I've got some crumpets, lots of butter and even a bit of your mother's strawberry jam which ended up in the wrong flat."

"Coffee and crumpets sound good," she said. "I'll toast the crumpets on the fire while you make the coffee."

She collected two packets of crumpets, a plate and the butter from the kitchen and settled herself on the pouffe by the electric radiator. With a knitting needle held at arm's length she toasted and buttered them one by one.

Tim put on the *New World Symphony* and she enjoyed the heat on her face and the music and the fact that he was in the kitchen. She smiled to herself and was thankful that life could sometimes give so much and that it wasn't always only the dreary day-to-day happenings of working in London.

Tim came back with the coffee, placed the cups in the grate and drew the two armchairs close to the fire. The chairs didn't look too brilliant but they were solid, high-backed, and when sat in, sank, and served to keep the draught away, which was always an advantage in an old house. The crumpets were hot and full of butter and they both ate hungrily, with the hot coffee warming them from the inside.

"You'd better go across the road and get changed, milady," he said, when the crumpets were finished.

"Where are we going, Tim?"

"Everywhere, you're only twenty once. We'll take a taxi into town. It's hell trying to park on a Friday night. How long will you be?"

"Give me half an hour and I'll bust myself to be ready in time."

"I'll call a cab for seven o'clock," he said, getting up.

He took her coat from the door and held it ready for her.

"Won't you tell me where we're going?" she asked in a low, persuasive little voice as she looked up at him with soft, hurt eyes.

"Nope, it's a surprise. But if you ask me again I'll tell you it's somewhere very cheap, rather nasty and very uninteresting, so you'd better not ask."

He buttoned the top of her coat, kissed her on the top of her head, and ushered her out of the door. She turned at the top of the stairs to wave before running down.

"You'll need a cocktail dress," he called after her.

He closed the door and went into his bedroom to change. His spirits were high and he longed to hear a knock on the door which would tell him she had forgotten something. He wanted to see her again, quickly, just for a moment.

He changed into his dinner jacket and left his bow tie hanging while he went into the lounge, poured himself a glass of sherry, and crossed to the stereo where he put on a recording of Chopin ballades. The music calmed his excitement and he was able to make a fair job of the tie in front of the large mirror which dominated the room from above the fireplace. He went out into the cold corridor and called a taxi from the public telephone box, returning to finish his drink. The minutes were long as he waited for seven o'clock and the time he would go across to collect Marguerite.

The taxi arrived, heralded by his doorbell. He went down and asked the driver to wait while he went across the road.

"Costs yer money, waiting on her," said the taxi driver in good humour.

"You can't hurry women," Tim answered back in the same tone.

"You're right," said the Cockney, "it's a ruddy shame, but that's 'ow it goes. Don't you worry, I'll be 'ere when yer get back."

Marguerite answered the door and stood back, still holding the handle, while he looked at her.

She looks perfectly lovely, he thought, and wanted to hold her. The dress was soft pink, falling to the knee and flared to make her waist seem even smaller than it was. The thin straps over her soft, cool flesh were exciting. Her auburn hair was brushed back and the tiny ears shone through. Her long, beautifully formed legs held everything to ransom.

"You mustn't kiss me," she said, with a smile, "or you'll smudge my lipstick."

They both laughed and she quickly got her coat from the hall chair. She called goodbye to Mrs Fenton in the kitchen who called back, telling them to enjoy themselves. Going out into the cold street they climbed into the taxi which had turned round and parked in front of the wooden gate.

"I call that pretty quick, considering," said the taxi driver with a chuckle. "Where yer want to go, guv? Say the name an' Bert'll have you there quicker 'n lightnin'."

"The Berkeley," said Tim.

"Couldn't 'ave picked better meself," said the Cockney, closing the glass partition and putting the taxi into gear.

"They're worth a pound a minute for laughs," said Tim, taking her gloved hand and squeezing it.

The taxi passed down the Bayswater Road and on into the galaxy of Hyde Park, down Park Lane and left into Piccadilly where it shortly stopped outside the Berkeley.

The doorman greeted them outside the swing doors and they went on in and to the left where they were shown to a table next to a piano. Their coats were taken from them and they settled into the comfortable seats.

"What are you going to drink?" he asked, as the waiter hovered close but with perfect discretion.

"Would a Pimm's seem fantastic?" she asked.

"Of course not." He turned to the waiter. "May we have a Pimm's and Gin and French cocktail, please?"

The piano music flowed lightly through the room, and the tall ceiling, held high by marble pillars, blended closely with the deep red carpet, the buttoned sofas and the Georgian chairs. There was a graciousness about the cocktail lounge, with its subdued murmur of conversation, the elegant dress of its patrons and the perfect understatement of its service. Such was the best which London could offer and it was magnificent, and yet as Tim absorbed it, a picture of Rhodesia came back to him and he saw the sun-drenched veld with its light, and the great expanse of nature at its most powerful which was Africa itself, and for a brief moment he wished he were home. With her, yes, but home.

They finished two drinks, along with a multitude of cocktail bits, and talked of little things: things that made them laugh, made them happy, requiring little thought that might otherwise have spoilt their mood.

"I think we had better go and eat," he said bringing them back to reality, and caught the eye of the attendant who had taken their coats.

Tim thanked the head waiter who showed them out and the doorman called a taxi. Walking quickly, they crossed the pavement and sought the comparative warmth of the cab. They were dropped at the Blue Angel and went down a flight of stairs into the basement, where she found herself in the famous night club with a table reserved for them.

Their meal began with smoked salmon, followed by a delicious red Tournedos steak. The light was low and candlelight flickered over their food; the red wine went to her head; they danced on the small, raised square around which clustered a galaxy of tables. She estimated a hundred people were seated in the room, their faces hallowed and made mysterious by the guttering candles. The soft light showed her a well-known society face and she whispered the name to Tim. The cabaret was excellent, if a little near the bone, but no one seemed to be embarrassed and she clapped along with the rest. The band played all the tunes she loved, and many more; the second bottle of wine took hold; she drifted happily from the table to the dance floor under the guidance of Tim; she was happy, they were happy, completely alone together even amongst so many people. The others didn't matter; nothing else mattered; they mattered a lot; they danced again and she wanted to bite his ear.

By two o'clock people began to leave and soon after he called for the bill.

They reached his flat and she dreamily agreed to go in for a cup of coffee. She was not tired or even worse for the wine; she floated up the stairs, drunk with happiness. They went inside and he pulled her close to him and kissed her nose, her eyes, and slowly settled on her mouth. His touch was at first lingering and then hard and earnest, and she joined her passion with his.

She went into the bedroom to leave her coat on the bed. He followed her, placed his coat on the chair and gently lifted her chin so that he could undo the button of her coat. He slid it off her shoulders and ran his hands over the soft warmth of her bare flesh.

"I love you, my Marguerite," he said.

A great surge of passion rose up within her. With a trembling hand, she reached behind him and pushed the door shut.

When she woke in the morning she was frightened, but he reassured her and, as she loved him so much, she believed and trusted what he said. He brought her tea and kissed her tenderly and once more she left the world of reality and soared high into the same realms of sweetness and ecstasy they had enjoyed together the previous night.

THE WEEKEND WAS over and she grew to accept the step she had taken in her life. The week went by and she lost the greater part of her regret and let herself enjoy the deep contentment of her new-found love.

February passed and they both remained cradled in the present, giving no thought to the future. She convinced herself that people spent too much of their lives considering the future and dwelling in the past and thereby failed to achieve the aim of life – to be happy and make others happy in the here and now.

For Marguerite this happiness had often escaped her. Violent depressions would take her very low for weeks on end, and yet, for all this, she was blessed in being able to rise to supreme heights of joy. When she reached those heights she would be desperately loath to fall back. She therefore clung to what she had and refrained from looking at the consequences.

Later, only much later, did she have cause to face reality once again. Fear took her heart and crushed it. She walked alone for a week; she had no one to run to apart from Tim and she was afraid to tell him. She feared it would break the bond between them; having given her soul in forging their precious love, she could not bring herself to test its worth.

The strain must have shown in her face, because on the Thursday evening, after they had finished dinner in his flat, she was staring through the window at the car headlights on the road below, thrusting their beams through the slanting rain, when she felt his hands on her shoulders. She covered his hands with her own and hoped he couldn't see her reflection in the window.

"What's the matter, darling?" he asked softly.

She couldn't answer as a hardness took hold of her throat. The silence was heavy for both of them; she turned towards him and buried her head in his chest. He felt the sobs run through the slim body and gently stroked the auburn hair, waiting for her to tell him what he feared.

She slowly brought up her head and he looked down into the tear-soaked eyes which were now so desperately unhappy.

"Tell me," he said again, in just above a whisper.

Her mouth quivered as she looked up at him.

"I'm seven days late," she blurted out and then clung to him, crying loudly, letting out the pent-up agony of the previous week.

"Don't worry, darling," he said, soothingly. "Everything will be all right; we'll think of something."

"I'm frightened," she said, "frightened, just frightened." And once more she could not speak for the choking sobs which coursed through her.

"We'll have a drink," he suggested, guiding her to the chair by the fire. "When you feel better we can talk about it."

He only had sherry in the flat but it cleared her throat and she began to calm down. He wiped her eyes with his handkerchief and refilled her glass.

She held the sides of her chair and brought her voice under control with difficulty.

"What are we going to do?"

"What do you want to do?"

She looked straight ahead and set her jaw. "I'm going to have it, Tim." And then softly, much more softly, as the tears came back again: "I could think of nothing more wonderful than having a child of yours."

He took her hands in his and waited till she looked at him.

"That is the sweetest thing you have ever said to me." He paused, and tried to draw a line between reality and sentiment. "But I can't let it happen like this. A shotgun wedding would ruin any future for us from the very beginning and that's no way to start the rest of our lives. In all probability it's a false alarm; nature is playing one of its tricks on us. The most practical thing we can do at the moment is let you soak in a very hot bath for a couple of hours and see if that does anything. If it doesn't then we'll have to think again."

Relieved that the responsibility was shared and thankful that she could rely upon him, she did what he said and her happiness returned.

Nothing happened on the Wednesday and by the Thursday evening her fears had come back.

"We'll have to get married," she said, "that's all we can do."

He came out of the kitchen; his face was drawn; his voice was measured, unpleasant. "To start with you are under twenty-one and we'd have to get your mother's permission; secondly, I couldn't possibly afford to get married at the moment."

His voice grew harder. Stunned, she listened to a side of him she had never seen before. "It would ruin my career; put a stop to any thoughts of going into politics. We'll have to find a doctor or something."

She waited to recover her wits and then screeched at him.

"To hell with your career and your politics, what about your baby?"

"We must be reasonable," he said, trying to change the direction of what he could see was a difficult discussion.

"Oh Tim," she said, "how can you sit there and only think of yourself?"

"I'm not," he said shortly, "I'm thinking of you, just as much. This way no one will know anything about it. Your mother and Mr Featherstone will not think any the worse of you. It's practical logic and not sentimental nonsense."

"Okay, okay" she said drawing in her breath. "So you want it this way. Well, you can have it, but when it's all over you can count me out. I'll give you a ring at your precious office and, if necessary, send you a bill.".

"Don't be so damned stupid." he said, taking her arm. "You can't walk out in a temper like this."

"Why not?" she demanded, pulling away from him.

"Because I say so!"

He manhandled her towards a chair and sat her down by the fireplace.

"Now let's both keep calm," Tim said, controlling his voice and speaking quietly. "We're probably still making a mountain out of a molehill and nothing will happen, so don't let's take it out on each other just because we're both worried. If you want it the other way then that's how it will be. Now if you hold your horses I'll go and cook a couple of chops and we'll both feel better for something to eat."

She did not argue; her energy was spent. Anyway, she had nowhere to run, even though he had hurt her more than she could have imagined.

He did not see her on the Friday and thought it best to let her think alone. He had just got up on the Sunday when she let herself in with her duplicate key. Her shoulders were hunched and her coat hung loosely.

"You can stop worrying," she said in a soft voice, full of bitterness. "It started late last night."

"Thank God for that," he said, sinking back against the kitchen sink, and then hurriedly and with too much brightness in his voice he asked her if she wanted a cup of coffee.

"I suppose so," she said, but there was no happiness in her voice.

"Cheer up," he said.

"How can I? When you hurt me so much on Thursday."

"I'm sorry, darling, but please don't let's go over all that again. I'm sure you'll see I was right in time."

"I hope so." Her voice was resigned. "But it will be many months before I can think of loving you again."

And there they left it. She returned to her deep depression. She was alone again, completely alone.

4

CHRISTMAS, 1959

*A*part from brief encounters in the street, Marguerite didn't see Tim till just before Christmas. It was the present which brought them together.

Her main wish had been to get away from everything, to be alone so that she could piece her life together and somehow regain her dignity.

She had become more of a realist, not so inclined to take people at their face value without looking a little deeper. She concluded that people were not as sincere as she had always believed them to be. To an extent she was disillusioned. She withdrew into herself and began to read books on a wide variety of subjects. Her view of life broadened still further and Marguerite began to understand things that before had passed her by unnoticed. The deeper she probed, the more she wanted to know, and slowly she was able to find the reasons for many things in life. For a while she thought she understood other people. It was like emerging from a very deep tank of water, for a brief moment, to catch a breath of air.

Instead of accepting the conclusions of others, she began to form her own, and started to build herself a set of values from what she had discovered. From the outside she appeared harder but this was only a protective coat that she had learnt to her cost was necessary.

The perfume was Marguerite's favourite and very expensive, inducing a longing to see him again. She tried to compose herself to write a letter of thanks but was unable to control the feelings which had been aroused. After half an hour of trying to read a book, she flung it on the bed, fetched her coat and was soon crossing the street to his flat with the coat buttons still undone. She rang the bell. When the door opened he took her in his arms and she began to cry and all he did was hold her closer.

They went inside and through a mixture of tears and laughter she thanked him for the lovely perfume and later, as they sat in the lounge drinking coffee, they realised that the last two months were behind them: it was as though they were back as before. They talked quickly and she asked him if his socks had been darned and when he said that they were, she felt cheated and looked forward to the time when he'd make another hole so that she could mend it for him.

"What are you doing for Christmas?" he asked.

"I was going down to Mirelton, but mother says that a lot of the family will be there, including Myles, and she thinks it best if I stay away. Quite frankly I think it's stupid, the whole thing was nearly four years ago, and anyway we're both very much older now and would probably laugh at the whole thing. Still, I don't fancy being looked up and down disapprovingly by his mother, so it's probably just as well. It wouldn't be much of a Christmas... Mother would be sure to think I was getting in her way while she was cooking."

"Well that makes two waifs with nowhere to go," he replied. "How about buying a turkey at the market and having it here? We could get wonderfully tight on gin and champagne."

"I don't know so much about the gin," she chuckled, "but the champagne sounds perfect. We'll have to hurry though, we only have tomorrow to buy things in."

"You'll do it then?" he said, getting up excitedly.

"Yes," she said.

"You're simply marvellous." He took her by the waist and lifted her up.

"Put me down," she laughed, "and don't be so silly."

"Not until you promise to kiss me."

"I promise," she said from her point of disadvantage. Whereupon he put her back on her feet so tenderly that she thought she would burst.

The next day they drove the car through the winding back streets to the Portobello Road and, after parking it in a side street, began the search for a suitable turkey. Tim had carefully measured the oven and they went from stall to stall trying to find a small enough bird. They bought one eventually which they thought would fit in the oven on the skew. They then bought parsley, sausage meat, breadcrumbs and chestnuts to stuff it with, after Marguerite had spent a few minutes trying to remember what her mother put in the stuffing. Dried fruit and walnuts, together with a plum pudding, were added to their basket before he made for the off licence and stocked up with the drink. Taking a handle each, they carried the basket to the car.

"Let's get some people in for drinks tonight," he suggested.

"Okay then. We'll get down to some solid telephoning when we get back to the flat."

Some of their friends were still in town and between them that evening they all got a little drunk. The next day being Christmas, Marguerite came across at eleven o'clock, both of them complaining of a hangover.

Preparations went ahead in a fever of energy. Eventually the turkey was ready to put in the oven and they could relax. They dozed in front of the fire, just managing to baste the bird at irregular intervals. By four o'clock the whole flat smelled of turkey and they opened the bar.

Tim carved, and arranged the roast potatoes around the plates where she added the Brussels sprouts. It was dark when they sat down to eat and the two candles gave a soft, tranquil light, enhanced by the glowing red of the radiator. The ice-cold champagne cleared their palates and seemed to encourage them to eat more. The black coffee and miniature bottle of liqueur filled the last gap. Tim complained of not being able to move.

The flat was quiet; outside the church bells broke across the still night. Later they went out for a walk to look at the many Christmas trees shining brightly through the open-curtained windows of the otherwise shuttered homes.

When they parted that night Marguerite thanked him for the most wonderful Christmas she had ever spent and he told her that hers could not have been more perfect than his.

She was happy again but refused to return to him under the same conditions, though very often she found it difficult to keep to her resolution.

It snowed at the end of January and for three days it lay on the rooftops. She found it very amusing when Tim explained it was the first time he'd ever seen snow.

It was the idea of snow which made him suggest a holiday in Switzerland. She laughed at first and jokingly said, "Wouldn't that be marvellous." Then Marguerite realised he was serious. She said it would cost far too much and that she couldn't possibly afford it.

"It wouldn't be so much if we went by train," Tim explained, "and anyway I'm being paid a Rhodesian salary. The cost of living is far less here than at home. I think I could squeeze enough money for the two of us."

"You're mad," she said.

"Would you like to go though?"

"Of course I would."

"Then that's settled. All we have to do is decide where we're going and when."

"I really do think you're mad, wonderfully mad," she said, putting her arms round his neck.

"I've collected some pamphlets together," he went on, breaking away and going over to his desk, "so you can decide where you want to go."

"You've already got pamphlets?"

Tim smiled, handing them to her. She took them one by one, reading out their names as though there was magic in every one of them.

"Geneva would be too commercial," Marguerite said, as a matter of fact, "there'll be too many banks, and probably a United Nations meeting with everyone going around with guns. I don't like guns so we won't go there." And she threw the pamphlet on the floor before taking up another.

"Ooh this one sounds nice. 'Small chalet, at high altitude, with exhilarating air and magnificent views.'"

"And what could we find to do up there for a fortnight?"

"Well, I've got some idea," she said knowingly as she looked up at him. "But that would break my resolution, so we can't very well go there." And she threw it alongside the Geneva one.

She looked through them all and finally returned to the one marked Lucerne. "This one sounds rather wonderful," she said excitedly and he knelt down on the floor beside her so he could see over her shoulder.

Lucerne in the spring, with the avenues of chestnut trees by the lake just breaking their buds; the tall snow-capped mountains thrusting up from the edge of the crystal-blue lake into the drifting layers of soft white cloud.

"Now how about that for a bit of romance?" she said, holding the pamphlet at both arms' length.

"I rather had my eye on that one as well, but more for its casino than the chestnut trees. I've never been to a casino."

"Do you know something?" she said with a puckered frown as she got up from the floor. He waited but didn't say anything.

Suddenly her eyes sparkled and she sprang towards him, took both his hands and began to dance him round and round.

"Half an hour ago," she laughed, nearly out of control, "I'd only heard of Switzerland and now I'm going there and what's even more wonderful is that I'm going with you."

"So Lucerne it is at the end of April," he said, catching her mood and whirling her around even faster.

"Don't let go," she shouted in sudden fear.

"What makes you think I'd let you go?" he called back.

"I don't know, but we're going awfully fast."

And slowly he brought her to a standstill and let her sink into the safety of the armchair.

It was such a wonderful surprise that Marguerite couldn't close her eyes that night without seeing miles of snow-capped mountains.

In the coming weeks everything was arranged. She wrote to her mother saying they were going in a foursome in the hope that what the eye didn't see the heart wouldn't grieve about. The return letter was a little puzzled as to how she had saved so much money. Marguerite responded by saying that she had been doing extra typing in the evenings.

They saved as much money as they could in the three months, forgoing their weekly trip to the theatre. Then they nearly lost it all when her mother came up to London to see Marguerite and Tim took them both out to dinner and on to the theatre afterwards. It was a very happy evening. Much to her surprise, her mother greatly took to Tim, and when they were alone, couldn't stop talking about 'that nice boy'.

Harriet spent one night in town and Mrs Fenton was kind enough to find her an extra bed in the house, saving a large hotel bill. She hurried back to Dorset on the Sunday afternoon train as she didn't like the idea of poor Mr Featherstone getting his own meals. She wouldn't have come up to see her daughter in the first place if he hadn't paid the rail fare and made her go.

They caught the boat train on the Saturday evening as Tim had to work in the morning. A taxi took them to Victoria station at six o'clock, with their two large suitcases stowed in the boot. She was so excited at the thought of making her first trip out of England that she was certain she had left a hundred and one things in her room. They arrived at the station a little early and drank a cup of coffee in the buffet lounge while they waited.

The loudspeaker called out above the heads of hundreds of travellers that the seven o'clock boat train for Paris was leaving platform one in ten minutes. A tingle ran through her as she realised it was their train.

They got their luggage aboard and found the two reserved seats. As the train moved out of the station she held his hand and sat gazing out of the window like an overawed schoolgirl.

They left the train at Dover and took their luggage through customs and onto the boat. Tim led her down the narrow steps of the cross-channel steamer to the lounge where he ordered them drinks. It was cold up on the deck and the warmth of the smoking lounge was very pleasant. Some fifteen minutes later the hooter sounded and they could feel the ship getting underway. The boat rolled a little in the Channel and Marguerite felt peculiar to start with till she got used to the motion.

At Calais, Marguerite's new passport was stamped for the first time. She quite expected them to open her case in the customs shed and had her key ready to oblige, but the official simply marked it with a chalk cross and they passed though as easily as Tim had said they would.

Having separate compartments on the train, Tim saw her into the sleeper which she shared with an elderly French lady who spoke not a word of English. When Tim said goodnight and went off to find his own sleeper, Marguerite tried to carry on a conversation with many signs and laughs until she decided it was impossible and went to bed. She couldn't sleep and spent the night in spasms of sleeping and waking. Awake, she listened to the rhythm of the train as it sped through the French night, until once again she fell into slumber. Waking early in the morning, Marguerite was already dressed when the attendant called something in French through the closed door that might have meant breakfast. She mimed to the French woman who confirmed with a smile and a vigorous nodding of the head that *le petit déjeuner* was indeed breakfast.

Marguerite stepped out into the corridor and slid the door closed behind her. Watching the countryside go by with its endless procession of damp green fields, she was surprised to find that it looked little different from England. During the night the train had stopped in Paris and now they were speeding on towards the Swiss border.

Tim joined her and she looked over her shoulder to make sure no one was coming before letting him kiss her good morning. They breakfasted on hot rolls and coffee in the dining car and just before lunch, the train stopped at Basel with the Swiss officials coming aboard. All passengers were allowed off the train for half an hour but before doing so, Marguerite persuaded the Swiss official to stamp her passport. He did so with a shrug and a gesticulation which plainly meant that it wasn't necessary; the implication was clear: 'Tourists'! She took the passport back from him and proudly dropped it into her handbag with a satisfied smile.

The train took a slower course through the winding valleys which cut into the Swiss mountains, arriving in Lucerne just after three o'clock. A taxi took them to the Luzernerhof where their rooms had been booked. The hotel was new and sparkling fresh. Here they encountered for the first time the genial welcome of the Swiss.

No sooner had Marguerite seen her case safely carried to her room than she ran down the corridor to Tim's room.

"Let's go for a walk along the lake shore," she said, taking his hand.

"Aren't you tired?" he asked, holding back.

"Of course not, and we'll have to hurry before the light goes," Marguerite said, pulling him towards the door.

They went down in the lift and across the road to the lake.

"Darling, just look up the lake at the mountains. They go on and on, so high and beautiful."

He turned from the mountains and looked at her, loving the

simplicity of her happiness. Slowly they walked along the footpath between the avenues of trees which sheltered the delicate spring snowdrops and daffodils. The air was crisp and penetrating, which made them glad of their coats; the late-winter sun held little advantage among the mountains. She snuggled to him and he drew her close. They wandered alone, sometimes turning to look at the mountains which rose from the shores of the lake. The sun danced on steel-blue water sparkling with a million jewels. Everywhere was perfect peace.

Dusk had fallen by the time they returned to the hotel and after bathing, they dressed for dinner. Tim telephoned for sherry to be sent up to his room.

She was surprised to hear the telephone ring, even more so when she recognised his voice telling her that a drink was waiting. Quickly she put a little of his perfume behind her ears and went across to his room where he gave her a glass of dry sherry and kissed her on the tip of her nose.

"How is the most beautiful girl in Lucerne?" he asked.

"Just fine." She watched him over the top of her glass as she sipped.

"What do you say to a sumptuous dinner, a bottle of wine and the most delicious brandy to follow?"

"I can't wait."

The food was excellent and they lingered a long time over dinner as their energy was spent. Only when they had finished a second cup of coffee did they go upstairs.

Alone in her room, tiredness conquered her and soon after drawing up the eiderdown to her chin, she fell asleep.

The next morning they rose late feeling fresher, and spent the day exploring Lucerne. She found a clock shop off a side street which charmed her into a world of make-believe. There was every size and shape of cuckoo clock and some which didn't even seem to be clocks at all till they chimed the hour. The sound of their ticking hung portentously in the shop, a thousand dials all showing different times, all working feverishly.

She was particularly entranced by a miniature clock tower which sent two horsemen against each other, lances ready and visors closed, when the hands reached the quarter hour. She was lost in a world of chivalry when the cuckoo in the clock behind sprang out at her. Clutching at Tim, she withdrew to a safe distance.

A cable car took them to the top of Mount Pilatus. A footpath, guarded by two iron rails, ran to just below the summit. They gripped the rail, dizzy yet exhilarated by the height. Around them were the tops of many mountains, slicing through the clouds, showing only their snow-capped peaks. They seemed to be looking out and over the very roof of the world.

Once back down via the footpath from the summit, they returned to the hotel, a log fire, hot cheese, and the warmth of hospitality.

Later, they went to the casino, were they were dazzled by the glitz, and even won a little money much to everyone's surprise, though no one was more surprised than Tim. They spent the money on wine and returned late to their hotel just a little worse for drink. Tim imagined he had supported Marguerite on the walk home and Marguerite thought the opposite.

For twelve days they lived amongst the freshness of Switzerland; she became entranced by its natural perfection and beauty. The days went by quickly and it was on the morning before their holiday was due to end that Tim hired a small launch-boat. Together they journeyed up the lake and once more left the world of reality to travel into a solitude and peace of their own. He drove the boat at a low throttle, cutting into the still water which went unrolling behind them. A wild duck flew low ahead of them before coming to rest among the silent reeds clinging to the shore. The engine throbbed and Marguerite wanted to apologise to the stillness for its noise.

"Are you happy?" he whispered to her above the engine.

"I'm going to burst with it," she said, and kissed him behind the ear.

But for these words they did not speak again before returning to the jetty in time for breakfast. Together they had achieved a harmony needing no words, and not for the first time their souls combined into one far out on the lake of Lucerne.

That evening they again took the launch and went out with the sun still showing above the mountains. Turning the boat into an inlet, Tim cut the engine and they drifted silently between the tall rock faces which plunged into the crystal water on both sides. An orange glow hung like fire in the sky as the sun dipped behind the snowy peaks. He let the wheel fall idle and turned her towards him.

"Will you marry me, my Marguerite?" he said.

His soft eyes watched her and saw the newborn tears roll gently down her cheek; and then, more softly, again: "I said, will you marry me?"

"Of course I will, you wonderful darling." And they clung to each other in that precious moment. Slowly he drew back till he could see her face and their laughter rang out across the lake and echoed in the mountains.

GOODBYES, 1960

*B*y the time they returned to London the world had turned upon Rhodesia's southern neighbour. South Africa was condemned from every quarter for the massacre of sixty-nine Africans at Sharpeville. Tim felt sympathy for all concerned, having lived all his life in a country of mixed races, and knew the tensions which had made such a catastrophe almost inevitable. When Marguerite asked him about the seeming brutality of it all, he merely asked her what the world's oh-so righteous attitude would have been had the European police been slaughtered in their place.

"But Tim," she argued, "there was no danger for the police. They fired at the backs of fleeing Africans."

"It's easy to be wise after the event. The first shots obviously turned the rioters about and the last prevented them from turning back again. Not for a minute must you think I condone such slaughter, on the contrary it sickens me. When it comes to killing, the colour of a man's skin counts for nothing."

"Where will it all end?" she asked.

"I sometimes dread to think," he replied. "When two forces, each certain in themselves that they are right and both capable of going to any lengths to achieve their aims, are thrown together in one country, the only thing to do is hope that sanity and reason will prevail."

"Darling, I'm frightened of Africa, even though I'm so looking forward to going there with you."

"There won't be any trouble north of the Limpopo." He was certain about this in his own mind, with the certainty common to those who lack first-hand experience. No matter what you read in the papers, he thought, the worst only ever happened to the other fellow.

He went on, "We're going about it from the other direction and trying to build a multi-racial society to prevent any outbursts of antagonism between the races. The police haven't shot an African in anger since the Matabele rebellion, before the turn of the century."

Going over to the chest of drawers, Tim found a reel of Scotch tape. Mechanically, he cut a length of tape and stuck the flowering end of the bright green creeper higher up the wall. As she watched him, her unconscious mind still wrestling with thoughts of Africa, she realized the creeper had grown a good six inches while they were away. She wondered if she would find such delicate greenery in Tim's country. Through the window, she leant out to touch the fresh green sycamore leaves which brushed against the building, the first warmth of summer bathing her face. From behind, Tim put his hands round her slim waist and followed her gaze through the window.

"It's just as beautiful at Macheke," he told her. "Different, but just as beautiful."

"How did you know what I was thinking?" she asked him wistfully, though not surprised.

He touched her hand, the one which was tracing the veins of the sycamore leaf.

"By the way you're fingering that leaf. It gives you away."

"Yes, I suppose it does." She ran her finger all the way to the tip of the leaf.

"Is it really as beautiful?"

"Yes, darling, it is." He enjoyed being able to talk about it; it made him miss the place even more, but it was worth it. "At first you will say it's just dry and empty, but as the months go by you'll grow to love the vast expanses and the constant excitement of it all. Crickets sometimes so loud they deafen you; birds and flowers so luxuriant that they startle you when you suddenly come across them in the waterless bush. And all blended together under a powerful, dominant sun creating wonder which must be experienced, felt on the skin and deep in the mind, bathed in, before it can be fully appreciated."

"Why is it," she wondered, "that we always love best the country in which we're born?" She paused and tried to find the answer. "I suppose it's what we're used to. I can take so much pleasure from looking at that one leaf, with its delicate veins spread out in perfect symmetry like a fish bone. And if I look long enough, I find it difficult to decide which is more beautiful, the delicate pattern or the softness of the colour." She gently let the leaf fall back into its place on the tree.

He wanted to kiss her. For some time they remained together with their separate thoughts and let their minds wander far from the summer afternoon in Holland Park.

Marguerite was the first to voice her train of thought.

"What's going to happen in the Belgian Congo when it gets independence?"

"Hell only knows, once all those charming little dark-skinned gentlemen are set free to snap at each other's throats. The various tribes are only waiting for the starter's gun on June 30th and then they'll be at it like a pack of bloodhounds. The Belgians should never leave," he said, moving away as his passion rose, "but what else can they do, with every little trumped-up country with a United Nations vote baying at them? Jan Smuts would turn in his grave if he saw the hypocrisy which has developed out of this wonderful dream of a so-called league of nations."

"The Gold Coast was all right," she said.

"If you mean there isn't any trouble, yes, I agree, but it isn't surprising with the opposition in jail. A splendid example of one man, one vote."

"You sound bitter," she said.

"Yes, I suppose you're right," he replied tersely. "But then it's so damned exasperating."

May gave way to June, and the evenings lengthened and the twilight lingered till after ten. They agreed to marry in Rhodesia, even though it meant waiting for Tim's firm to send him home.

Having realised that her months in England were numbered, she grew to appreciate the small things in her home which she had previously taken for granted. She began to store up her memories to provide a source of comfort in the years to come. She would always be thankful that a memory would invariably evoke happiness as an antidote to anything unsavoury.

In the evenings, when they had both returned from the turmoil of the City, with its never-ending urgency and clamour which engulfed and saturated the soul, they would grab with both hands the peace which was so perfect in the summer evenings. And there was so much of it to be found in the tree-lined back streets of Holland Park. Each holding a finger of the other's hand, they would meander beneath the trees, not speaking, content in the perfect tranquillity of their surroundings and the intensity of the love which flowed between them. The publican grew to know them well in the William and Ann, as they often found a secluded bench in the beer garden to dawdle over a shandy and a glass of beer.

IT WAS two days after midsummer. The day had been hot throughout, with Tim complaining at the discomfort. After dinner they sat out on the flat roof which overlooked the back gardens of haphazardly strewn blocks of semi-detached houses. The bushy green tops of trees broke up the barren brownness of the bricks which contrasted with the grey of slate roofs. A pigeon, breast blown full out, cooed proudly from the top of a chimney pot and vied with the sparrows and starlings.

To get onto the roof they had climbed through one of the windows of Tim's flat, taking the wicker chairs with them. The iced coffee was delicious and ran cool down their throats.

"Why don't we walk into the park for a change?" suggested Marguerite. "It isn't very far."

"All right," he agreed. "When you've finished your coffee we'll make a move."

It was too peaceful to hurry and she idly picked a delicate rosebud from the sprawl of foliage that had climbed the latticework and grown over the wall onto the lead roof.

"It flowers like that every year," he said, "all thirty feet of it, and with the first frost, the blooms will fade away until next summer."

"Nature is rather wonderful," she reflected.

Returning the chairs back through the window, they rinsed out their glasses and closed up the flat.

When they slammed the tall Victorian front door, the knocker bounced in retaliation. Laughing hand in hand, they went down the steps and through the iron gate which led onto the pavement and the street beyond.

Apart from the Poodles and Pekineses on their evening walks, there was little life on the streets. Sundays were usually quiet.

"Oh darling, did you see that?" She giggled and squeezed his arm. "I bet its tummy gets cold in the winter."

They both turned to look at the receding Poodle as it tripped along beside the staccato tread of two stiletto heels.

"Poor little thing," said Tim. "It looks more like a half-shorn sheep than a dog."

They crossed the main road and some ten minutes later turned into Holland Park. They chose a path which seemed more secluded than the others and ventured between the avenue of towering elms whose branches spread a cover of foliage many feet above them; yet, where they walked, they could see between the straight and slender trunks of the tall trees. Further on, a clump of lime trees gave out a sweet, delicious scent and thousands of industrious bees droned in amongst the white tassels of flowers.

As they moved further into the park, they heard waves of orchestral music and, like the children of Hamelin, followed the sound as the floating notes, which spread like balm through the trees, became clearer. Closer to the source, more people appeared along the various paths, all intent on the same quest.

"What do you think it is?" asked Marguerite.

"It must be a concert in the park," he said. "Everyone else seems to know where they're going, they can't all have just been attracted by the sound of music, there are too many."

They followed the people and as the music became clear and magnificent, they came to the gateway which led into the private grounds of Holland House. He paid two and sixpence and they moved on, drawn by the power of Richard Wagner. At last, they came out onto the lawns where a multitude of people were clustered on the grass, motionless and completely wrapped up in the music. On a high piece of ground had been erected a large bowl which projected the sounds of a full orchestra. A great crescendo from the overture to *Rienzi* boomed out and spread over them all.

They found a small patch of grass and sat down, falling completely under the spell of Wagner. The notes fell like rain, purifying them. A fanfare heralded the strings, and the strings heralded the trumpets, which in their turn brought in the drums, and as all the instruments surged forward together, the music mounted and drove to a pitch of exhilaration, powered by the conductor. Still higher Wagner built his overture, then down, down and then, gathering all its strength, it mounted again, higher and higher, to another summit, and then down again, ready for the final ascent to majesty, beyond which there was no further to climb.

The ruined house gave a back drop to the simplicity of the music bowl and round the green lawns the elms, the limes and the chestnut trees stood sentinel, large, deep and soothing to the eye. The summer evening hung tense and poignant without a breeze to blow away the notes or the sweet scent of a delicious warmth. Without thought she found his hand and they intertwined their fingers. For an hour and a half the music continued and finally it was dark and even then the music continued as the pale sky gave way to the early stars.

The perfection of the setting and the way in which they had found it left Marguerite in a state of supreme elation as they walked back through the darkness. Even the occasional bat, which circled in the open spaces between the trees, seemed to fly in harmony with the music which still coursed through her mind. The street lights attracted a wealth of summer moths which dashed at the glass panes and patterned the road with their shadows.

All these things she would treasure in her memory when she was thousands of miles away in Africa.

The Big Continent was going through the most terrible birth pangs. Between March and the end of July the people exposed their most grisly characteristics to public scrutiny. The slaughter of Sharpeville was still fresh in the minds of all the nations of the world when it was followed by the agony of the Congo. Many who had lived their lives amongst the African tribes had foretold the exact nature of the immediate aftermath of independence, but even they had not imagined the extent to which inter-tribal and European hatred could be taken when driven by the stupidity of the super powers. They fanned the flames first one way then the other, while the international game of chess continued with the Congo as the board. Each nation tried to turn the disaster to its own advantage and while they bickered and haggled over their own petty advantages, the mass of the Congolese people surged one way and then, with equal fervour, back again.

At last the world powers were able to stand back with self-righteous hypocrisy and see the results of their all-conquering, selfish, dollar-ridden deals play out – starvation, disease, rape, murder and the very worst of human depravity.

As the tragedy unfolded and the various nations preached their condescending, self-interested sermons, Tim felt sick and bitterly indignant as more and more first-hand reports flowed into his office from Northern Rhodesia.

Soon the trauma overtook him personally: widespread rioting

broke out in Bulawayo and Salisbury, the twin hearts of Tim's country. The violence continued day after day and in desperation the police opened fire. Several people were killed, and the 1896 record for the highest number of protestors slaughtered had been broken.

The Congo fire seemed to be spreading in every direction and Tim determined to go home, wanting to be in Rhodesia at such a time. The public relations firm agreed to release him from his contract and in great haste he prepared to fly back to Salisbury.

"Darling, I think the best thing is if I fly ahead and get everything arranged so we can be married soon after you arrive. It will take time to have the banns read. How long do you think it will take for you to sort everything out before joining me?"

"I must go down to Mirelton for at least a week, to say goodbye to Mother," she said.

She was full of excitement, uncertainty and genuine fear for the unknown, but if Tim went, she would follow. Now it was upon her she was ready to go.

"I'll have to give them a couple of weeks' notice at the office," she went on. "Book me on a flight in three and a half weeks. I don't think I could take being away from you any longer than that," she ended unhappily.

The tarmac of London Airport shimmered in the heat. Planes taxied and took off, their destinations known only to those who flew in them. Marguerite and Tim stood together in the departure lounge without speaking.

For Marguerite it was the beginning of an unknown future, a dark future which seemed to hold so many terrors. She gripped his hand harder as the pictures piled up in her mind and he returned the pressure.

Tim fidgeted and tried to suppress the constant churnings of his stomach. He heard the flight to Nairobi announced and his mouth dried. He was conscious he was embarking on some vast adventure but was unable to give a definitive reason for the surging excitement he felt building up inside.

"It won't be for long," he told her.

"I know, I know," she said. "But it's still horrible."

He kissed her eyes to stop the small flow of tears and drew her with him towards the barrier.

"Keep your chin up," he said, "and in three and a half weeks I'll show you my country and in no time you'll love it as much as I do."

"Yes, I'm sure I will," she said, but the choking of her throat prevented any more words.

"I love you, darling," he whispered into her ear and hugged her close before turning to the gate and the long walk across the tarmac to the Comet.

She watched his back retreating into the distance and the breeze from another aircraft tousled his fair hair and blew it out of place. He walked up the flight of steps into the tail portion of the aircraft and turned at the top to wave a last farewell.

The aircraft doors closed and soon was deafened by the roar of four jet engines. The plane moved forward to its place for takeoff. She watched it race down the strip and lift into the air. Moments later it was out of sight.

For over seven months she had lived close to him and being alone now seemed to Marguerite like a vacuum, with nothing to snag her interest.

She went by train and tube back to Holland Park, and her spirits revived a little when she returned to her room which even now she still loved.

She gave in her notice and two weeks later she was not sorry to leave the office and the materialism of London. She had decided not to return to Holland Park after her stay in Dorset, coordinating her departure so she could catch a plane for Rhodesia directly.

Saying goodbye to Mrs Fenton proved to be very difficult as the old lady had grown more than fond of her. She always seemed to have time to spare for Marguerite, often cooking her evening meals. Even with Tim so close she had cheered up many of the otherwise dull and never-ending evenings, but then again, as Marguerite would say, 'you couldn't help but be fond of the dear old lady'.

The ageing gentlewoman wished her God speed and a wonderful life which she so richly deserved. Marguerite kissed the gaunt, wrinkled cheeks and wanted to say something more than thank you, however sincerely she meant it. The old eyes grew lonely and moist, and Marguerite understood that there was no need for further words. The old lady was speaking anyway.

"I think that must be your taxi, my dear," she said, taking command again of her voice. "You'd better not keep him waiting."

Marguerite turned away. She knew the thoughts that were passing through the wonderful old lady's mind: even if she and Tim returned to London in three years' time, as they planned, they would be unlikely to find Mrs Fenton still alive. They both knew this was adieu and not au revoir, but how could one put such thoughts into words without them sounding pathetically inadequate? No one likes to face old age but sometimes it turns and stares.

The cab driver loaded her cases into the front luggage compartment and Marguerite got into the taxi. She leant forward to wave through the window to the slender, fragile Mrs Fenton, who had closed the old wooden gate and was standing behind it, using it as a support. She was leaning over and gently waving to the taxi as it drew away. She didn't move as the taxi turned into the Bayswater Road, and Marguerite finally lost sight of her friend whom she was unlikely to see ever again.

She was close to the end of her journey and the taxi, a rather old Humber, ground its way into the drive and she was again in the beautiful setting of Mirelton. The car managed to crawl up to the front of the house in first gear and she saw Mr Featherstone on the terrace calling into the house with his deep, military tone.

"Harriet, come out to the front, it's Marguerite." Without waiting for an answer he made his way down the terrace steps to greet her as she stepped out of the taxi.

"My goodness," he said, "you have changed. Not surprising after two years." He gave a throaty chuckle. "Even prettier than before, methinks." And having taken her outstretched hand he patted it.

"How nice to see you again," she said, with a deep smile.

"Ah, here's your mother," said the retired District Commissioner, as Mrs Stearle came bustling out onto the terrace and down the steps to greet her daughter. The years and the good food of Mirelton had played their havoc with Mrs Stearle, who had grown considerably more homely in the last few years and now sported a splendid girth.

Marguerite was enveloped by her mother and drawn up the steps in her wake.

"Would you be good enough to bring the cases through?" Mr Featherstone called to the taxi driver.

"Where shall I put 'em, Mr Featherstone?" The man had an almost intelligible brogue.

"On the terrace for the time being. We'll find somewhere better when Mrs Stearle is organised."

It was late afternoon and Mr Featherstone invited them both to join him for tea.

Marguerite answered many questions – about Tim, London, what she did, and the most important one, on how she was going to enjoy Rhodesia.

"Mark you, I envy you going to Africa," the elderly gentleman was saying. "Probably not the same as it was in my day. Still, it's Africa. Fine place, yes, a fine place. Kind of takes a hold of you... can't explain...tried...many times... In fact, it won't have lost that, nothing could take it away. It's in the atmosphere, intangible. You'll see."

"I think I'll stick to Dorset," put in Mrs Stearle.

"You wouldn't have thought that at Marguerite's age," he chuckled.

"I would, you know. All those black men... Why, you can keep them. Don't like the sound of the place and that's a fact."

"But Mother, they're just the same as us," Marguerite protested.

"Got nasty habits, I daresay," replied her mother firmly, "you mark my words."

"You must have had a nasty dream about them at one time."

"No I didn't. I saw one of them, during the war. Horrible he was. Great big man, and black, jet black, and what was more I couldn't understand a word he said!"

A great burst of laughter from Mr Featherstone cut her short and then Marguerite joined in. Mrs Stearle looked from one to the other disapprovingly, with an aloof expression of 'some people'.

After tea they took her cases through into her old bedroom and Marguerite asked her mother if it would be all right to swim before dinner.

Changing into a pale blue bathing costume, a bathing wrap drawn tightly round her waist, she walked out to the top of the cliff and down the path leading to the sea. She had one small bogey to lay to rest and she was going to do it once and for all.

The path she took was the same one she had used so often with Myles. As she walked slowly down through its twists and turns, memories of five years ago returned, as is so often the case with the wonder of first love. And soon she found herself yearning as deeply for Myles as she had been, but half an hour ago, for Tim.

When she reached the sand she had lost the preceding five years and was once again sixteen, thinking of the intoxication of her first kiss at this same spot. She had cherished the moment for so many years, and now she let herself dwell in the sorrow it had caused. Standing here, the picture of Myles would not fade. She saw every feature of his face and in her dream she waited breathlessly to hear him speak. Surely he would say 'Let's go sailing,' and yet he didn't and slowly his features began to blur and when they became clear again it was no longer the face of Myles Featherstone but Tim Carter and he was saying to her, very gently, 'I love you, my Marguerite,' and even as he said it she heard his voice echo in the mountains.

Throwing off the wrap, Marguerite ran down to the sea in her joy and swam deep out into the calm blue water. After swimming hard for a long time, she returned to the beach and lay down to let the evening sun slowly warm her glowing body. The close-cut auburn hair, which clung to her ears, began to dry. Where she lay the sun shone deep into her eyes, but she ignored it because her heart was beating so fast and her soul was so happy that nothing could distract her from the bounding joy which engulfed each vestige of her mind and body.

THE WEEK PASSED QUICKLY and she and her mother talked much of her father, and again she realised how deep a void his loss had made in her life. She went back to the old farmhouse, to say goodbye, and to remember all that had been wonderful about the place.

She took the same paths which always seemed to lead to Dancing Ledge and there she spent a beautiful afternoon by herself well away from the families she found ensconced on her beloved cliffs. All was so peaceful and not a ripple broke the mirror-like surface of a totally becalmed sea.

She didn't return to Mirelton till late in the evening as she waited to watch the sea smile at her and swallow a sinking sun. She once again imagined herself to be the guardian of this wonderful setting. The most practical minds are often capable of becoming the instruments of ethereal thought and for a while, as Marguerite stood high up on the cliff, she left the world of reality and stepped out into the ether. She was floating amongst the small billowing white clouds which drifted beneath the pale blue sky. Without any difficulty she found her father amongst the clouds. He was so happy to see her and she to see him, and as they drifted between the wisps of cloud they met Tim and she introduced him to her father and when he had gone away, her father said that she had made a wise choice and that she would always love him... It was a lovely dream while it lasted, yet even when Marguerite awoke from it she retained a glorious sense of solace, and as she turned away from the sea and the cliff her soul was warm and she found herself loving even more powerfully her life to come.

When she left Mirelton, the District Commissioner took them to Corfe Castle station where they said goodbye. Mrs Stearle was so prostrate with tears that she told Marguerite it would be better if they didn't wait for the train to come in.

"It would probably be much better for both of us," Marguerite agreed. "It could well be another half hour as it is. Goodbye, Mr Featherstone." She extended her gloved hand. "And thank you again for all your wonderful kindness."

"Ah well," said the DC brusquely, in an attempt to overcome his 'rather ticklish sentiment', as he always put it, which tended to pervade such occasions. "I expect we'll hear from you, and you know where to write if you need any help."

"You're sweet," she said, and before he could recover from the surprise she had stood on tiptoe and kissed him lightly on his well-tanned, leathery cheek.

"You'll be giving me ideas," he said jovially, and obviously greatly pleased by the small show of affection from the girl he had known since she was twelve.

Mrs Stearle's sobs only deepened, and she barely managed to send her love to Tim and wish them every happiness on their wedding day before her employer took her gently but firmly in hand to guide her away.

And suddenly Marguerite was alone and her journey to Africa had begun.

She looked up at the tall hills which rose gracefully on either side of the railway track. On top of one stood the ruins of the castle which her ancestors must have seen in its prime, and she became conscious of the majesty of her heritage. Even though the castle was no more than a ruin now, she was deeply glad to be English. Such reflections bolstered her courage, and when the train finally arrived to take her away, she boarded eagerly, with a sense of excitement and anticipation, scarcely able to believe that in twenty-four hours she would be in Southern Africa.

PART II

Rhodesia, 1960 to 1975

6

A THURSDAY, 1ST SEPTEMBER 1960

"*B*elow is the Zambezi River and shortly we will be flying over the Mozambique border into Southern Rhodesia."

The captain's voice jarred Marguerite back to consciousness and she sat up quickly to crane round and peer out of the window, down through the light pattern of clouds, at the unwinding ribbon below which sprawled across a brown wilderness.

'It looks so small,' she thought to herself, and then was glad for being twenty-five thousand feet above the river. Tim had said it was infested with crocodiles and she didn't like anything creepy-crawly, especially reptiles. She watched the pattern of gentle hills and plains pass slowly below, unbroken, uncultivated, as they had been for thousands of years and more. Later she picked out a straight line which ran out into the distance.

"It's a road," explained the woman in the next seat. "We're now over Rhodesia."

Marguerite looked harder and tried to pick out more detail in what was going to be her home.

From the brown earth below, rolling everywhere into the distance, patchworked by specks of trees and occasionally broken up by a splash of green, a flash of sun suddenly jerked upwards from a tin roof. It wasn't the reflection of water because that would have been softer, a shimmer rather than this jagged display of sunlight. And then she could make out a building, and then another, and then a cluster, a matchbox farm, made up of straight lines, submerged in the bush.

Further into Rhodesia, cultivation became apparent and the roads more numerous.

"They only opened up this area six years ago," volunteered the pleasant, middle-aged woman from the next seat.

They only talked when they wanted to and found each other relaxing company. Both were flying alone. Mrs Greene was the wife of a civil servant in the Agricultural Department in Bulawayo. She had stayed on alone in England with her parents after her husband's leave had expired.

"George," that was her husband, "says the land is good and some of the people who opened it up are beginning to make a lot of money; so is the tax inspector. It's a really vicious circle. The more you make, the more you have to give away, and if you have a couple of bad seasons," she ended with a laugh, "they don't give you any back. When you're making good money they help you spend it; they only sit back when you go bankrupt. If they ever tell you that tobacco farmers make easy fortunes you can call them liars from me. For every one that makes a fortune, a hundred are struggling to make a living. If they do get rich, you can be sure they've earned every penny. You're lucky your fiancé is a city man – much safer."

"I'm not sure what he is at the moment," Marguerite replied. "He gave up his job when he left London. At the moment he's staying with his mother on their farm at Macheke. I expect he'll be broke by now. After we're married, we'll be living on this *sadza* he says the Africans eat."

"You won't have long before you see him. We should reach Salisbury in half an hour."

"I can't wait. It seems so long and yet it isn't even a month."

"A good sign," said the woman, laughing as she patted Marguerite's arm. "There's nothing more glorious for the middle-aged to see than a really good overdose of young love. And if I may say so, you seem to have got a pretty severe case."

"It seems silly doesn't it?" Marguerite said, and blushed a little at the sharp perception of her companion. "You know, we've been like this on and off for over a year. It's mentally most exhausting."

"It's good to see. There should be more of that and less of the bickering. A word of warning for married life – never nag and never bicker. Neither of them gets you anywhere, and after a long enough time they can build up to a living purgatory."

"I'll remember that," said Marguerite, "but I don't think we're the types who would nag and bicker at each other."

"You're lucky."

Marguerite strained for her first glimpse of civilisation for many a mile and the conversation fell away. The plane dropped lower and the farms became clearer and she could pick out the homesteads with the outbuildings clustered around them.

Through the heat haze she began to make out what seemed like a small village. The central cluster of buildings thrust up and away from the clutch of smaller buildings which fanned out and faded into the bush.

"What village are we coming up to?" she asked her neighbour.

"Village?" said Mrs Greene, leaning across and looking out of the window. "Oh my goodness," she said, laughing when she saw what it was, "you won't find anything bigger than that in this part of Africa. That's our capital Salisbury, with all its eighty-seven thousand European population. About the same number as the labour MPs win their seats by in Ebbw Vale."

"Oh" said Marguerite," considerably deflated, "I thought it was a city."

"It is," said Mrs Greene. "It's got a cathedral and at least three cinemas. It's not as nice as Bulawayo, it's too big."

"It doesn't look very big to me," said Marguerite, despondently.

"They never do from the air. Nairobi only looks a speck in the dust when you're flying over, but when we landed it seemed quite big. You'd better fasten your seatbelt as the landing light's just flashed on."

Marguerite withdrew into herself and watched, fascinated, as Salisbury grew larger. She saw the airfield was some distance from the city and thrilled at the thought of Tim waiting down there in one of those buildings.

The plane dipped and straightened, level with the long strip of the runway which rushed towards them. The wheels smacked at the tarmac and the aircraft was thrown up again. It bounced once more, had another go and finally settled firmly on the ground. The speed decreased and the blurred rush of the runway coming towards them and passing out of sight under the wings gradually became more solid and stable.

They taxied towards the large airport building with its clock tower. The whole was lost to her as the plane turned onto the apron and came to a halt. She tore off her safety belt and leaned across in front of Mrs Greene to look through the window on the other side. She could see little apart from the engine and impatiently waited for the aircraft door to be opened so that she could find Tim in the crowd of people she had glimpsed before they turned onto the apron. She hurriedly said goodbye to Mrs Greene when they stood up and crossed the aisle and knelt on the opposite seat to look out of the small window. People seemed to be in two groups, one at ground level, lounging on the barrier which separated them from the aircraft, and the other clustered out on the balcony, underneath the large clock tower.

She couldn't see Tim and her impatience wouldn't allow her to wait in the plane any longer; she irritably followed the other passengers down the aisle towards the door.

The burning sun seared at the back of her eyes as she broke into the sunlight. It was hot, but not as hot as she had feared. She stepped down onto the tarmac and felt Rhodesian soil under her feet for the first time. Till her eyes became accustomed to the sun, Marguerite was unable to focus on the faces. Then she caught sight of him to the right of the crowd by the barrier. He was waving to her and her heart leapt in excitement. She quickened her pace towards the gateway nearest to where he was standing and she saw him work his way through the crush to greet her. They hugged each other before she was told quite brusquely by an official that she had to go through into Immigration first.

"See you outside in a minute," he said with his wonderful smile.

The minute stretched into half an hour before Customs and Immigration were satisfied.

She had sent some of her luggage by sea: books, a typewriter, in fact everything bulky she could do without for a few weeks. What was left she and Tim put into the shooting brake. Then they were away and the waiting was completely over.

"Everything is arranged for Monday," he said taking one hand from the wheel and squeezing hers.

"Three days or so will be fine," she said, leaning across to kiss him behind the ear.

"You'll have me driving up that msasa tree," he said laughing and trying to press her head between his own and his shoulder.

"Don't do that," she said with a purr and a playful nip at his ear.

They didn't talk a great deal, being more than content to enjoy each other's simple presence. The road from the airport led along a good tarmac road and, driving fast, they quickly covered the seventeen-odd miles into the city.

She was conscious of everything being dry and flat. There was little colour to be seen in any direction, save for the crystal-blue sky, barely broken by the unmoving flecks of white cloud which alone seemed to brave the heat of the African sun. The car slowed down to go through Salisbury and Tim drove into and around the centre to point out the places of interest. A limp Union Jack flew from the pioneer column in Cecil Square, and behind it the fountains vied with the dry air. The trees around were green and so was the grass, in patches. As they drove by Meikles Hotel she was introduced to the second home of all tobacco farmers. In its youth the hotel had known dirt roads and horses, hitching posts and dung heaps; now it saw gleaming cars, a department store and droves of people trying to hurry along the pavements in the lunch hour. Tim turned up Jameson Avenue, passed the dominating statue of Cecil Rhodes, and joined the four-lane road signposted 'Marandellas and Umtali'.

"It's all so clean," Marguerite remarked, "and there isn't much traffic around."

"You should see it on a Saturday morning, you can't move for cars."

"Some of the buildings are enormous," she went on excitedly, "and much bigger than they look from the air."

"I like Salisbury," he agreed. "Plenty of air in the centre and plenty of space a few yards down the road."

The Umtali road soon left the clusters of neat bungalows behind. They passed enormous balancing rocks which seemed to be held in place by the hands of invisible giants, the points of contact no larger than a man's palm. Flat-topped trees showing a little green, never more than twelve feet high, sped past as the road cut its way through the open bush. Hills shimmered in the distant heat. Forty minutes later they turned off the main road onto a dirt track.

"Twenty-five miles of this and we'll be home," he said.

The corrugation was bad and Tim drove fast. The jolting force of pounding wheels on rough road became all-pervading. The speeding car hurtled on ahead of a blanket of dust, which settled on the already covered grass and trees which converged on either side. Tim swung to the left of the road and they passed another car going fast in the other direction. They ate each other's dust for a while.

Tim stopped the car, having gently edged it onto what might have been a soft verge.

"You can really feel the place in the middle of the day," he said.

She agreed with him. It was poignant, hushed, full of expectation, yet alive with the sounds of Africa – crickets, harsh and searing – birds, discordant yet mellow; and always the burning sun, pressing down on the stationary car.

They drove on and she began to realise what he meant about Rhodesia, but for the moment she was frightened. It was so big, and they were so much alone, just a spot, a tiny dot engulfed in its all-embracing grip.

She was looking forward to seeing the farmhouse and was a little surprised when Tim turned off the road down an avenue of tall gums which rose high and green-leafed above them, their thick trunks obviously long-established.

"Here we are," he said. "Welcome to my home and what shortly will be yours."

"But I had no idea everything was so developed from the way you spoke in London."

"We have been here for nearly forty years."

The avenue was long and cool, with the tall gums lacing together high above them. The road curved, and through the trees loomed a house, its colour making a sudden splash amid the well-watered, green foliage around them. Tim drove onto the circular driveway, enclosed by trelliswork which was itself engulfed and suffocated by heaps of bougainvillea. Four Bullmastiffs rushed down the steps which led from a long veranda, barking, not knowing who had arrived. Tim yelled to them to shut up and the barking subsided into the wagging of four imaginary tails; the stumps were all they had left.

He went round to the other side of the car and opened the door for Marguerite. She stepped out a little bewildered.

"Why, it's beautiful," she said.

"I suppose it is," he replied, and to convince himself he scanned the nearby scenery. "I must have got used to it."

"But there's so much colour."

There was: it seemed like a purple, yellow and green oasis, surrounded by dry grass away from the homestead.

"One of the boys will bring the things in, so don't worry about that," he went on, drawing her towards the steps with his arm around her waist.

A moment later his mother came out onto the veranda to welcome her future daughter-in-law. She was tall and thin, and the taut, papery skin of her face highlighted the hollows of her cheeks and bore witness to a lengthy sojourn beneath the African sun. Her movements and bearing were elegance itself.

For her part Mrs Carter was pleased, and very relieved at her first sight of this Marguerite her son had talked so much about. She looked young, fresh and healthy, pretty without make-up. She was not very fond of the painted girls that seemed to have come to prominence of late. She had always put this unwonted phenomenon down to a superfluity of spending money. There weren't enough young women in the country either, which no doubt enhanced their egos well beyond their normal bounds. This one at least seemed different, so she smiled a warm if slightly aloof smile as she turned to greet her.

"Hello, my dear. I do hope you're not finding it too hot... England, I believe, is still very cold, even in the summer."

"Hello, Mrs Carter," replied Marguerite, warmed by the reception which she felt was genuine. It made her less nervous, a little more certain of herself. "My idea of a beautiful day has always started with a clear blue sky overhead. It always makes me happy. So long as the sun shines, I don't mind how hot it is."

"We only have one bad month," Mrs Carter went on as she took Marguerite by the arm and led her into the house. "October can be unpleasant, but it's very soon over. In the forty years I have lived here I've never found it completely unbearable."

The lounge was a continuation of the veranda, only shuttered by two large folding doors for protection at night. Inside, the thatched roof rose steeply, suspended on thin, straight gum poles with no flat ceiling as such, and the coolness of the room was immediately apparent. The wooden block floor shone from many hours of polishing and reflected the stout gum beam which ran the width of the room above their heads. The fireplace was deep, and crossed below the heavy mantelpiece were two native spears. They looked like they would be excellent weapons in the right hands. The room was lightly furnished; a zebra skin rug, curling at the edges, held court alone in the centre. The chairs were covered in fresh white linen and a silver rose bowl, spilling over with yellow roses, sparkled on the highly polished bureau.

Mrs Carter rang the bell by the fireplace and an elderly, barefoot African, dressed in immaculate white uniform topped with a red fez, entered from the interior of the house. He matched the crispness of the surroundings perfectly.

"Shake hands when I introduce you," whispered Mrs Carter, fearing to embarrass Marguerite. "He's been with me for thirty years and I know he'd be pleased."

"Ah, Madazi," she said, turning to the African. "This is Miss Stearle, who will soon be Boss Tim's wife."

"Hello, Madazi," she said, going towards him with a smile and an outstretched hand.

Madazi gravely took the hand before replying. "May I welcome you to Urangwa for me and my people here. We all hope you will have much happy. God be with you."

The unexpected welcome, the gravity of it, and the sudden depth of feeling, brought tears to Marguerite's eyes.

"I'm sure I shall be happy," she replied simply but with genuine warmth.

"Would you bring us some tea, Madazi?" asked Mrs Carter.

"Yes, madam," he said and retreated calmly and gravely to make the tea.

"There aren't many like that left," said Mrs Carter, having half-read Marguerite's mind.

"The younger generation are somewhat the reverse," put in Tim. "Give them an inch and the next week they're asking for your house and car, but never your job. That would mean work and the younger Africans don't like work. The adage of getting married and sending your wife out to work is very much practised."

"I hope the idea hasn't spread to the European Rhodesians?" asked Marguerite, looking up at Tim with a wicked smile.

"I haven't heard of it recently," put in Mrs Carter, joining the joke.

"Personally, and from the male point of view, it's the answer, especially when you're allowed more than one wife to do the work," he said, trying not to laugh.

Marguerite took in everything, and even before the tea was served she felt at home. There was nothing forced, the atmosphere was gentle, and even the dogs, now resting by the fireplace, had calmed down. It was hot, and so they lay down, recovering from the intrusion of the car. There was no need to jump up and make a nuisance at Urangwa.

"How would you like to be married in this house?" asked Tim as he sat down in the white linen chair with a dish of tea held in both his hands.

"But I thought it had to be a church?" Marguerite said.

"The vicar makes an altar in the house and conducts the service. It's very common in the farming areas for Sunday services. With the nearest church sometimes sixty miles or more away, it wouldn't be possible to go very often."

Mrs Carter interjected, "A beautiful wedding dress would be perfect in this room. We could make everything look so lovely."

"I didn't know it was possible," answered Marguerite excitedly, "but I think it's a wonderful idea. And I already have my wedding dress brought with me from England."

"Oh, how wonderful... Many of our friends will be here," went on Mrs Carter. "They will be able to spill over onto the lawns and still hear the service. Tim has asked Steve Ritter to be his best man. He's a very old friend of Tim's – his father began Karilla at the same time as my husband opened up Urangwa. The Ritters and the Carters have always been more than good friends. It wasn't easy in the early days, and without each other's help they would never have survived. Many returned to civilisation, beaten by the heat, disease, the loneliness, but above all by the lack of water."

"It was ox wagons then," Tim put in, "tractors had barely been thought of in these parts of the world."

"To reach their farms," his mother continued, "they travelled along the old game rangers' route as far as it went in their direction and then they cut a way through the bush, along game tracks, and, when the compass bearing made it necessary, through the tall six-foot grass, bypassing msasa and sugar bush trees till eventually they pinpointed first Karilla and then Urangwa. Then with the six men they had each brought they split up to survey the farms. Once they'd found the easiest path for a roadway, and recruited a nucleus of local labour, they cut a track to the game rangers' route. They then brought up supplies on the wagons and separated again, fanning out to their farms, to build a pole and dagga in which to live. That was how they started."

"What's a pole and dagga?" asked Marguerite.

"Virtually a mud hut," replied Tim for his mother. "You build a framework of poles and then seal the gaps with mud."

"It sounds rather primitive."

"Even today, when new farming areas are opened up, the farmers live in a pole and dagga for a couple of years while they get themselves established. The first job is clearing the lands and building barns to cure the tobacco in. After that come grading sheds, for sorting out the cured leaves. Then workshops, wells, boreholes, roads and right at the end of the list a brick house in which to live."

"Is it worth it?" asked Marguerite, already knowing the answer.

"It's a way of life which you either like or you don't," Tim said with a shrug. "If you like it, the initial hardship and possible wealth at the end are incidental."

"It made rather a tyrant of Jock Ritter," said Mrs Carter, smiling, "but Steve is completely the opposite. He is as charming as his father is gruff. I've often thought he would make a magnificent surgeon. His hands are so sensitive."

Tim brought the conversation back to the main subject.

"You think it'll be a good idea to have the wedding in this house?"

"I think it's a wonderful idea," Marguerite replied.

"We hoped you would like it," said Tim's mother. "To be frank, I'm rather relieved. The invitations have already been sent out and the thought of phoning over a hundred people is frankly appalling."

"The next problem is a bridesmaid," said Tim.

"I didn't realise there were so many problems," answered Marguerite, laughing, "but I think you're doing a wonderful job."

"As a matter of fact I bought a book on the subject," replied Tim, a trifle embarrassed by the admission.

Both Mrs Carter and Marguerite were unable to control their laughter and only when it had died down was Tim able to get a word in edgeways, to recoup a little of his fallen ego.

"It's a magnificent little document. Why, it even tells you who you give presents to; a rather too comprehensive list, I might add. It has everything, in fact, for the bachelor turned bridegroom."

"And does it say bridesmaids are essential?" asked Marguerite.

"Most definitely."

"Well then, bridesmaids it must be. How many does the book require?"

"At least three."

"Do you think the publishers collect commission on the number of bridesmaids?"

"I don't think so. Why?"

"I just wondered." She loved teasing him, especially when he was trying to be frivolous and serious at the same time.

"The thing is, they all require presents."

"I thought they might."

"Have you got anyone in mind?" Marguerite asked.

"Well, I thought of one tall and two tiddlers in the form of Steve's sister Jenny and two of the Grant children."

"Who are the Grants?"

"They live on the next farm."

"That explains everything," she said, laughing. "How many children have they got?"

"Four, last time I counted."

"Ages?"

"Between two and eight."

"Boys or girls?"

"A mixture."

"Really, Tim," interjected his mother.

"I meant, of course, boys and girls."

"Never be afraid to say what you mean," Mrs Carter said with a wink at Marguerite. "You will always be faced with the problem of keeping him under strict control, I'm afraid."

"I think I can manage," she replied.

"Getting back to the matter at hand," Tim said somewhat stiffly, "you still haven't picked your bridesmaids."

"Why don't we walk round to the Grants and then I can take my pick?"

"Well to start with, the house is five miles away."

"But I thought you said it was the next farm?"

"So it is."

"Large farms," she replied, pulling a face.

"You'll have to make a lucky dip."

"Does the book allow for page boys?"

"I think it does, but I can check," he said, putting down his tea.

"Let's not check, but just assume. What do you say to Jenny Ritter, a child bridesmaid and a page boy? You can pick the Grant children as you probably know the ones least likely to tread on the hem of my dress."

"Settled. The next problem is time."

"I put eleven o'clock on the invitations," interjected Mrs Carter quickly.

"We'd better stick to eleven then," replied Tim, "we don't want to upset the guests. Time eleven o'clock... Marguerite's dress: a dress soon to be revealed... Tim: morning coat, without top hat, patent leather shoes, as I can't afford leather... In attendance: two bridesmaids, one long, one short, also a Grant boy who should never be underestimated as his size and weight, though small, provide a considerable amount of nuisance... The date: Monday 5th September 1960. And that gives me three and a half days of bachelorhood," he finished hurriedly.

"I think you'd better call it off," said Marguerite, teasing.

"No, no, I'll stick it out."

"Are you sure you can manage?"

"I have every hope of sustenance."

"All's well that ends well: Shakespeare," she replied.

"With a little bit of luck: Lerner and Loewe."

"Shaw."

"Quite, thanks."

"Bernard, you idiot."

"Another cup of tea?" asked Mrs Carter.

"If I may," replied Marguerite.

"Of course you can."

And as Mrs Carter passed the fresh cup of tea, she said, "I thought it would be nice if you met the Grants and Ritters before the wedding, so I invited them to dinner for tomorrow." Her mind went forward. "I wonder if the vicar could be persuaded to join us? I'll ask him anyway. He's an absolute dear. And that reminds me, he must be nearly fifty."

"Are you referring to his girth or his age?" asked Tim with a laugh.

"Come, come," said his mother, "he isn't that large, not quite anyway. No, I was referring to his birthday." Turning to Marguerite she added, "He's been a good friend of the family for many years, so we take a little licence occasionally."

"He sounds great fun," said Marguerite.

"He is, he is."

"Mother, do you mind if I take Marguerite to the club for a drink? I can't wait to show her off."

"We dine at eight o'clock. We always eat later at this time of year," she added for Marguerite's benefit, "to avoid the heat. When the sun has been down for a couple of hours it is very much cooler. The temperature can drop by as much as fifteen degrees." And turning back to Tim: "Shall we say seven-thirty then, to provide time for a cocktail before dinner?"

Tea was finished and Mrs Carter rang the bell for Madazi to collect the tray. The dogs got up and walked out onto the veranda. They looked bored with the conversation.

"May I show you your room?" asked Mrs Carter, rising. "I expect you would like to wash and change before going out."

"I'll have a quick look at the seedbeds while you're getting ready," said Tim.

"I'll be about half an hour," Marguerite told him as she rose to follow Mrs Carter.

And, as they went, Tim heard his mother telling Marguerite about seedbeds: about the small, delicate tobacco seedlings which would shortly be put out in the lands with only a pint of water slopped on top of each one to last till the rains arrived.

It was only five-thirty when they met on the lawn half an hour later. She was wearing a bright yellow cotton dress. He had just found time to change into a clean shirt after making sure the seedbeds had been watered properly. They walked close to a gardenia bush and the perfume from the white, rose-like flowers was strong and fragrant. She looked up at him and smiled. He squeezed her waist and they walked on round the well-kept garden, now bursting with colour. After a while he said, "I didn't mention in my letters that the manager left three days after I got back."

"Who's looking after the farm at the moment?"

"I am, with the assistant, but he's only twenty and doesn't know much about tobacco. It takes at least four years' experience before you can grow a crop alone. The manager had been with us for ten years, in fact ever since my father died."

"Why did he leave?"

"He'd been married four years and couldn't see any future here for his two young children. He was young enough to start again elsewhere, so he took the plunge for the children's sake and went off to a ranch in Queensland. He was offered a job through some friends and asked mother if he could leave straight away. The new tobacco season had only just started and as luck would have it, I'd just arrived home, so off we went."

"Are you looking for a new manager?"

"Yes, but it's very difficult to find a good one who will stay for any length of time. If they grow a couple of good crops for you, their bonus can give them enough money for a crown land farm. The Government loan you the land, and if you've got five thousand pounds the Land Bank will lend the same again. With credit for fertiliser, there's enough money in the kitty to build a dozen barns and grow a crop. If we change the manager every couple of seasons we're sure to get a bad one sooner or later, and a bad manager can lose the previous five years' profit in a couple of seasons."

They found two chairs nestling in the arbour at the end of the lawn. The trelliswork of the arbour was saturated in tumbling red bougainvillea. They sat down and rejoined their hands.

He looked into her eyes.

"Would you like to live here for good?" he asked seriously.

"How do you mean? You could never get to an office in Salisbury every morning from here."

"What I'm trying to say is, I don't think I ought to take a job in Salisbury, I think I ought to run this farm."

She looked around her without speaking. She took in the beauty of the thatched roof, the tall trees, some of which were trying to bud, the flowers, the well-cut lawn; but above all the peace which surrounded her.

"I could be very happy here," she said at length.

"I hoped you'd say that."

He pressed her hand.

"I never thought I'd be a farmer's wife."

"You'd better have some time to sleep on it."

"If you've slept on it, that's enough for me."

"There are lots of problems of course, starting with the fact that I've only done three years in tobacco and anyway I'm out of date. Steve Ritter says he'll help me as much as I want. Then there is where to live when we're married. I don't think mother will want us on top of her. She's far too independent, and however well you get on, it would be a two-sided argument."

"Don't let's worry too soon, darling. I'm sure we'll be able to solve these problems as we come across them."

"You're the most wonderful thing in my life," he said, hugging her. And then holding her at arm's length he added, "Can I go and show you off at the club now?"

"I sound like a prize tobacco plant, off to the Agricultural Show," she laughed.

"You're teasing again," he said as they walked away, arm in arm, towards the car.

The bar was empty save for the club manager, a man in his late fifties, tough, sun-scorched, and outspoken.

"Hello, Tim," he called, "it's nice to see someone. I thought you farmers had all lain down with your seedbeds to keep the caterpillars away."

"Come off it, they're not that bad," Tim joked back as they reached the front of the bar. "This is my fiancée, Colin, Marguerite Stearle. Marguerite, meet Colin Mandy."

The formal introduction having been completed, the manager leant across the bar in a mock attempt at ensuring no one, including Tim, could hear that he was about to confide.

"May I say in the strictest confidence that, unknowingly, you have been the saving of my sanity. I arrived at this club from Kenya six months ago, and during that time I have heard talk of nothing but tobacco, babies and houseboys. The first I know nothing about and cannot, therefore, add a grain of intelligence to the conversation; the second, fortunately, I have forgotten about, being as it is a distant relic of my youth; and the last are bloody natives we have no cause to mention. In the depths of my melancholia your name came through, and for three weeks Tim has held the floor while tobacco, babies and houseboys took a well-earned, or should I say flogged-out, rest."

She was laughing.

"But surely there must be other sources of conversation?"

"I've never heard them."

"You make us out to be a terrible colony of shop-talkers," Tim grumbled.

But still, he knew Colin was right. Everything did centre around tobacco: it had to, it was their livelihood. Any information was continually being gleaned from friends to provide possible answers to the many problems of growing a profitable crop.

Colin Mandy changed the subject to a more fertile area which he knew well – some said too well. He spoke again to Marguerite.

"Be my guest for your first drink in the club. What will you have?"

"A gin and tonic, please."

"Coming up." He turned to the bar. "What's yours, Tim?"

"A beer please, Colin."

He set down the drinks, completed his own execution of a double whisky – Marguerite was sure he only used four mouthfuls – and then:

"Will you excuse me for a while? Without my wife around anymore I find bachelorising a little difficult to manage. Food, for instance, though essential, is often a damn nuisance when you have to organise it yourself. Help yourselves to another drink if you like and just let me know if the bar gets too full."

He pushed up a section of the bar counter and the heavy, now fat-covered shoulders eased their way through.

The club was serviceable but not elaborate. Tall stools were ranged below the solid timber bar. Wicker tables and chairs were scattered inside, and beyond the large French windows they spilled onto the red polished concrete of the stoep. Two large overhead fans, the size and weight of old aeroplane propellers, turned lazily in the heat. A few photographs of people holding cups and spoons were dotted around the walls and from behind the bar, the rows of bottles, mirrored by the glass behind, looked down on it all.

When Colin's footsteps had died away, Marguerite asked, "What was he doing in Kenya? He doesn't look the kind of person to have run a club all his life."

"Cheers again," said Tim before replying, and they raised their glasses silently to each other.

"No, you're right about the club. He certainly hasn't been a barman all his life. He ranched for thirty years."

"For someone else?"

"Oh no, he had a ten thousand hectare farm of his own. Still has, for what they're worth."

"Why did he leave? I thought everything in Kenya had been settled when the Mau Mau Rebellion was put down."

Tim played with his glass before answering.

"'Put down' is probably right, as in 'down underground'. Colin left because of a culmination of threats, blackmail and a lack of incentive to fight anymore. It all started when the Mau Mau killed his wife and carved marks on his back while they drank her blood. Oh don't shudder, it's all true. If only a few people would wake up to reality, a further tragedy in Kenya might be avoided."

She seemed to want to hear more, so he went on.

"He wanted legal revenge for his wife at first, but no one outside the Europeans in Africa was interested, so the months passed into years and nothing of value came about. His labour force became too frightened to work for him. If they did, their huts were burned, or worse. The situation became more and more unpleasant, so Colin, having unsuccessfully tried to sell his ranch for any price he could get, put as much as possible in his car and drove south. He had little in the way of money, just the price of thirty very thin cattle, all that were left out of what had been thousands of healthy black steers. He got to Salisbury and someone put him into this job and he's been here ever since. His only failing is the bottle, but who could blame him?"

Slowly, the words took shape in Marguerite's mind. The picture became real, not just something that had happened to someone else. The man who she had just seen drink a double whisky in four gulps had been through all this. His agony and frustration suddenly snapped into full, horrifying focus.

At length she spoke some of her thoughts out loud.

"It all seemed so far away in England."

There was a bitter tone in his voice when he replied, "Yes, and what the eye doesn't see, the man in the street doesn't grieve about."

"Couldn't he ranch here?" she asked hopefully.

"What with? He's no money and his next birthday puts a nought on the six."

"It doesn't seem right." She wanted to mitigate the situation somehow.

"No, it doesn't, but that's part of the joy of living in Africa." He grinned mirthlessly. "Shall we have another drink to cheer ourselves up?"

She tried to smile.

"I think we'd better."

Tim pushed up the flap in the bar counter and reached for the gin bottle, took a tonic from the fridge under the bar, deftly cut a slice of lemon, joined the three together in a glass and handed it across to Marguerite.

"You make a wonderful barman," she laughed.

"I always knew I'd missed my vocation." He promptly disappeared from view to forage for a cold beer in the fridge.

After he had removed the top, she watched him quietly pour the beer down the side of a large glass and expertly end up with an eighth of an inch of froth.

"Tim?"

"Yes, darling?"

"How long have I been in Africa?"

He looked at his watch.

"About four and a half hours."

"Incredible, it seems more like a couple of years."

"You don't feel lost away from England?"

"I suppose I should really – feel strange anyway – but I don't. Let's hope it stays that way."

"I'm sure it will," he replied, and just had time to squeeze her hand before someone came into the bar. He turned to see who it was.

"Hello, Steve," he said. "You couldn't have timed it better. Darling, this is Steve Ritter, our best man-to-be. Steve, meet Marguerite Stearle."

"Hello, Marguerite. I feel I know you well enough already from Tim's conversation these past weeks."

She smiled at him happily.

"Tim and his mother have been telling me all about you as well."

"I hope they were nice about me."

She shook his strong, sensitive hand. "They were."

He was tall, over six foot, though never held himself to his full height as if not wishing to embarrass people who were shorter. The most striking thing about Steve Ritter was the sensitivity of his face: each angle of the nose and cheeks, the chin and mouth, the hair and forehead, was gentle.

She liked him immediately.

Without asking, Tim poured him a beer in a pint tankard and returned again to the right side of the bar.

"Have you cleaned me out of liquor?" Colin Mandy demanded, reappearing.

"Not quite," said Tim, laughing. "You came back before we could drive the truck up to the back door." He paid him for the drinks and a double whisky, the whisky he had more than probably come back for.

They explained their plans for the wedding to Steve and as the time drew closer to seven-fifteen the bar filled. All the customers knew each other and seemed more than pleased to meet up again. Marguerite was introduced to a lot of people but couldn't remember a single name. Seedbeds were discussed from all conceivable, and some inconceivable, angles. The wives seemed to ignore their husbands and seated themselves at the tables. Marguerite couldn't hear their conversation but assumed it was about babies and houseboys after a further soliloquy from Colin Mandy on the subject. The manager was nearly drunk but nobody blamed him for it.

"We'd better get back," Tim said to Marguerite, "it takes ten minutes for the drive."

"That's a very good idea. I don't want your mother to think I keep you late at the bar." She nudged him playfully, nearly causing him to fall off the stool.

"I think I'd better make a move as well," agreed Steve.

"We'll see you at dinner tomorrow?" Tim said.

"Seven-thirty."

"Fine."

"Cheerio, Colin."

"Goodnight."

They waved to a number of others as they threaded their way to the door. Outside they took leave of Steve at the door and walked across to the car. Marguerite was surprised to find how cool it was after the heat of the day. The dry heat of Salisbury airport seemed far away from the freshness of the night around them. The car started and the noise thundered into the darkness. Their headlights thrust a strong beam between the parked cars. Steve went out in front of them and they waited, not wishing to eat his dust. Two minutes later Tim let the shooting brake roll forward through the gate and gather speed along the dirt road. To Marguerite, they seemed to be driving through a dark tunnel which forged on through the grass and trees, their way picked out by the powerful lights. A rabbit, mesmerised by the headlights, jerked from side to side at great speed before flashing out into the darkness again. Insects splattered the windscreen. The car pounded on through the blackness and for them their only world was the car and the speed at which they travelled.

Soon, the car beams circled towards the house and lit up the veranda. They were home. A light glowed from the inner sanctum and Marguerite felt happy to be back at Urangwa. The sight of the house was big and comforting; something solid amidst so much nothing, so much unknown, either side of the car's headlights. Tim killed the engine and they were plunged into darkness. They left the car in the driveway and as they climbed the steps, the lights of the veranda came on and Madazi welcomed them home.

Mrs Carter joined them. Drinks were served and later, by the light of candles, they enjoyed an excellent dinner. Soon after ten they retired.

Alone in her bedroom, Marguerite wondered about her future years in Africa. As she started nodding off the picture became hazy, the problems receded, and the general feeling was only of warmth and happiness. By the time she fell into a sound sleep, she was content. She didn't dream.

7

THE FIRE, SEPTEMBER 1960

"I'd make an exhibition of them," Jock Ritter said. "For every riot take a batch and shoot them."

"But you can't, Father, it goes against all the ideas we're trying to convey to them."

"I know we can't, but it still doesn't alter the fact that it's a damn good idea... That fellow Hsoudedi I'd shoot."

"And if he knew you, he'd probably say, 'when I run this country, I'll shoot that man Ritter'."

"He'll run this country over my dead body," thundered Steve's father, the colour running to his already red face.

Tim interjected, "But there must be a civilised way of convincing them they are only defeating their own ends."

Jock Ritter gripped the edge of the dining table and thrust forward at Tim. "When in Rome, my boy, do as the Romans... These people are not civilised and if you want any proof have a look at Colin Mandy's back... Civilised! That's barbarism! Savagery is the only thing they understand. Ten years ago I never reasoned with a *munt*: when he stole I just hit him and the harder it was, the longer it prevented him from trying again. Now I have to drive him thirty miles to a police station to charge him, and three days later do the same journey to be a witness, while the darling little savage understands not an iota of what the hell's going on... When they let him out of gaol a couple of weeks later they send him back to me with a little bow, love and kisses and the sweetest note saying he's cured, and when I kick the little bastard off my farm they wonder why. If I'd hit him in the first place he'd have understood, respected me, not lost his job, and his fellow workers would have thought him a fool to have tried. 'Got what he deserved.' The whole thing would have been over and done with."

"Progress has a number of teething troubles, Dad," Steve explained patiently.

"Progress! You sound like a first-rate propagandist for the progress of the mighty American dollar, the root cause of every trouble in this country."

He turned to Mrs Carter and put his hand on hers where it rested lightly on the table's edge.

"If Jack had been alive I'd have had a real ally in such arguments, eh Clara?" And turning to his wife, without waiting for a reply, "Don't you agree, my dear?"

"There are probably truths in both arguments," suggested Mrs Ritter calmly. She was used to interceding between her husband and her son. A placid and practical woman, she was the perfect counterpart to her bombastic husband. Someone once asked if she minded his outbursts: 'Of course not. It's always better to get rid of such things than to hold them in.'

Her husband went on as he pushed away his coffee cup.

"Clara, your dinners are always excellent, quite excellent."

"You always appreciate them, Jock." She had always found his nickname a little hard to use but Jock Ritter answered to nothing else and once, when he had asked her to 'call me Jock', it seemed such a breach of confidence not to do so. Thirty years of use, however, had not changed the hardness of the word.

"Shall we move onto the veranda?" suggested Mrs Carter. "The chairs are so much more comfortable." She made to rise.

"The Romans certainly had the answer for mealtimes," agreed

Steve as he helped to move the chair away from Mrs Carter. "Eat, drink and recline on a full-length couch."

"It must have been awfully messy using their fingers," spoke up his sister Jenny, a rather weak-minded girl who had few ideas of her own. She was pretty, which helped, but it didn't help enough.

The vicar had fallen silent, which was surprising. He was well fed, a feeling he greatly enjoyed and wished in no way to disturb. He was forced to rise and cover the space between the dining room and the veranda. He made the journey at last and eased his ample proportions into the chair next to Marguerite. He leant slowly across and addressed Tim who had found a comfortable chair on her other side.

"You're a lucky man."

"I know I am," said Tim, taking her hand.

"Yes, I thought you did," mused the vicar, subsiding back into his place.

Mrs Carter was still preoccupied in her role as hostess.

"Tim, I think the men may like a brandy. Vicar, can my son pour you one?"

"Well, since you suggest it, my dear Clara, I think I am forced to accept, though I do so willingly." This last was said with a small turn of the head and a twinkle in his eye which even the subdued light of the veranda could not suppress.

"Jock, will you have a cognac?"

"I don't think it will take up much room so I'll join you."

Steve took one as well and after Tim had handed them round, a satisfied silence fell on the veranda. As they all contentedly digested their meal, cigar smoke curled high in the still night air from the chairs of the vicar and Jock Ritter.

Mrs Carter broke the spell; her mind had broken on a vivid picture of her husband and she wished to talk and ease the pain.

"It's amazing how a family diminishes for a while and then grows again." She was looking at Marguerite and her voice betrayed her feeling.

"I know what you're thinking," said Mrs Ritter kindly, and added, "It always happens that way. We can't alter it."

"I know, but it's such a pity he can't see his only son married."

The vicar spoke. "There are many things that bring unhappiness in our lives, but to give us strength in our wanderings there is also happiness. God willing, the two will balance out over the span of a lifetime."

The sound of his voice ran gently over the company and out into the night, but what he said had left comfort in its wake. Mrs Carter smiled.

"You are always so right, vicar. You have dispelled any thought of self-pity and made me thankful, once again, for all the good things in life."

"It's never easy to isolate a problem," went on the vicar, "and view it in its complete context. As is often the case, however," and here he laughed, or more exactly he rendered a gentle, vibrant chuckle, "it is easier to solve other people's problems than your own."

"Come now, vicar, you haven't any problems," put in Tim. "I've never even seen a worried look on your face."

"You do me a disservice, Timothy. You must agree that life would be very dull without problems, and for myself, I have never found life dull for even a moment, which only goes to show that I must have problems."

"On second thoughts, I can see you do have a problem. Your glass is empty."

The vicar took with both hands the glass which was handed to him before going on.

"There you are! My world is full of problems."

"I wish all problems were the size of yours," said Marguerite, smiling.

"Come now, young lady, we should not have talk of problems from such a pretty person at such a time. And anyway" – and here he mock-whispered in her ear – "if you have any problems after Monday you can turn them over to Timothy."

They all laughed.

"I'll remember that," said Marguerite.

"And so will I," Tim added.

The trees outside began to move and a cool breeze broke unexpectedly over the veranda.

Jock Ritter commented, "If it was December and not September I'd say rain was close." He was always alert to any changes in the weather, an essential quality for a successful tobacco farmer.

The wind subsided and once more complete stillness prevailed. It didn't last; a stronger wind bent the trees and plucked at their clothes, and even in September made them think of cold.

Subconsciously Tim had smelt burning, brought in by the wind, but failed to let it register in his conscious mind.

Jock Ritter, always restless, rose and went to the steps to take in as much of the cool wind as possible. His voice cut sharply into the evening.

"Tim, come here."

He could smell it now and knew before he reached the steps.

"It's the Grants' farm, isn't it?" Jock Ritter said without turning.

By this time they had all left their seats and were looking towards the red glow of fire which spread between the gum trees, probably four miles away.

"Madazi!" It was Tim's voice, loud and urgent.

The African answered immediately; he too had smelt the burning bush.

"Sound the *simby*," Tim told him briefly. "Tell the men to get down to the barns as quickly as possible, I'll meet them there with the five-ton truck."

Jock Ritter spoke to Mrs Carter.

"Can you look after my family for a while? We won't have much time with a wind like this behind it."

"Of course. You must do what needs to be done."

He spoke again to Tim.

"Where is the straightest piece of road between here and that fire?"

"About a mile down the road to the club, there's a turnoff to the Grants' farm which cuts sharply to the right. That's probably our best bet."

"Steve, you go and get the men," ordered his father, "I'll go with Tim. We'll meet along that road and burn a fifty yard wide break along the side nearest the fire. Get all the boys you can lay your hands on."

Then, "I hope to hell Fairburn's seen it as well." He turned to Mrs Carter: "Can you phone him in case and tell him what we're doing?"

Without a word Tim's mother hurried into the house.

He looked at the fire again as Steve brought the car out of the driveway, the engine revving at high pitch. "It must be half a mile long at the front. The Grants will be lucky tonight not having a thatched roof. Let's go."

He led the way determinedly down the steps, his chin forced hard to one side.

The vicar, having resigned himself to indigestion, followed remarkably quickly. For once the size of his proportions failed to impede his movement.

The metallic clang of the *simby* broke into the night. The four Bullmastiffs moved out onto the veranda, down the steps and onto the lawn. One cocked up his leg at the tree in the centre of the lawn while the other three bayed at the night in anything but unison. Satisfied, the straggler lowered his leg and began to howl along with them.

By the time Tim's car reached the barns, the first of the men had begun to assemble. Tim went for the truck after telling Philip, the young assistant, summoned from his bed by the *simby*, to get as many of the men out of the compound as possible into the truck and bring the stragglers in the car to the crossroads.

Five minutes later the truck moved off with over sixty men packed on board and ground its way towards the crossing. Jock Ritter stood on the running board, holding on with one hand through the open window. With the vicar inside, the cabin was seriously cramped.

The vicar shouted above the engine noise.

"You'll have to excuse my ignorance but why don't we make for the fire and try to beat it out?"

"It's going too fast," Tim shouted back, half turning his face, "probably moving forward at bursts of up to ten miles an hour with this wind. You'd be hard pressed to run ahead of it, let alone try and put it out. If we burn a break we may have a chance of stopping it jumping the road."

The vicar fell silent and thought about it doing just that. He had seen bush fires, many of them, and with quite a number he had joined the beaters in putting them out, but he'd never been anywhere near one travelling at ten miles per hour. He was quite sure he would never be able to run at such an inordinate speed. He estimated his normal walking pace at one and a half miles per hour at best, and the thought of increasing this by nearly seven times was indeed ludicrous. The vicar cast the impossible from his mind and set about a determined concentration of mind to stop the fire jumping the road.

The truck swung right at the intersection and Tim brought it to a standstill. The headlights beamed along a straight, clean road until they faded in the distance.

As the engine stopped, the sound of the fire took hold and the wind deposited ash in its flight. The red gash in the night flared and hurled a cascade of burning sparks into the air.

Jock Ritter took command.

"We'll fan the men out along the side of the road nearest the fire and burn up towards the main inferno; it'll burn slowly with the wind against it."

In Shona, he ordered the men to each cut a length of brush from the trees. Most had already done so – they knew the ravages of fire as well as the boss.

"If the men can stop our own fire jumping back across the road, we should be all right. We'll have to burn a mile. With another hundred men we could do it."

He made three fire brands, handed one each to the vicar and Tim, then posted the men behind the proposed new fire line and on its wings. They started to burn with the main fire less than an hour away.

The dry bush, in parts waist high, dotted with msasa trees, caught quickly. Fire ate its way into the wind. A dry-as-tinder patch flared high and the wind showered the other side of the road with sparks. Smaller fires started; the wind fanned these pirate fires while the men beat at the flames. The boss boy, Shadrac, wheeled five men onto a fire getting away from the beater; sheer weight of numbers put it out. Tim grinned at the boss boy who over twenty years had taught him most of what he really knew about Africa. Shadrac grinned back. He too had no intention of letting that fire catch a hold on the wrong side of the road.

The car arrived with the assistance and six more men. Jock Ritter waited anxiously for the sound of his own truck. It would take time, that he knew; seven miles had to be covered there and back. From the opposite direction, above the sound of the fire and the wind, he heard a truck; a thread of light jerked from side to side on the rough road, stopped, ejected African men, went on and ejected more.

"That'll be Gary," he called.

"Yes," shouted Tim, without looking up from the firebrand he was methodically drawing along the grass.

He couldn't shake off the constant feeling of ineffectiveness. Hell, the damn fire was moving towards their puny little firebreak too fast; they'd never burn a mile. If it jumped the road it would get the house, it must, there was nothing else to stop it. He tried to conquer the heavy feeling in his feet. He had to get the fire out; they had to get it out. He seemed to be working so slowly, so damn slowly. Everything was so much bigger than them. He looked up; everything seemed to be standing still except the oncoming fire, and that was moving faster. Damn the bloody thing, he wanted to rush at it in his frustration, with his bare hands. But, when he wanted to, his legs seemed rooted to the ground.

"We'll make it yet," called Jock Ritter as he passed on forward to burn another patch.

'The old boy looks as though he's enjoying it,' laughed Tim to himself and felt better, much better. The heavy sensation in his legs left him. His body responded more quickly, more urgently, to the dictates of his mind, and with the upsurge of confidence his pessimism vanished.

The vicar was puffed; a little too much bending over was inclined to prevent air circulating properly through the considerable chest.

They each burnt a patch, caught up with the other, jumped ahead. Behind, a line of fire advanced slowly away from the roadside. Africans were lit up by the patches of fire they thrashed at; the Europeans moved steadily forward, from the light into the darkness.

The truck had disgorged its cargo and rattled itself to a halt alongside the three white men.

"I say, vicar, don't you think you might do yourself a permanent injury? I mean, it's a bit out of your sphere." Gary Fairburn could never have been mistaken about the identity of the crouched figure rolling from side to side with a firebrand in its hand.

"My dear fellow," bellowed back the vicar – he loathed extending his larynx but wished to defend himself – "if you remove yourself from the sanctity of that truck, it'll be my pleasure to do *you* a permanent injury."

"What will you do?"

"I'll roll on you."

"I take back all I said under such a threat."

"Well might you do so." And the vicar broke into a little run before burning a fresh patch ahead of Tim.

"How many did you bring, Gary?" asked Jock Ritter as the other farmer took a light from his firebrand.

"About forty."

"Thanks for coming."

"Don't be damn stupid, what did you expect me to do, sit on my arse?"

"Such words," interposed the vicar, as he moved forward again, "and I always thought him a gentleman."

The wind freshened and the ash from the oncoming fire thickened. The proliferating mass of flames seemed to be moving faster. Tongues of flame seared into the sky and started fires forward of the main mass.

Twenty minutes had gone by and Jock Ritter gauged that the main conflagration would meet them in less than half an hour. One third of a mile was burning behind them and the strip of burnt, smouldering stubble was growing wider. In patches the charred ribbon of scorched earth widened to fifty yards, and within that ribbon and the five yards of the adjacent road, there was nothing left that would burn. But there was still no sign of Steve, and the line of beaters was getting thin.

Tim became anxious and his loathing of the relentless power of the oncoming fire renewed; it never wavered, simply came on, seemingly faster, coughing, spluttering, and emitting a deep roar full of menace.

They worked faster and Shadrac, seeing the fire was winning, swung as many men as he could from the far end of the line to the front and himself took a firebrand and joined the Europeans.

They sweated in the heat.

Suddenly Steve's lights swung in from the crossroads and the big truck gathered speed again.

"Drop them off up ahead; start burning a line opposite the other end of the main fire," bellowed his father as the truck went by.

"I've got about fifty," shouted back his son.

"Good."

"Are you all right, vicar?" asked Jock Ritter.

"Fine."

"We should win now."

Steve began to burn from the other direction. A thread of fire sprang up and forged into the wind. Three fires: if the two smaller ones joined they could put out the larger.

Steve dreaded fire, not because of the crops but because of the animals. They would be frightened ahead of that hideous wall of flame; the weak encircled by the crackling inferno, growing hotter and hotter till it burnt first their fur, then their flesh, and blessedly, at the last, their life.

The main fire gathered speed and it was soon obvious that the two smaller fires would not have time to join. The heat became intense and the air grew full of ash, rather than sparks. The noise mounted and there, in front of the fire, between that and the smaller one, a leopard. It stopped in the face of the oncoming flames, uncertain of its path. The heat grew closer. The leopard tried to move away but then it was nearer the smaller fire. There was no way out. The gap shortened; the heat intensified from both sides; the animal stood stark against the fire. Steve was sick, not even bothering to turn his back from the boys. Flames grew on the leopard's back and it sank slowly. The two fires raced towards each other, drawn by the suction of hot air above. A great rush at the end and flames shot fifty feet into the night sky and then, as suddenly as it had flared up it finished, and the only flames came from the gap where the two smaller fires hadn't joined.

The fire had shrunk, but soon, if they couldn't beat it out, it would grow again.

"Get the bloody trucks out of here and pick up the men," bellowed Jock Ritter. "We're going to win even if we have to suffocate it with weight of numbers. Concentrate on putting out the patches away from what's left of the main fire." He spoke the last in Shona as he led the way.

They had only delayed the fire as it jumped the road and caught hold on the opposite side. More men ran up to help and then the trucks came back and the business started in earnest.

If you concentrated on your own bit of fire for too long, you'd find another burning at your back and then you ran for it.

The Europeans moved along the road, keeping track of the fire, shouting here and there at an African about to be encircled by flames.

Shadrac and Tim saw him at the same time. A *piccanin* probably about fourteen, kneeling, petrified, in the centre of a fire. His black skin shone with the sweat that was pouring off him. The fire was zeroing in on him steadily, methodically, relentlessly, a solid wall rising six feet high in parts. Tim saw a gap where the flames had dropped, seemingly to catch their breath in preparation for the final scourge. He started to run and Shadrac tried to stop him. He sidestepped; the African only clawed at his sleeve. Tim ran into the twenty-feet-wide lane of fire. His trousers, a good pair from the dinner party, caught alight and the pain stabbed into him. He was through the flames, now himself burning. He grabbed the *piccanin* who screamed in terror. Tim hit him, hard, picked up the limp body and began the slower, more painful journey back. The flames flared up around him and his eyes were red and blinded. He stumbled on, staggered. Hell, he wasn't even sure which way to go...was he walking away from or back into the fire? His mind was clear, too bloody clear, but all he could see with his eyes was a red wall of fire. Then the heat began to press on his lungs and all he could breathe was smoke, harsh, pungent and suffocating.

Strong black arms took the *piccanin* from him and he followed the dim shape out of the fire before losing consciousness.

They rolled him in the grass and tore off his smouldering clothes; underneath he was as black as the Africans. They put the flames out on Shadrac and the *piccanin*. Jock Ritter sent Philip back to Urangwa with Tim and the two Africans. Few had seen the incident and those that had, turned back to the fire to find that it hadn't waited for them to finish their rescue mission.

Off to one side, the vicar was convinced he had lost a stone in weight and tried manfully to remind himself that there was always good in any evil. Where an African began to lose ground he helped, and if it wasn't enough, he concentrated even harder.

Further round, Gary Fairburn continued to encourage the beaters in Shona, spoken with an immaculate Oxford accent.

Steve fought the fire as if it were his personal enemy... He was bent on revenge, and angry, very angry, something he hadn't been in many years.

Jock Ritter kept track of the burning front. Slowly they were stopping its spread, containing the fire in islands surrounded by burnt stubble. The islands burnt lower and then only glowed; but as yet they were not out, only cowed, watching for a chance to rise again.

Jock posted a gang to watch the smouldering bush and the rest climbed into the trucks. They were singed, sweaty and exhausted.

Steve was conscious of the effort involved in taking his foot off the clutch and the truck, in sympathy, kept its speed to ten miles an hour. Steve's mind was so dull, now that it was all over, that he failed to change gear. They rolled on at the slow speed, the human cargo in the back lurching gently from side to side. Many were lulled to sleep by the rocking motion. They were all content, whether awake or asleep, at having beaten the fire. Beside Steve, the vicar sat staring through the windscreen, seeing nothing.

Gary told his driver to take the truck back and organise some food and drink for those left behind. He then told his span there would be no work the next day. He drove back to Urangwa in Tim's truck, with Tim's men in the back completely silent, an almost unheard-of state for Africans. In the other seat, Jock Ritter was asleep.

Tim regained consciousness in the car and the pain sliced into him.

"How are you doing?" asked the assistant.

"Bloody awful."

"We're nearly there."

"Where?"

"Urangwa."

"Do I look a fright?"

"'Fraid so."

"Can we drive to your place first and clean the mess up a bit? I don't want to frighten Marguerite." His mind wandered and then came back again.

"What happened to the *piccanin*?"

"He's in the back. So's Shadrac."

"What's he doing there?"

"Same reason."

The pain caught him for a while and he concentrated on getting the better of it.

"How did he get burnt?"

"Fishing you out."

"I couldn't see who it was."

Tim couldn't turn round so he called instead.

"Shadrac?"

"Yes, boss?"

"Thanks."

Silence fell in the car and Tim began to pinpoint the sources of pain. His feet and ankles were the main offenders, his elbows too. There was a scorched patch between his thighs.

"I can't smell burning flesh, so it can't be too bad," he joked.

The car swung into the driveway and drew up below the veranda. The lights were still on.

"I thought we were going to your place?" Tim said, registering where he was.

"They'll look after you better here."

"That wasn't the point." And then he couldn't be bothered to argue anymore, everything hurt too much.

Inside, Marguerite heard the car and ran from the kitchen where she was helping Mrs Carter prepare a large drum of cocoa for the boys when they came back from the fire. Mrs Carter had seen a number of fires on or near Urangwa, and knew how exhausted the boys would be. At such times it was possible to show a softer side and be able to let the hard exterior of employer fall away. She never missed such an opportunity.

Marguerite reached the veranda as Philip the assistant climbed out of the car. She went to the top of the stairs as he called to her.

"Can you get Madazi to give me a hand? Tim's got himself a bit burnt and his feet aren't too good."

She ran down the steps, forgetting anything about Madazi, and continued to the other side of the car.

"Darling, are you all right?" she cried. "Oh darling, please say you're all right." And then she opened the car door and would have put her arms around him but recoiled at the sight of his sooted face, his burnt hair, and the tattered remnants of his clothes.

"Hi," he said.

"Darling, what have you done?" she said, trying to recover from her shock.

"Nothing that a bit of soap and water won't put right." And then he forced himself not to wince as he tried to step out of the car. He wanted to reassure her but he wasn't able to, and she saw all this and found it hard in her turn to stop the tears forcing their way through her eyes and onto her cheeks and down her face. They were tears for him, for his pain.

"Can you get Madazi?" he said weakly. "Shadrac and a *piccanin* are in the back, a bit scorched as well."

"Yes, yes, of course I'll get him," and she backed away and then turned, ran around the car, up the veranda steps and through the house into the kitchen. "Mrs Carter," she burst out, "Tim's burnt himself and he looks terribly ill."

Mrs Carter, alarmed, didn't show it. She put down the big wooden spoon she was using and spoke quietly to Marguerite. "It always looks worse at first sight."

"Philip wants Madazi to help him bring Tim into the house."

"Can't he walk?"

"I don't think so."

At this Mrs Carter realised it might be serious and her manner changed accordingly. Firmly she ordered, "Madazi, come with me."

The three went quickly to the car and after some difficulty, and a lot of pain for Tim, they managed to get him up the steps and into the house.

Mrs Ritter and Jenny had been resting in Mrs Carter's bedroom and Marguerite went to wake them. Mrs Ritter heard the story as she patted her hair into place.

"I will look after Shadrac and the child; you and Clara will stay with Tim." And without any more words she bustled out of the room with Jenny in her wake.

Philip was waiting by the car.

"Go and pour yourself a drink," said Mrs Ritter. "I expect you know where to find the cabinet. I'll drive the car to the compound. Shadrac's wife will want to be in on this." She had known Shadrac for many years and knew that his wife specialised in herbs. Their curing capacity was often remarkable when applied to Africans.

Mrs Ritter spoke Shona, an unusual achievement for a European woman. She turned to the car and addressed the African in his own language.

"How bad is it, Shadrac?"

"Not so bad, madam."

"We'll take you straight to your wife."

"That will be good." He wasn't as badly burnt as Tim, neither was the *piccanin*, but the pain was just as acute. He had faith in his wife's healing herbs and the thought of them was easing his pain already. He was glad that the madam knew where he wanted to go.

Some of the people had said the European medicine was good but at times like these he preferred the medicines in which he had faith, in this case, his wife's herbs.

She would make a small ceremony of preparing the ointment; their hut would be strong with the scent of herbs for many days afterwards but the cure would work. When she placed the ointment on his burns, the pain would go; he was sure it would go, as he was sure his wife's herbs had made pain go from his ancestors, the ancestors buried in the mounds, even those buried in the small, dumpy mounds, the mounds that had shrunk with age, the mounds that had been there the longest.

Ah, this is unusual, thought the African, they are taking the car into the compound. And even with his pain he was able to hope they would miss the chickens... There were so many of them and some so small that they hid behind the mealie cobs and then they were not easy to see. He had run over such a *huku* with his bicycle only that same week. He thought then that the boss method of putting them in coops was a good one...but then he had thought of his tribal customs. Customs which had grown with his ancestors, customs which were never broken, and he realised that chickens always ran free in the village, and who was he to think of changing, anyway? One small chicken had been a sacrifice, but then it was only two weeks old; it was just one of those unpleasant things that had to go with the pleasant things in his people's way of life. No, he wasn't going to change anything.

There were no men in the compound, they were all still fighting the fire; but the *piccanins*, pot bellies protruding over half-mast pairs of trousers, and the women, draped in faded European dresses, came to the doors of the small, round, pole and mud houses badly thatched with *vlei* grass. They stared, some having just woken up. They were all dressed; they never took off their clothes, even to sleep.

The car stopped outside the largest of the huts. It was certainly well appointed: a neatly thatched fence of grass circled three sides of the house and the edges of the vegetable patch. The entrance comprised packed earth, leading up in two well-cut steps. The hut was square, the thatch strong and waterproof. To Shadrac it was the only place in the world he wanted to live.

The old boss had always tried to persuade him to live in a large, brick house, with a tin roof and concrete floors. The boss had even gone so far as to offer furniture in an attempt to give him what he, the boss, thought would be nice. Shadrac feared the space, the light, the coldness of the floor and walls, but above all he feared change. He knew how to live in a pole and dagga and he didn't want to change, to draw away from his ancestors. All his people were the same: none of them wanted to live in a house like that of the boss – it was too shiny, too light, and there wasn't any earth to touch in the depths of the night when a spirit was heard. The boss boy at Karilla had let Boss Ritter build him a brick house and when it was finished the village had laughed very much, but to themselves, because the boss boy had only let the house be built to please the boss. The house, of course, had windows, so he couldn't sleep in it. In the day he used it sometimes, but never at night. When the boss asked why he didn't live in the house at night he was surprised that the boss didn't know: the spirits, the people, anybody could look in at him while he was asleep and that was bad, very bad, as the evil spirits could enter his body while he slept and while he slept he couldn't fight them. That was why the village laughed as they saw that the boss boy could never sleep in his new house. So the house remained and the people stayed as before.

Shadrac heard Mrs Ritter speaking to his wife. He was always pleased to hear Mrs Ritter speaking his own language; he knew how much trouble it must have been to learn.

"Your husband has been burnt, together with a *piccanin*," Mrs Ritter was saying. "I have brought them straight to you."

"I will take away the pain from both," replied Shadrac's wife, an elderly woman, wise, respected by all the races. She never stooped to anyone and no one expected it.

Quietly she helped her husband from the car and into their hut and then again the *piccanin*. She did not expect the Europeans to go into her hut even at such a time, and would have been offended if they had tried. Mrs Ritter knew the customs and formally wished Shadrac well outside the hut and then drove the car slowly out of the compound. The next day a small bowl of tomatoes or eggs would arrive at her house, without any explanation and, unless she happened to see the bearer, without any indication of who the gift was from. That was the custom and she would take the gift without sending anything in return – if she did, she would offend.

Inside the hut Shadrac's wife selected herbs and roots from the branches hanging from the roof. She then went out into the night, into the bush, and searched by the moon amongst the dry grass which ran through the silent msasa trees. She found first one plant, then another and then, after looking in six places where she knew it grew, she found the third plant and took away its leaves to the hut.

Her two smallest sons had restarted the fire in the middle of the hut and the thick smoke was hanging in the air, sometimes making a lazy exit through the hole in the roof. Shadrac rested but the *piccanin* was frightened at finding himself in the headman's hut.

She took the herbs and the green leaves and ground them together in a bowl with a round stone, a relic from far distant times. She kneaded them together and then added a large clot of sour goat's milk, to give the ointment a base. She heated the bowl just a little on the fire which made the milk thin out; then she ground till the paste became firm and finally removed the stalks.

Shadrac had watched her all this time; and now the pain was such that he longed for the touch of her ointment and as she knelt beside him and gently laid the paste on his burns, the ecstasy made up for the previous pain. While she was laying more ointment on the *piccanin*, Shadrac fell asleep; he had told himself there was no more pain.

Mrs Carter and Marguerite had cleaned him and sealed off the burns with dry bandages. Lying between the clean sheets, Tim found the pain less cruel and felt it subside into a steady throb. The hot tea was welcome. He began to feel more like himself. When Mrs Ritter came back he enquired after the Africans.

"His wife has got it under control," she replied. "He was as happy as a six-year-old when he got home. I expect the herbs will have done the trick by now."

"Do you believe in herbs?" asked Marguerite.

"No, but Shadrac does and if you believe in a cure as strongly as they do, it's fairly certain to have an effect."

"It's psychological then."

"A bit of both."

"Incredible."

"It works and that's all that matters."

They waited for the others to return. The cocoa was kept hot, ready to be taken to the compound.

Marguerite sat on the bed holding Tim's hand, and a great warmth flowed between them. They were happy just to be close to each other. Soon they were to be married and her heart beat excitedly at the thought. The others left the bedroom and they were alone.

"Darling, this may put our wedding off for a couple of days."

"That doesn't matter," she said, "a few more days from that evening on the lake at Lucerne won't be too bad." And then she said with a serious face that tried hard to break into a smile, "I think it's worth waiting."

They were quiet again, everything was quiet, and with the bedside lamp turned away from them to cast shadows high in the rafters, she curled up beside him on top of the bed and let herself doze gently on the fringe of sleep.

She didn't even see the long band of fire far out in the dark convulse and in its convulsions finally consume itself.

A while later the sound of heavy trucks in low gear brought her back from the world of dreams... She'd got married, but she'd married Steve Ritter and after the wedding in the bush, they had got back to a house that looked like Mirelton to find that he was already married to his sister Jenny, so she had to go away again.

She got off the bed.

"I'll go and help your mother. Shout if you want me."

"Fine," he replied sleepily, the codeine having had its effect.

"Did I hear somebody mention brandy?" It was the vicar, inevitably.

"You'll find it in the lounge, you know where the cabinet is, surely," laughed Mrs Carter.

"My dear Clara, don't you think that is rather a rash invitation? In my present state of health I would only be able to repair my stamina after half a bottle."

"And when the half bottle had its way, you would be impeded again." It was Gary, leaning nonchalantly through the window of Tim's truck.

"Why, my dear chap," replied the vicar, "what a masterpiece of thinking."

"Think nothing of it."

"I rarely do, I rarely do," reported the vicar as he heaved himself up the veranda steps on his way to the cocktail cabinet.

"I'll take the men back to the farm," Steve called to his mother. The truck ground away, headed for Karilla.

Gary mentioned, to no one in particular, "I say, I wish you'd do something about this thing in the seat next to me."

"Why, what's the matter?" demanded Mrs Ritter in a worried tone, having seen from the top of the steps that the thing in the next seat was her husband.

"Well, I'm not really sure what the matter is, but it's making the most extraordinary noises."

By this time, Jock Ritter had commenced to snore, jaws hanging open, head slewed on one side, chest pumping great volumes of air. The noise, now that the truck's engine had stopped, was alarming. The sound drifted up to his wife and the others on the veranda and their laughter ran from a trickle into a torrent. The noise woke the gentleman in question.

He sat himself up straight and, still half asleep, opened the door and fell nearly flat on his face. His right leg had gone to sleep. Fortunately, this graceless trip was hidden from the onlookers. He stood below the steps and blinked up at the lights and the mirth.

"Well, eh, what's the matter?" he asked gruffly, and then commenced to rub the leg which didn't seem to want to wake up.

Gary, having seen this clumsy exit, now lowered himself from the truck, his face purple and his sides painful from the laughter which, owing to lack of breath, had failed to make a sound.

He put an arm round the older man and helped him up the steps.

Mrs Carter collected four men from the back of the truck. They went into the house and came back with the drum of cocoa which they deposited on the tailboard. She told the driver to take the truck into the compound: there would be no work for anyone the next day.

Back in the lounge the vicar said to Gary, "You'll have one with me?"

"If you insist."

"But I do."

"In that case I have no alternative."

Jock Ritter had collapsed in a chair.

"Hell, that was quite some fire."

"You can say that again," replied Gary, not daring to sit down with all the ash still clinging to his clothes.

"Where do you get your energy from, vicar?" asked Jock Ritter.

The vicar had found his second wind and his second brandy.

"I have been told the process is something like a camel," he replied. "With all this fat." And here he put down his glass and gathered up his girth. "My reserves are unlimited. Why, my dear" – and here he turned to Marguerite – "I even broke into a run at one stage during the fire, something I haven't done for a considerable number of years."

They were all laughing so much, Marguerite felt able to join them without being rude to the vicar.

And as he took up his glass again he went on, "Yes, it must have looked a little amusing, especially from the side." And once more the large twinkle shone out across the lounge.

"My goodness," thundered the vicar, "here we are relaxing in the perfect company of a glass of brandy and we haven't even asked after the patients, let alone investigated the situation."

"The Africans are being looked after by Shadrac's wife and Tim is fast asleep."

"Good," said Jock Ritter in a tired voice. "I don't think I could have done much more tonight. I must be getting old."

"On the contrary," said Gary, having braved the ash and Mrs Carter's wrath by sitting next to him, "you've just done three men's work."

Mrs Carter joined them.

"I've had enough beds made up for you all, so there's no need to drive home tonight."

"That's kind of you, Clara," said Jock Ritter.

His wife and daughter returned from having helped out in the kitchen.

"If you make the effort now," Mrs Ritter said to her husband, "you'll appreciate the sheets even more when they close around you." She knew her husband well.

He agreed.

"I'll say goodnight then, Clara." And as his mind wandered in his tiredness, he mumbled, "I hope the Grants are all right, the telephone won't be working, that's for certain, the copper wires will have melted. There isn't much bush close to the house so they should be all right." He wearily made to follow his wife; it seemed a long way, across the lounge and then down the corridor, to the bedroom; undressing; the raising of hands above the head to remove a shirt; then finally the sheets and no more effort required. Yes, he was certainly tired.

"Goodnight," they had called after him.

"The Grants will be all right," Gary said firmly. "The house was certainly surrounded by the fire but inside, and without a thatched roof, it would only have been hot, not dangerous. I'll bet they were more worried how far it would spread, especially being unable to do anything themselves."

There was a silence, a very tired silence.

"I think sleep will be the best thing for all," prophesied the vicar.

And with these words the dinner party came to an end and they made their way to their separate rooms, their beds, their sleep.

Alone in her room, Marguerite pondered. She had seen how swiftly Africa can react. From a dining room table in the best of taste, to a raging fire in less than fifteen minutes; and at the end, burns, not even anticipated when dinner was served. She was not frightened, only determined to be alert, to be able to avert a sudden danger, to be able to come to terms with the unaccustomed. This was Africa and not England, a fact which the evening had taught her in no uncertain terms.

8

SIGNS AND PORTENTS, 9TH DECEMBER 1961

*T*im rose to consciousness and then subsided again into sleep. He was dreaming about the telephone bell, and yes, it was giving two short rings and one long: that was their number. Someone was trying to call. He answered the phone and there was no one there, but when he put down the receiver the bell went on ringing.

He was awake, and for a moment lay still, with Marguerite fast asleep at his side. He was unable to differentiate between the dream and the telephone, now pumping out two shorts and a long; then two longs – that was Gary they wanted; three shorts – Lance Grant: three shorts and a long – the Camphers, Afrikaners on the next farm. A party line telephone made it plain who was popular with the calls. After counting the rings with academic interest, mingled with curiosity, he came fully awake, saw it was two in the morning, and then he knew what it was about. Hell, he thought, and quietly but quickly got out of bed. Torch in hand, he made for the corridor and the still ringing telephone.

In the corridor he picked up the receiver.

"Hello, Tim Carter speaking."

"Hello, Tim. It's Steve."

They were interrupted by a frightfully English voice proclaiming annoyance.

"What the hell's going on?"

"Morning, Gary. It's Steve Ritter."

"I see you have the decency not to preface the morning with a 'good'," and then more seriously, "What's the trouble, Steve?"

"The government are banning the NCP from dawn this morning. Msondedi's in Tanganyika, waving an independence flag, but his little friends will probably want to do a damn sight more than that."

Tim interjected; he was awake, alert.

"I thought that would come. They've been advocating violence for months. The PM has probably had a bellyful, that's all."

"The reason, in fact, is a little different," went on Steve. "There's been violent intimidation in the African townships around Bulawayo and Salisbury. It's a case of, if you don't join the party and pay your membership, we'll beat you up, and if that doesn't work we'll have a go at your wife."

"Nice people," put in Gary.

"Quite. So much so that now their own people have got fed up with them and the PM is in a stronger position to do something about it."

"You're also forgetting that the British Parliament agreed his new constitution only a few weeks ago," Tim suggested. "It's only now that he's free to move."

"That may be so," agreed Gary. "But it doesn't alter the fact that Msondedi and his gang are a damn menace to everyone, black or white."

"You think there'll be trouble?" asked Tim.

"I don't know," replied Steve, "but it's quite likely unless we do something about it. If there's a big enough show of police strength they'll get cold feet. They only like making a noise when the numbers are ten against one in their favour."

"What time are we out on patrol?" asked Gary.

"Three-thirty. That gives us an hour before dawn. Time enough to pair up and spread out. Meet here with batons and riot shields, but no guns."

"See you at half past three," finished Tim.

"Hell, you'll never wake that fellow Grant with a telephone," mused Gary.

"I know that," put in Steve, "so could you get over there and wake him up?"

"Trust my luck to be caught in the Police Reserve with a man who sleeps like a rock, breeds sleepers of the same masonry and even indoctrinates his wife. I'll ring off then, and run round the ruddy rockery."

"Cheers."

"How's Marguerite?" asked Steve after they heard the click of Gary's replaced receiver.

"Fine. The doctor says she has another couple of months to go, so there shouldn't be any trouble tonight. I don't like leaving her though."

"Can't you get your mother to come across?"

"Yes, I'll do that."

"See you at three-thirty."

He went back to bed: there was still an hour's sleep to be had. He tried to relax but the tension had gripped.

'Let's hope this is only another scare,' he thought; it can't be too bad if they don't want us to take rifles.

Should he go and wake his mother or should he wake Marguerite first? With the child so close, sleep was difficult for her and he didn't want to disturb her unless it was absolutely necessary.

He was sitting up, arms circling his knees under the bedclothes, only half of him covered, his mind racing through all the possibilities, the probabilities, the uncertainties. It was dark outside, black; the only light was being thinly spread by a three-day-old moon. It's dry anyway, he thought, no rain for two weeks, and that set him off worrying about his tobacco crop.

"What's the matter, darling?"

"Did I wake you?"

"Why aren't you trying to sleep?"

"We've been called out at three-thirty. Steve's just been on the telephone. They've banned the NCP."

"Sounds fun." She was still half asleep and failed to register the significance of what he said.

He slid down in bed so he could lie flat and put his arm round his wife. She snuggled close to him and he talked gently into a sleepy ear.

"Do you mind walking across to the cottage when I go? I think if you and mother are together it would be safer."

She was awake now, caught hold of his arm and strained to see the expression on his face through the darkness. But it was too dark, too black.

"What do you mean, safer?"

"There's no cause for alarm – the whole thing is an exercise in precaution, from banning the NCP to calling out the Police Reserve and sending you across to mother in the cottage."

"You will be careful on your patrol?" She was worried, but then, he thought, women often see danger more vividly than men. They see its product, misery. A man goes out to meet it but if danger meets him, that is the end, he is not left behind to suffer. He is dead.

"I'll be out with Steve. Between us we know this part of the country as well as anyone."

"As well as the Africans?" she put in apprehensively.

"As well as the Africans," he confirmed. "We were born here too."

They lay in silence, close to each other, with their separate thoughts. Tim could never understand why women always built up such a small situation. This was routine, like the other patrols he had done in the past. They went out on foot and plodded up and down a few farm lanes. The Africans saw them and the ones that might have wanted to cause trouble refrained from doing so. There was no ill-feeling generated. The peace was kept, that was all.

After a while, when he had stopped trying to convince himself, his wife spoke.

"Shall we go across to the cottage now? I can make you some coffee before you go. How long are you going to be out for?"

"Probably a three-hour stretch."

"Would you like some sandwiches to take with you?"

"I'll have breakfast when I get back." He smiled without seeing her in the dark, but knew her expression without seeing it – very serious, nose turned up, eyes flashing. He loved it and found her mouth in the dark and swallowed her next remark in its infancy.

They began to laugh and no African in the vicinity would have guessed the truth from it – that their Nationalist Party was to be banned at dawn. Tim changed into his blue denims, boots and the Police Reserve bush hat.

They walked the short distance to the cottage, the cottage they had built for her mother-in-law after they were married. The door was locked and they banged loudly till a very agitated Mrs Carter let them in.

"My goodness, you frightened me banging on the door like that. What on earth's the matter? It's only half past two."

As they went inside he explained. The bright electric light cut deep at the roots of their eyes.

Coffee was brewed and drunk. By three-fifteen, Marguerite had made herself comfortable in the spare room and Mrs Carter had gone back to sleep. The elderly woman was not in the slightest bit disturbed by the NCP or any other NP or PDN; at three o'clock in the morning she expected to be asleep, and it was only her weakness at such an hour which gave her any cause for consternation.

Marguerite let Tim out and locked the door behind him before returning to the spare room to try and sleep.

The beam of his torch picked out the path and he followed it to the main house where the shooting brake was parked below the veranda. Two of the dogs padded down the steps to investigate, then, satisfied, they went back to their baskets on the veranda. He began the drive to Karilla to join the others.

Gary had arrived with Lance Grant and was holding the floor with Steve as his only audience.

"My dear chap," he was saying as Tim made his way into the lounge, "I damn nearly had to knock the door down before they heard. It's not surprising he nearly got fried last year with the whole family in bed fast asleep. Thank goodness I was there to extinguish the flames."

"Were you alone?" asked Tim from the doorway.

"I have vague recollections of some superfluous helpers; one who was rather large and fat, another who got his pants burnt, but for the rest I regret my mind only retains important facts."

In the next moment three rather large men silently converged on the slightly more modestly proportioned Gary Fairburn, late of Eton and Oxford (the latter having dispensed with his services after a ridiculously short stay).

Slowly and with great precision they turned him upside down and started shaking him, rhythmically.

His quivering voice floated up from four inches above the floor.

"What are you doing?"

"We are sifting from the bottom to the top of your brain all those facts you consider unimportant," explained Lance Grant while at the same time increasing the speed of the shakes.

"The blood's all running to my face," Gary stuttered between jerks.

With one accord they put him down and turned him upright again.

"You're a fraud," proclaimed Lance. "Your face is red, not blue – so much for the aristocratic content of your veins."

"Must be something to do with the heat," explained Gary through the disapproving silence. "Makes your blood go thin."

They all laughed and would have sat on him if the victim hadn't taken advantage of the respite to crawl behind the sofa.

"Good morning, all." It was Jock Ritter, freshly awake and looking as healthy as ever. "Who are we waiting for?"

"Campher and Colin Mandy," explained his son.

"Where's Gary?"

A head appeared timidly from behind the sofa, obviously not sure whether it was yet safe to grace the room with its presence. Seeing there was no immediate move to suffocate him he braved their mood to announce himself.

"Well, actually, I'm here."

More laughter ensued, this time followed by a flight of cushions. The speaker subsided into his sanctuary.

"We'll wait for the others before I explain what we're going to do," went on Jock Ritter, ignoring the interruption. They irritated him in their present mood. There were more important things to do. Nevertheless, it was probably the younger generation's method of conquering their nerves. A damn funny way of doing it; had it too soft in their childhood, he concluded.

A car drew up outside, followed by another. Colin Mandy came into the room with a Sten gun hanging by its steel bar butt from his right hand.

"What the hell are you going to do with that?" Jock demanded.

Colin Mandy was obviously tensed up and, dangerously, sober. He was looking for trouble from black faces.

"I was dreaming about my wife when your telephone call woke me," he said to Steve.

"Have you got a licence for it?" Jock persisted.

"No."

"You don't need that in Southern Rhodesia, this isn't Kenya."

"You never know," was all he said.

Jock Ritter could see trouble ahead and was determined to prevent it.

"Our orders, Colin, are not to take arms, especially things like that," and as he completed his sentence he caught sight of the Afrikaner in the doorway: full beard picking out a set of rotten teeth, a sawn-off shotgun held in a large, heavy hand; a big man, rather magnificent in a grotesque way. "Christ," he said under his breath, "we've certainly got the bloody lot this morning."

Louder, he addressed the Afrikaner.

"That goes for you too, Van. All artillery is to be left behind."

"Artillery, now you're talking," put in Colin Mandy, a smile creasing his sour face. "A nice old 25-pounder set up at the back of the club would suit me down to the ground. If the bastards got obstreperous I could lay into them by the hundred."

Jock Ritter made a mental note not to call out Colin Mandy on their next Reserve duty, but for the moment the damage was done and they had to live with it.

"I'll take that gun myself, thanks Colin."

Their eyes met fiercely: one was a fanatic and the other was just not used to being defied.

"I know how you feel," went on the Scotsman, "I'd probably feel the same in your circumstances, but it still doesn't alter the fact that you can't go round stirring up trouble on a private grievance. During Mau Mau maybe, but this isn't Mau Mau, and never will be as long as we keep our heads and realise that for every one who wants to cause trouble for their own political ends, there are many thousands more who want to live and prosper alongside of us. All right, my views might have changed from a few years ago, but since then I've looked at the problem as a whole and not in isolated instances. There's bad in every race but there is also good."

"I've never seen any good in them."

"You should have been with us at the fire on Lance's farm last year. An African saved Tim's life at the risk of his own, for no other reason than Tim was another human being in trouble. The colour of the skin didn't enter into it. I wonder how many Europeans 'back home' would have had the guts to go into the middle of that fire?"

"Tim went in first." Colin was losing the argument and knew it.

"So did the African, and that's my point."

The tension had been lost and after a short silence Jock Ritter put one hand on Colin's shoulder and beckoned the Afrikaner into the room.

"Here's a baton," offered Steve. "If it's not exactly fair exchange there isn't any robbery in it, of that I'm certain."

Uneasy laughter followed but the guns were exchanged for

batons and they all seated themselves, Gary tentatively on the arm of the sofa, while Jock Ritter stood with his back to the unlit fire. He started from the beginning.

"We're not going out on patrol as told to you on the telephone. Our instructions have been kept as quiet as possible, so as not to put the wind up the NCP. Our job is to go and sort out the local NCP office at the back of the native store on the road to Marandellas. We impound everything except the personnel. I don't think there will be much trouble but we're going in force just in case. We leave here at four-fifteen, that's in twenty minutes' time. We'll take two cars, mine and yours, Tim, if that's all right."

Steve had organised coffee; the houseboy was in the compound and there he would stay until it was all over. The starched blue police uniforms were incongruous in the domestic setting of the Ritters' lounge; the heavy boots were inclined to mark the polished wood floor.

What a mess the whole bloody world was in, pondered Jock Ritter to himself. It wasn't only his own country, it was everywhere. In the Congo, black killed black; in Algeria, white killed white; in England, one itchy Russian finger could finish everything; in Australia, millions of Chinese and Indonesians just waiting to flood the place; and in America there were Americans.

At four-fifteen, with a faint glow of light showing in the morning sky, they filed out of the house, one wicker shield and baton apiece.

A small bird called encouragement to the new day and then a crow, more sure of its authority, summoned the sun and it rose, rays daggering into the night, deposing the moon. Slowly the fiery orb heaved itself above the line of flat-topped trees that spanned the horizon.

The reservists kicked up the dust into the freshness of the morning as they drove, their two cars well apart to avoid the other's cloud.

At first light there was no colour. Then that gave way and the colours came: reds, crimsons, gold, orange and still more orange

and at the centre of everything a ball of fire. The light spread
through the vegetation and silhouetted a line of scarecrow trees on
the side of the hill, away to the right of where Tim was driving.
The cold air made him put up the car window a little. The beauty
of the African morning almost made him cry, he loved the place so
much.

Ahead of them Jock Ritter let the needle of his Buick hover
around the seventy mark. There wouldn't be much traffic about at
this time of the morning.

He talked to his son.

"We'll park the cars a half mile away from the store and circle
the place. If we drive up to the front they'll bolt like rabbits out of
the back and take as many of their membership lists as they can
carry."

"Is there a compound anywhere near?"

"Yes. That could be a snag. The Roads Department houses over
two hundred men a couple of hundred yards away...hence the store.
If we do it quickly, and without giving anybody time to think, it will
all be over before they wake up."

The road ran along a ridge and from the hills on either side the
two cars could be seen, a good distance apart, tiny dots with long
dust tails, moving fast.

On the flat ground the two cars cut their way across the plain.
Cultivated tobacco lands spread away on either side. Cattle browsed
in large herds, well fed and healthy.

The flat-topped msasa trees, bathed in full light, no longer
scarecrows, fled past quickly and the tall grass at the roadside was
momentarily disturbed.

The leading car stopped and Tim caught up and brought the
shooting brake to a standstill just behind. The reservists got out,
took in the fresh air of the morning, and congregated around Jock
Ritter.

"Tim, will you and Colin Mandy go off first? Circle round to the
back of the store. At exactly five, move in.

"Steve, you and Van get between the store and the compound.

Face the compound, not the store. If we get any trouble I think it will be from that side. It will be up to you to calm them down.

"Gary, Lance and myself will tackle the front. Check your watches. The time is now exactly twenty-seven and a half minutes to five. Let's go, it's cold standing here."

Tim and Colin moved off at a fast pace to give them time to reach the back of the store. Then came Steve and the Afrikaner, then the other three.

"I hope one of the little bastards tries to make a run for it," muttered Colin, his baton swinging lightly by the strap. Fiercely he gripped the wood, holding it at the ready in front of him. "If he does, I'll knock his bloody brains out."

"We're not after the people, Colin," Tim warned him, "only their documents so that we can see who's causing the trouble. Then we can quietly prevent them from repeating it in the future. The people running the store are probably stooges, doing it because they're too scared to do anything else."

"They've still got black curly hair," replied Colin, menacingly.

"If anything needs to be done, we'll do it together, but you're not starting trouble on your own account."

The animal hatred in the Kenyan's eyes as he pronounced 'black curly hair' had stabbed fear into Tim. Could a man really hate that much? As they skirted round to the back of the store and his expression grew even harder, he knew that Mandy, for one, could.

They had five minutes to wait, Colin nursing his hatred and Tim preoccupied with his thoughts.

Tim was thinking about the other man. How would he feel if they did to Marguerite what they had done to his wife? The idea swelled before him and he began to hate also. He didn't hate the colour of the skin, only the people who could do such a thing; for that they deserved such hatred.

From the foot of the kopje where they sheltered from view they could see the back of the store between the trees. The heavy boulders hid them. They waited. The second hand moved on, and then it was time and they broke cover quickly, darting towards the store with the living quarters at the back. It was quiet, deathly quiet, and the long, dew-wet grass swished against their boots.

Tim could only see one door. There was a window too – someone might try and get out that way. He beckoned Colin to cover the window and himself took the door. They waited for Jock Ritter to go in from the front.

A loud, harsh tone in Fanagalo, the local pidgin dialect, could be heard: "It's the police, open the door." Silence again, quieter than before.

Again in Fanagalo from Jock Ritter: "I'll knock the bloody door down if you're not quick about it."

A short pause and then they started on the door. It didn't sound very strong.

There was a scuffle inside. The back door suddenly burst open. An African, not more than five foot one inch tall, bolted through the opening with his head down, straight into Tim. The speed of it surprised and winded Tim who was unable to stop the African making a dash for it.

With a growl of excitement, Colin Mandy detached himself from the window. He stepped over a fallen tree which he didn't even look at; he had eyes only for the African who thought he could get away. That same black twisted hair, black skin. He would do it slowly, savour the pleasure. He caught up with his quarry and, as he ran, slowly raised the baton above his head. Then with powerful force, he brought it down, hard, onto the man's skull.

Tim saw the blow, heard the crunch, saw the African fall forward. He was on his feet. The bloody fool would kill him if he didn't get there quick. Colin, up ahead, was standing over his fallen prey, gloating. He was raising his baton for a second, pleasurable stroke.

"Let him be," shouted Tim.

But the process had been started and his distant words had no effect. The baton moved once more above Colin's head, paused, ready; this time, if it hadn't already done so, it would kill.

Coming up behind him, Tim tried again.

"Put the bloody thing away, you've half killed him already."

Colin Mandy, with the baton still poised, slowly turned his head and shoulders to survey with puzzlement the interruption from his rear.

Tim stopped short. The eyes were glazed, mad; the head was tilted awkwardly. They stared at each other in horrible silence.

The madman broke into a thin, high-pitched whine. As he spoke, his head twisted further sideways into the shoulder.

"You wouldn't stop me, Tim. You wouldn't stop me. No, you'll let me have my revenge. Tim, they killed my wife. They should have killed me too but they didn't and now I shall take my revenge. You won't stop me will you, Tim? You'll let me have my revenge." This last was followed by an animal noise, part howl, part laugh, part lust.

The man kept looking at him and Tim's mind raced to find a solution. For the moment it was obvious, Colin Mandy had gone insane, something had tipped over inside his brain.

He tried soft words.

"Come on, old chap. I know how you feel but this one isn't a Kikuyu."

He had said the wrong thing. The man before him started, as if he'd been slapped across the face. The hand holding the baton aloft tensed till the knuckles were white and the arm shook. Taut silence hung in the air between them.

A hysterical reply whipped at Tim.

"Get away, get away, let me do this, I must do this, I must, I must." The eyes grew more wild, more liquid, more lunatic.

Sharply Mandy turned back to his victim. A pause, then in a the thin, soft voice: "It's all right, Judy, I'm doing this for you at last."

Tim tried shouting again.

"Give me that baton."

"I won't."

Louder: "Give me that baton!"

"I won't, I tell you, I won't, I won't, I won't."

The back began to tremble, then the whole body standing

poised in front of Tim began to shake. He moved forward to grapple with the baton but the hand gripping it uncurled and the three-foot piece of wood slowly came loose and fell. The hand still remained aloft, but the baton fell. Colin Mandy, five foot ten and one hundred and fifty pounds, began to cry like a baby and walked away with his right hand still in the air, the fingers still uncurled.

Tim knelt beside the African, looked at his head and felt grateful for the thickness of the man's hair. The blow would have killed a European but the African head had vied with the African sun since man began and the result was a thick, solid cushion which had probably saved this man's life. His breathing was all right and apart from a break in the skin, to an inexpert eye he seemed undamaged.

After a while the man opened his eyes, saw the blue uniform, and shut them again. There wasn't much wrong with the African, Tim concluded. His brain was working in the normal, illogical way. Having seen Tim, he was going to feign another sleep in the hope that the European would go away and give him a chance to escape. Tim laughed with relief. He had feared the one blow might have been sufficient.

A police whistle cut into the morning air. More trouble. It was from over by the compound. He quickly searched the African for papers and spoke to him in Shona. "*Hamba manji.*"

A second request to go was not required. The eyes shot open and the African clambered to his feet. He moved off to the right of the kopje with an uncertain gait and a hand held firmly to his head. He'll probably have a headache for a week, Tim surmised.

He left Colin Mandy leaning against a tree. He had nothing to say to him. The violence had gone out of him like a light switching off, and all that was left was an elderly man who should be left alone. If he was going to gather his wits, Tim thought it better for him to gather them by himself. Anyway, there was trouble elsewhere and he hadn't any time to spare.

He ran down to the open back door, through the empty house and out onto the veranda which flanked the road. There was nobody there either. Noise came from beyond the bend in the road but the kopje obscured his view. He knew the compound was round the corner. He ran down the steps and onto the road, making for the noise. The other five patrolmen were lined up across the road, batons and wicker shields at the ready. Hell, he had left his shield behind in the fracas. Coming towards them from down the road was a crowd of some fifty Africans. Someone had tipped them off.

He joined the line between Steve and his father.

Jock Ritter talked without taking his eyes from the mob.

"Where's Colin?"

"I left him looking after the store." He had no intention of entering into a long discussion at such a point. Anyway, he himself needed time to think. If Colin recovered, there wouldn't be anything much to think about.

"Where's your riot shield?"

"I left it at the store."

"You make a bloody fine policeman."

A couple of bricks were thrown, which fell short. It seemed that two people were goading the rabble on; the local NCP probably, thought Tim.

The whites watched the mob as it drew closer. It was swelling too. The NCP were gaining confidence; they taunted, threatened, and from a loose assembly the mass gradually grew into an ugly mob. As their friends arrived they found more courage too, especially when the word was passed back that there were only six bosses ranged against them.

They didn't see him move till he was on his way. He had no baton or shield. In fact, halfway between the police and the mob, Gary Fairburn put his hands in his trouser pockets. The remaining police watched apprehensively. Jock Ritter had no idea what the bloody idiot was going to do until it was too late.

The mob stopped. The slightly-built Englishman continued to saunter towards them. The leaders lost an element of their conviction. Gary was walking with his eyes fixed firmly on the largest NCP member. The fellow looked to his right and his left.

He didn't like it on his own. He yelled to the others to move forward but they didn't and he was afraid to move forward alone. Gary walked straight up to him, looked him in the eyes and told him to *voetsak*, a word which Gary used only very rarely on his fellow human beings. They stood looking at each other for some time. The mob was silent and then from the back it began to melt away.

Jock Ritter started breathing again.

"Come on," he said, "now's the time for us to join him."

The five moved forward. It was too much for the Africans, who just turned about and made themselves scarce.

Gary was left alone, with the one NCP member rooted to the spot in front of him.

"After you, Claude," he said in English with a gentlemanly smile.

And that was that. It was too much for the African; he could never understand these Europeans. If they had tried to fight, his people would have been too many for them, but this way he had no answer. So he turned and followed the backs of his companions.

For a moment there had been an incident and then there wasn't. Jock Ritter, responsible for the patrol, was relieved. He put a large hand on Gary's shoulder.

"You're a bloody idiot."

"Thanks."

Jock Ritter, roughened by over thirty years in southern Africa, had a marked disinclination towards what he called 'piss and wind Englishmen', but sometimes Eton and the Guards were just the sort of things one had to bring to bear in these circumstances. And he had just seen that occasionally the 'piss and wind' had something underneath it. He spoke to them all.

"I want that one big bastard. He'll be given a few months to remember that it doesn't pay to cause trouble."

They all moved off in pursuit of the receding backs. The NCP member turned his head, caught sight of them, and tried to force his way between the people in front. But the people in front were also trying to be inconspicuous and wouldn't let him pass. He shouted at their backs but to no avail.

Tim, Lance and Steve handed over their accoutrements and broke into a run. The African glanced behind in his fear and saw them running him down. He was off like a startled rabbit into the bush. He was going well but so was Lance and Lance had recently finished a profitable rugby season. It was something of an obstacle, race – fallen trees, rocks, clumps of tall grass, a stream. They both took them all in full flight.

The other two were well behind but the gap between Lance and the African was still the same. They broke onto clearer ground and the gap began to close. With a final burst Lance came in hard and low at the knees. The African, who with his friends had been so ready for a fight, was now afraid to get up. Lance, forcing air into his hard-worked lungs, grabbed a flailing arm and bent it behind the other's back.

"Get up," he said in English.

A second request was not required. He walked him back towards Tim and Steve Ritter and then together they took the prisoner to the store and the cars.

The others were transporting the contents of the NCP office into the cars. They slid the sulking African into the Buick.

Tim slipped away and went round to the back of the store.

Mandy was lying face down in the coarse grass, still crying. Tim knelt beside him.

"How are you feeling?" But Colin Mandy gave no sign of recognition.

Tim shook the limp form, then tried to lift him up, but the dead weight was too much. Still the sobbing continued. He turned him over and glazed eyes, full of tears, looked without seeing. Tim hoped it was only a nervous breakdown.

It had become too much for one person so he left the crying hulk to tell Jock Ritter as much of the story as was necessary.

"Poor bastard," commented Jock Ritter. "Lance, will you take the others back to the house in my car and then run the prisoner and the files into Salisbury? Tim and I will come on behind in the shooting brake." Aside to Tim, he added, "The fewer people who know about this the better."

They saw the other car move off and build up its tail of dust. In the ensuing silence they went into the store. It was empty, not only of files and people but of the spirit which one hour before had been a part of the bricks and corrugated iron.

Between them they carried the remains of Colin Mandy, a spent force, to the car. The sight of him hunched in the back, still crying, made the older man feel his age and for a moment his old loathing of the African races returned. He forced himself back to the present and at length the feeling went.

"We'll take him to my wife," he said to Tim. "I don't think doctors can do anything. Rest and gentle understanding may bring him back again." He made the pathetic sight comfortable, climbed into the passenger seat next to Tim and then proceeded to brood on the last ten years of Colin Mandy's life.

"I'd better lock the store," said Tim, breaking into his thoughts.

"Yes, yes," he replied, unconscious of the question.

How the hell can a man get himself into that state? Then he thought of the Mau Mau, the deep fear they had provoked, and the constant readiness to fight that had necessitated; then he pictured the fight itself and the half-naked savages, crazed with their bloody oaths, overpowering then killing the man's wife and drinking her blood in front of his eyes.

The sobbing behind him wasn't really so surprising after all.

9

NEW LIFE, 10TH FEBRUARY 1962

Marguerite had determined to have her first child at Urangwa. A midwife had moved into the spare room a week ago. Tim would have been far happier if she had gone to the Lady Chancellor, but anyway it was only sixty miles to Salisbury and if anything looked wrong – and the nurse ought to know – he could get into town in little more than an hour.

The reaping was going well. The three-week drought had really worried him but when the rains came, the result had been rapidly growing tobacco. A few leaves had been sun-scorched but not many. It looked like being a good crop.

Tim kicked off his heavy gumboots at the top of the steps and carried them into the house. It was still drizzling and the lands were muddy. As usual at that time of the day he was hungry.

"Do you mind?" he said, stopping and addressing the four Bullmastiffs in line abreast who were making a delicate pattern with their muddy paws on the polished floors. The dogs stopped, looked a little crestfallen and turned on their tails.

He went straight to their bedroom where Marguerite was resting: nurse's orders. He put his head round the door.

"Hello, darling."

"Hello. There was a letter in the mail from Mummy this morning."

She was unable to say anything more because he had had time to cross to the bed and kiss her.

"Why did I marry a farmer?" she asked when he stood back and she was able to survey the wet clothes thick with good red African mud.

They both laughed.

He drew up a chair, having half sat on the bed, been frowned upon, and seen the error of his ways.

"And what did Mummy say?"

"Well," and then she looked up and saw the laughter in his eyes and they laughed again.

"We'd better not make too much noise," he managed to get out. "The Gorgon midwife will have me writing lines." And added in his best mistress voice, "I must not excite my wife."

"Sounds wonderful."

He forced mock severity into his expression.

"My dear, Miss Trump would not be thinking of it in that way."

"She's not that bad, in fact she's very sweet."

"I know, but it still doesn't alter the fact that she frightens me."

"You poor lamb."

"I know, and just now I'll be ready for the slaughter. By the way, what did Mummy say?"

"She doesn't want to come out for a holiday but she says it's very kind of you to offer to pay her fare."

"Why won't she come?"

"She doesn't say so in as many words, but I think it's the old man. She's been looking after Guy Featherstone for more than ten years and they're very fond of each other. He's nearly seventy and I suppose she can't imagine anyone else looking after him properly for six months."

"Ask the old boy to come as well."

"I'd love that, he's a wonderful old chap, but I don't think you'd get him to come to Africa. He's got himself well tuned to Mirelton after a lot of difficulty adapting back to the English climate. Six months in Africa would make him unsettled."

"Provided we don't have any more trouble out here, we'll make a trip to England and bring off the whole reunion thing in reverse."

"We'll have to make sure it's in the summer as I couldn't face an English winter again."

"You now know what I suffered in that flat. The overcoat was not affectation."

He had been trying to make that point for two years. She ignored the sally.

"There's a whole page about the career of Myles Featherstone."

"And what, pray, is your old heartthrob up to now?"

"Jealousy will get you nowhere."

"I know," and he kissed her again.

"He's in the Colonial Office, following in his uncle's footsteps."

"After the American missions to Africa, they come next on my list of untouchables. Where is he stationed?"

"He was in Sierra Leone, but after independence they sent him back to London."

"Is he married?"

"No."

"How old is he now?"

"A little more than twenty-five, I should think." Time certainly goes quickly, she thought.

"He hasn't wasted much time with his career."

A knock on the door. Miss Trump had arrived with the pills.

"It's one-thirty, Mrs Carter, exactly four hours after the last dose."

"What are they?" He wished he hadn't spoken. The look he received in return was gross disapproval, redirected quickly to Marguerite when she was unable to control the beginnings of laughter.

"Your lunch is ready, Mr Carter."

"Oh yes, yes, thanks, I'd better go and wash." He fled towards the door.

"I'll see you at lunch, Miss Trump."

"You will," the lady replied.

Miss Trump had her back to the door, her outstretched hand waiting for the glass Marguerite was using to down the pills.

Tim went out like a good boy, all but closed the door, half opened it again, poked in his head, winked at his wife, and just had time to withdraw before Miss Trump wheeled to squash the challenge to her authority. Marguerite had burst out laughing, dribbled a large amount of water and given the game away.

A crack of thunder split the drizzle and then the drizzle was rain, African rain, a great sheet of water driven by the wind, and within minutes the pathways and lawns were lakes; the thatched roofs gushed waterfalls and the lightning struck again. African storms are rarely frightening; there is nothing mysterious about them, they are clean, big and majestic.

Half an hour later the storm ceased, as quickly as it came. The sun burst through the clouds and the rain rose this time from the paths as steam. Two feet in the air it was eaten by the sun, drawn up in preparation for it to be thrown back down again.

Juliet Carter was born that night. The midwife proved herself and delivered the baby without any difficulties.

The child cried but couldn't know why. Was it against the world it was being born into, against the heap of chaos on every side? It knew nothing of Algeria to the North, the Congo, Angola, British Guiana, Indo-China, the Russian cold war, the incredible short-sightedness of the Americans, the perpetual British dithering, the bombs getting bigger and bigger.

She wasn't crying about these things, but well she might; well might she have asked to be returned from whence she came.

There was to be little future for a baby girl in the world of 1962, especially if she was born a Rhodesian.

10

THE DISSENTER, APRIL TO AUGUST1968

*I*n 1968 they were still on their farms: they were Rhodesians and had nowhere else to go. The situation could have been worse: they still controlled their own government. It had meant breaking all ties with Britain but then the ties hadn't been worth very much for the last ten years. The Federation had gone and Southern Rhodesians were alone. She had South Africa as a friend but the other nations found her an embarrassment and preferred to pour their money down the drain, currying favour with the here-today-and-gone-tomorrow black nationalists further north.

The province of Katanga in the Congo had paid the full price for their American-style democracy: the American dollar controlled the copper and the Katangese controlled nothing. The Central Government thought they did but they didn't. It was colonialism without using the naughty word.

Colin Mandy, still weak in mind but able, with help, to make a show of running the club, had been revenged. Black Kenyans had slaughtered each other in their thousands with the ugliest savagery the world had known for centuries.

To the south, the Afrikaners stuck to their guns, literally, and anyone who violated their borders was shot at. Few of them tried again. The African areas within the Republic were internally self-governing and the country was prosperous; South Africa controlled too much of the world's gold to be otherwise. There was internal dissention – there always was – but generally there was peace and race relations were much improved.

Nehru had shot his bolt and withdrew from what was left of the British Commonwealth, which wasn't very much.

To all intents and purposes, the British weren't the British anymore, having lost their financial identity in a greater Europe. It had had to come, but when it came it wasn't very pleasant. You can't have your cake and eat it too.

There were lots of things orbiting around the earth but people had grown used to them and failed to comment. The same had happened with the aeroplanes twenty-years before, when people had stopped looking up at the noise in the sky.

Mrs Fenton died in 1964; Marguerite had heard two years later from a mutual friend. She hadn't been able to make a trip to England, and as the picture of gates and fences and an old, white-haired lady came back, she became depressed. So much had been lost in the last five years.

Growing tobacco became more difficult as their labour force, paid three times as much as in 1962, still gave trouble and went on strike when they should have been reaping, so good tobacco rotted in the lands. There was little Tim could do about it but he still continued to make a living, not a good one, but a living, and anyway he loved the life more than anything else so as long as he had that, it was enough.

The Sunday afternoon sun was hot and cut a sharply defined shadow across the veranda. Tim and Marguerite had retreated into the shade where it was cool in contrast to the sun.

"More tea?" she asked.

"Please, but with one slice of lemon."

She passed the third cup of tea and talked again of what had been uppermost in their minds for the last six days.

"He didn't have a bad innings."

"What...sixty-eight you mean? No I suppose not."

"Better to go that way, like your mother did, quickly, when you're still strong. The business of just getting older and older with one thing less functioning every year doesn't appeal."

Tim's thoughts went on and reached a sad conclusion.

"It may be very selfish, but we just couldn't afford to lose him at a time like this. I don't believe anyone in this block realised quite how much we all relied on Jock Ritter. He'd lived here for thirty-seven years, he'd known most of the locals' grandfathers. To the Africans he was a legend – if they didn't like him they were frightened of him – but above all, they respected him."

Their six-year-old daughter came into their line of vision, riding a tricycle at speed.

Marguerite's heart ached for the child; being a mother had made her realise that the cares of the children rest with their mother. Lately, they had multiplied alarmingly. She looked away from the child, now racing her tricycle round and round the tree in the centre of the lawn.

Tim had watched both of them. Their eyes met, hers frightened, his understanding but determined. She broke the silence.

"Do you think we ought to send Juliet to England? I think I'd be happier without her knowing she at least was safe."

He leant forward in the wicker chair and took his wife's hand.

"No, darling, that's not the answer. She's a Rhodesian and belongs here. We can't be cowards and let her run away."

"It's not a question of cowardice," she snapped. "It's plain common sense."

"You're worrying too much. Every time there's been any trouble the police have prevented it from getting out of hand."

"What you mean is, when we had any trouble before, Jock Ritter stopped it getting out of hand, and now there isn't any Jock Ritter!"

'She's only wound up for the moment,' he thought. He didn't talk for a while and gently stroked her hand. After a while she smiled and covered his hand with her own.

"I'm sorry," she said at length, "it's just the old props seem to be falling away one by one and we're more and more on our own."

"At first we may not be able to do the job as well," he said, "but we can't just run away from it. I'm thirty-four next June and Steve's a year older. Gary is damn nearly forty. You see, it's coming round to our turn. Eventually it will be Juliet's generation and she can't run away from it just because the going gets a little hard."

"It's easy to theorise," she said.

"Darling, haven't you found in life that problems which seem so vast till they are beaten become small afterwards? Looked at theoretically my father's problems, while different, were far greater than ours. He only had to be bitten by a snake and that was that. These days, thanks to the work of this herpetologist, Mr FitzSimons, down south, a single injection and in five minutes you would be right as rain."

She got up sharply and crossed the shadow line into the sun. She leant forward on the terrace parapet and everything twisted even tighter inside of her. For a moment she loathed the hot sun, the house, the very smell of Africa, and if those damn crickets didn't stop that interminable crunching with their back legs she'd scream.

She had to vent her feelings on someone.

"I don't care whether it does prove to be a quirk of history; I don't care if eventually we all go to tea parties together and scratch each other's backs. All I know is at the moment I can't stand this continued war of nerves."

He didn't reply but waited for her to work through as much of her tension as possible.

There was silence for a while. Marguerite remained motionless with her back to Tim. The child continued to circle the tree.

And then she asked him in a strained voice, "Couldn't we get out, Tim?"

He had hoped she would never ask the question, but now it was out he had to address it squarely so it could be put away for ever. He would let her talk about it. It was better she got it all off her chest.

"Where would we go?"

"Why not Australia?"

"And in ten years' time face the same problem with the millions of Chinese and Indonesians who are certain to flood the country before long."

"All right, let's go back to England."

"If there's an atomic war we'd be much safer here! Besides, we'd get claustrophobic in England. A semi-detached house in a satellite town; trains and tubes; millions of people seething around each other, around us; a cold, wet layer of drizzle instead of the African sun. No, darling, you'd hate that even more."

"Well, we'll have to find somewhere," she shouted hysterically.

He got out of his chair and went across to her to put his suntanned arm around her shoulder.

He spoke very quietly.

"I could never leave this country and live again; I'd slowly wither, and then you'd wither with me, and at the end of it all we'd have nothing left but a bitter memory. Even our own love would die in such a climate.

"It's been said that once you have lived two years in Africa, you always come back again, and I think that after eight years you would find the same. There's something in the ether, something which enters your soul and takes a hold and never lets go. The whole place breathes, not just the people. Everything, pulse after pulse.

"It isn't money, authority or anything material which prevents me from pulling up my roots, it's something far stronger. I just can't leave this country, the cork won't come out of the bottle."

He stopped, as a lump had come into his throat. She turned to look at him; he gazed far into the distance, between the tall gum trees, to the brown, waterless country that waited for the rains. The sun made a jewel of the tear which coursed down her cheek. Tim found words again and made himself speak them.

"I couldn't leave because, after you, I love this place with a deeper feeling than anything else."

He felt better now. He'd never expressed himself in such words before and now his convictions took on a greater strength.

"You do understand?" he said softly, looking down into her eyes.

"Yes, my darling, I do. I used to feel like that about Dorset when I was a child."

"So few people know that feeling today."

He wanted to talk about it more, so he went on.

"If you live in the country, you can have that feeling. To a smaller degree you can love a beautiful city, but all the millions of people who live in suburbia are lost to such feelings. I don't envy their security. I feel so terribly sorry they give up so much for it. They're not free people in a free country but units of humanity divided off brick by brick, wall by wall, house by house. No beauty, there's no beauty."

She looked out through the gum trees too; saw the whispering heat haze on the distant hills; heard the tune the crickets were playing. She had seen off her fear.

"I suppose you're right, darling. I'd only want to come back again."

They stood together, bathed in the African sun; it put strength into the arm which rested on her shoulder; it made perfection of her auburn hair.

"Oh just look at that child," she said.

Juliet had become bored with circling the tree and instead had tried to drive her tricycle over the rose bed, without success, and was now extracting herself with considerable difficulty from the thorns. Having made a satisfactory retreat she crossed the lawn to her father.

"Daddy, could you get my tricycle? I don't like those bushes, they prick."

They shouldn't have laughed but they did.

Her father did what he was asked then promptly completed a couple of fast circuits round the tree, crouched in a curious position with his rear well protruded and his shins in constant, painful contact with the handle bars. Juliet followed him round, shrieking at the top of her voice. Madazi, now white-haired – a singular achievement for an African – came out, attracted by the noise, and added a toothless grin to the general merriment.

Juliet spied Madazi and scampered away to him. Simultaneously, the two Bullmastiffs, offspring of an earlier generation, decided the temptation of Tim's seat was too much and gave chase. Tim increased his speed but so did the dogs and the general noise level rose considerably.

Over to the right, at the edge of the lawn, a little way away from the main fracas, Juliet looked up at Madazi.

"Do you want a ride?" she asked in his own language, which she spoke far better than her parents.

"I'm too old," he complained, but she tried to drag him over by the hand to the still rotating tricycle.

Tim stopped and joked with the old man.

The largest of the Bullmastiffs took a playful nip at Tim's hand and got playfully clouted round the ear. The two animals withdrew from the engagement, their expressions conveying their conviction that the other chap didn't know how to play the game.

"I guess we're a little past this," Tim said to Madazi, getting off the tricycle.

The old man grinned again and put his hand on Juliet's shoulder as he had done to Tim thirty years before. All Africans have a very deep affection for children; it was Shadrac, the boss boy, who had taught her Shona, with the help of his seven children.

For the moment their troubles had been forgotten.

They walked round the garden, father, mother and daughter. The African watched them, still grinning happily. The bougainvillea were at their best and, as on previous occasions, the scent of gardenia was strong.

"It was nearly eight years ago to the day that you showed me this garden for the first time."

"And I'll still be showing it to you thirty years hence," he replied before kissing her ear.

Instinctively they walked to the same arbour they had walked in eight years before. Juliet ran off to investigate a large butterfly: red, with gold tips to its wings and an ability to keep just that little bit ahead of her.

"Do you remember our wedding day?" Marguerite asked.

"I don't think I could very well forget," he replied.

They laughed together.

"I didn't exactly mean you might have forgotten. I was reminded of it by looking up at the house from here."

Their minds went back eight years.

"When Jock Ritter gave you away I thought he was going to ask for forty cows in exchange. The expression on his face certainly seemed to say it. He only remembered just in time that he was standing proxy for your father."

From light jubilation she became serious. She spoke quietly and looked more closely at her surroundings.

"Daddy would have loved to see all this. He loved beauty. We used to walk for miles through the Purbeck Hills. I'd make him pick old man's beard from the tops of the hedgerows, then we would top the hills and see the glitter of a still sea, go down to the water, bathe in it, let the sun warm us, drink pop. Yes, he always remembered I liked ginger pop. And then we would eat enormous sandwiches with large bits in them from Pincher the butcher's. Such a pity he couldn't have lived to see beauty like this."

She choked at the end, but Tim was glad it was sadness of another kind she was feeling.

"Better to live and be loved for a while than live forever by yourself," he told her quietly.

She forced herself to change the subject. A false gaiety came into her voice.

"I forgot to tell you the vicar phoned yesterday to say he had gout."

Slowly the picture of a gout-ridden vicar came into his mind with large white bandages swaddling the ends of his legs, rivalling in size the girth above.

He burst out laughing.

"Poor man. It's probably the price of saying he never had any troubles."

"But darling," she said, "it's very painful. You mustn't joke about it."

"I know I mustn't, but I can't help it. The very thought of a gout-ridden vicar makes me laugh."

Sentimentality fled and she joined in with his laughter.

"We ought to go and see him," suggested Tim. "No doubt we'll be chastised for not having attended his last service at the Camphers', but that will have to be. We can't let him lie alone in such agony."

"Fine," she agreed. "Let's go tomorrow afternoon, when the boys finish work."

"They'll be through by twelve o'clock, there's only a small part of the *vlei* left to be cleared. Shadrac will watch the seedbed watering."

They slowly walked back to the house, collecting their daughter on the way.

"I'm not surprised he's got gout."

"Why?" she asked.

"He turned down the sixth glass of champagne at our wedding with the profound excuse that he never had more than one, and he wasn't going to change his practice, even at a wedding."

"I don't think you can blame him for that," she laughed. "I was watching and every time he put down his glass, Jock Ritter would materialise from behind and top it up. The vicar's only puzzlement with his one drink was the fact that it took him two hours of solid drinking to finish."

"There were certainly lots of people in the house that day."

"Even Steve ended up a little worse for wear. And I thought you Rhodesians prided yourselves on your iron discipline and self-control?"

They arrived at the vicarage a little after two-thirty, having made quick work of the thirty-seven miles. The house was modern, green-tiled, new-looking, nestling close to the newly built church.

"You can't get away from them," said Tim, as they swung into the drive.

Steve's car was parked just outside the front door. He had married just before Mrs Carter died in 1965. She was South African, sensitive, like him. Evalyn was still overawed by the elderly Mrs Ritter but that had been her only problem.

They hadn't met up since the funeral of Steve's father, held on the farm, a week before.

The two boys had dug the old man's grave; that had been his wish. A codicil to his will read: 'My son and my greatest friend's son shall prepare my resting place on the high ground at Karilla where I can see the country, the Rhodesian country, all around me. I looked at Karilla first from that place with Jack Carter and I wish to continue looking once I'm gone.'

They knew what he meant, had carried out his wish, and the vicar had stood on the high ground with hard tears in his eyes and laid to rest forever a great friend. In fact he'd laid to rest far more.

Tim stopped the car next to Steve's and together they went into the house. The front door was open.

"Well, well," cried the vicar, his voice as deep and resonant as ever. "So, you've come also to see the lamb, sacrificed for the over-indulgence of others."

They greeted the Ritters and the portly invalid.

The patient was ensconced in a large chair, its size appropriate to his bulk. The offending foot lay delicately placed amidst a large pile of resilient cushions.

"How are you, vicar?" asked Marguerite.

"My dear child, if I didn't know better I'd say I was dying... There's nothing more excruciatingly painful than gout. My father had it, poor man, and now it's my turn. What it is to be a father's son. If he were alive I could atone for many a misdemeanour committed when the old gentleman was similarly attacked, for now I could offer him knowledgeable sympathy in his affliction."

Timothy was unable to restrain a smile.

"Young man," said the vicar, his twinkle growing to a mammoth size, "you do me wrong by laughing. But may I add that if it wasn't so painful I'd laugh myself, as a more ludicrous position in which to be found I find hard to visualise."

"How long will it last?" asked Evalyn Ritter sympathetically.

"We have a lady in our midst," pronounced the vicar and proceeded to ignore the rest. "The doctor, I regret, was not very helpful and suggested a period of months."

"Are you sure he wasn't pulling your leg?" asked Tim.

"Timothy, the very suggestion of touching my leg is exceedingly painful, the thought of having it pulled forces me close to a swoon." He turned away from the disbeliever and back to his new-found ally.

"The length of time seemed a trifle preposterous, and then again his judgement did happen to be accompanied by the merest flicker of a smile."

The vicar would have continued had he been able, but at this juncture his four guests burst into uncontrollable laughter and to save face the vicar joined in with the merriment. In so doing he moved his leg and a look of agony contorted his face. Steve tried to stop laughing.

"I have heard that it only lasts a few days," he said consolingly.

Through the pain, the vicar forced a reply.

"It is kind of you to say so, kind indeed. A month of this could lose me two stone of weight."

"I don't think that would happen," interjected Tim seriously.

"Improbable, but not impossible," surmised the vicar, gathering up his girth where he sat.

The vicar turned again to his ally.

"Evalyn, my dear, would you be so kind as to repair to the kitchen and procure some coffee for ourselves and these unwelcome guests? Anything harder than milk, tea or coffee is prohibited in this house for the moment."

"Why's that?" asked Tim.

"Don't know," replied the vicar off hand. "The doctor laid down such a law, but for the life of me I can't see why as he knows well enough I am a total abstainer."

Evalyn heard the laughter from the kitchen.

When it had died down, the vicar went on. "As a matter of fact, he pocketed the key to my drinks cabinet, remarking as he did so that my absentmindedness and force of habit might find me with glass in hand and no recollection of its coming. If anyone had been witness to such a remark, I would have found it my bounden duty to enter the lists and take him to court."

The coffee was served and the vicar eased himself into a less painful position.

"How's your mother?" Tim asked Steve quietly.

"Not too good. She seems to have closed up and there's nothing we can do about it. I'm going to ask Jenny to come back from London and look after her for a while."

"That should help a lot," agreed Tim.

"It's going to be a slow, slow process. You can't force it. Time will be the only real consolation. If only she would talk to Evalyn and me it would help, but she won't. She'll sit for hours on the stoep, just gazing out at the farm. She can see the high ground from there."

"It's only been a week, Steve, you can't expect anything to happen in a hurry."

For once the vicar was silent. He also was remembering Jock Ritter.

"Only a week yes, but Tim, it feels like another age. Seven days of interminable length. It seems damn ridiculous but for thirty-five years of my life we've always had someone there to turn to. Latterly, for the last ten years, I've made my own decisions, but it didn't alter the fact that I had a second opinion waiting to be asked. We all feel unbalanced, as if we were all missing something vitally important."

"We do," Marguerite agreed quietly. "That's something we all have in common."

The vicar leant forward in his chair. It hurt his leg but he didn't mind.

"There are always times like this in our lives, times when it is difficult to look forward, but the great thing is we always do look forward, and go forward too. And it may seem callous to say it but often we go on just the same, poorer in spirit but the same in body."

"That's what Tim was trying to tell me this morning," Marguerite said.

"It's not always easy to follow in practice," Steve observed soberly.

"I know it isn't," agreed the vicar, "but neither is life. When my foot is better, I'll come and stay at Karilla for a few days, during the week if I may, and talk to your mother. And though I shan't show it, I'll find it equally painful to be in that house without your father."

No one spoke for a while. They all thought of the dead man. Intermittently, Marguerite thought of her father and Tim of his. Their hearts were heavy.

The vicar broke in to lighten the mood.

"Is no one going to get me a second cup of coffee?"

"I'm sorry," said Marguerite, "let me do it this time. Would anyone else like any more?"

"Please," said Tim, for something to say and do. Steve agreed and Evalyn helped to carry the cups into the kitchen. The men were left alone.

"I was going to ring you when I got back," Steve told Tim, "but with the girls outside I can tell you now. There's a Police Reserve meeting in the club at seven-thirty tonight to decide who should be put up in place of my father. At the same time we want everyone's views on these intimidators being filtered into the farms. It's got to stop and quickly. My boys are becoming impossible. One of their huts was burnt down last night because the boy wouldn't pay his dues to the Party. They don't mince their words. If those bastards get control of this country they'll soak their brothers to the last drop of blood and leave them writhing in the ensuing mess with a wave and a 'Thanks very much, you suckers. We've had our fun and your money and now you haven't got anything left you can go to hell'."

"The boys are easily frightened."

"So would you be if your wife and house were at stake. These self-styled liberators have nothing to lose and everything to gain, and to achieve their ends they'll go to any lengths."

"You'd think the boys would kick them out of the compound." Tim was thinking out loud.

Steve leant forward in his chair.

"Again, it's fear. They don't know who belongs to the Party and the majority won't stick their necks out. Would you?"

"Hell, it makes you sick," agreed Tim. "It's like chasing a phantom. It frightens to death everyone who is superstitious but you can't catch it. Superstition, physical danger, both are exploited to the limits in order to play on these simple, rural minds. The only way you can get near to competing is by using force in return and then every paper in the world howls like an offended maiden aunt, indignant because someone has told her it's the proper thing to be. In the next breath she's talking about the impropriety of sex. And for both discussions all she has to rely on is second-hand information. It's a case of 'Come on Maud, we'll be late for the sheep run'."

Tim turned to the vicar.

"Does Christianity completely expunge superstition?"

"Do you walk under or round a ladder?" asked the vicar in return.

"Why, that's merely to avoid the pot of paint that might hit me on the head."

"That is what the surface mind tells us. Will you walk into an old house at night by yourself and not feel uncomfortable? No. The answer is superstition remains latent in all of us, black or white, and it only requires unscrupulous misappropriation to have it turned against us."

Tim shook his head bitterly.

"If we didn't call ourselves civilized, and therefore above such things, we would use superstition in return. These infiltrators would fall easier than their own victims since their minds are steeped in black magic. But both ways our hands are tied. We just stand back and watch our own men suffer."

The girls came back with the coffee.

"You all look solemn," observed Marguerite, as Evalyn set down the tray.

"We've been deliberating the troubles of a much troubled world," explained the vicar. "The solution for such a grave state of depression is a drink, not a lot, just one, or maybe two."

"Or three," came from Tim.

"Ignored," continued the vicar. "But unfortunately we shall have to continue with our melancholia as the doctor has the key and last time I sent an envoy to negotiate its return I neither saw return of key nor envoy. I have every hope, however, that my envoy still lives – the doctor is an appalling shot. I decided to send no more parties of peace as I consider them to be useless."

When the vicar perceived that the company were regarding him accusingly, he decided to forgo any further explanations.

At four-thirty they bade farewell to the vicar who had continued for the rest of the afternoon to jest about his gout in a determined campaign to relieve the company's minds of other troubles.

The light was particularly bright when they crossed the threshold into the sun.

Tim and Marguerite saw the others into their car. Tim closed the driver's door and leant his hands on the bar above the wound down window.

"See you at seven-thirty."

"What's happening then?" asked Marguerite, overhearing.

"A routine Police Reserve meeting," replied her husband.

He had no intention of causing her alarm. The whole thing was likely to blow over.

"Don't be late," said Steve as he let the car into gear.

The sun had lost its power; in barely two hours' time it would lose its light. Tim increased his speed to seventy and together they enjoyed the cool wind forced into the car through the side window flaps. The dust trail behind curled high and wide, hanging poised in the still air.

"Three months without rain is a long time," commented Tim as the tinder-dry bush slipped past them on either side.

"I like it though," she replied.

"So do I." And they drove on.

After a while Marguerite broke into his thoughts. "The vicar is wonderful, how he laughs at himself."

"Gout is certainly no respecter of people. I doubt, if the truth be known, whether he ever has more than two drinks in an evening."

"Unless someone spikes his champagne," she laughed.

"Yes, it's just as well he doesn't have a wedding once a week."

"Gout has nothing to do with drink?"

"It may aggravate it but it certainly doesn't cause the trouble. The vicar is a case in point. He always gives the impression when you offer him a brandy or a glass of wine that it's the most exciting thing in the world, but then he does that with everything."

"He's a great man," concluded Marguerite.

"Many would say wasted, so far from the madding crowd. But the vicar would laugh in a jubilant tone and then quietly explain that here people had other problems, some far more pressing than mysterious wavy lines on television sets."

By seven o'clock they had finished an early meal.

"You'll come with me, darling," he said, putting down his coffee cup. "They won't let you into the meeting but I expect some of the other wives will be there. I don't like the idea of leaving you here by yourself."

"Neither do I," she replied. "Juliet can sleep in the back of the car." The latter was normal practice for farmers' children; for kids it was always a great treat.

The wives were left on the club veranda. In the small lounge at the back, doors and windows were closed and the large overhead fan turned on full power. Colin Mandy, no longer a member of the Reserve, agreed to keep an eye on the wives, and at the same time look out for any eavesdroppers who might want to hear what the farmers were discussing.

At sixty-seven, Colin Mandy was completely white-haired and still unable to marshal the full ingredients of his mind. In patches it cleared and he was himself, but never for long. The club he ran automatically; he never thought or made decisions, the committee did that for him. As he closed the door he concentrated hard to remember if he had left the table and three chairs, with the water and the three glasses (yes, it was three, three of each), where they had asked him to leave them. He couldn't remember.

Inside, thirty-four reservists seated themselves at convenient points facing the top table and its three chairs, two of which were filled. The middle chair was empty in body but the spirit of Jock Ritter still prevailed.

An elderly man, the vice chairman, rose to his feet on the right of the empty chair. He came straight to the point.

"The person who fills this chair has got to be young. The police have given us complete authority to choose our own chairman. There is too much to say about Jock Ritter so I will say nothing. There are pieces of paper on the desk here. Will you each write down your nomination and return it to the box. There must be no personal feelings. Just the name of the man you think can do the job."

It was done quickly, the ballot counted efficiently by the two men behind the table.

The vice chairman looked up from the pieces of paper placed into piles. One was very much bigger than the others.

"Tim Carter, will you come and take Mr Ritter's place?"

Hell, he thought, as he mechanically propelled himself towards that vacant chair. I can't fill it. Why the bloody hell couldn't they have chosen someone else? He wanted to go up there and tell them all not to be so damn ridiculous. He was thirty-four, Jock Ritter had been sixty-eight, double his age. How the hell can one catch up on half a lifetime in five minutes? The others were clapping in a businesslike manner.

He suddenly realised that if he didn't take the job they would think he was frightened. Well he was frightened, frightened of the responsibility, but if they wanted a young chairman they could have one, but only on his terms.

He took his place, standing, gripped the edge of the table and braced himself to talk. The clapping stopped. They were hushed, waiting, expectant. Tim spoke quietly.

"This is not a political meeting so I shall say little. I cannot fill this chair as it was. I don't think I can half fill it, but as a body, as a joint unit, with everyone assisting me with ideas and criticism, we can go on as before. Can, no, that's the wrong word, *must*, is what I meant. Jock Ritter has gone. It has left us all stunned. But we have got to knit the security of the block together again."

He felt as though his mind was floating well above the body saying these words, as though the body were a puppet and his mind the puppet master pulling the strings. From up above it didn't seem as though the puppet was making much sense. And then he felt a deep belief in what the puppet was saying and his mind didn't want to merely pull the puppet's strings, it wanted to go down there and say a lot more. He went on, this time knowing exactly what he was saying, what he was going to say.

"Many of us have been jittery of late. Our wives especially. There is only one way to combat this fear and that is by organising ourselves so well that any danger can be quelled at its source. Prevention, prevention and still more prevention is the only practical solution to the problem. If we are always prepared, the problem will never materialise. Jittery panic is a sure sign of failure and failure breeds fear and insecurity. Security can be provided and if it is, and properly, there will never be the question of fear driving any of us from our farms."

He was going to stop them floundering in self-pity, right from the start.

He'd been given a job, though for the life of him he couldn't see why – in fact to him it seemed bloody ridiculous. But it had been done and now he was going to get on with it; punch the whole bloody thing back into shape. If he did it wrongly, they would tell him about it as he had asked them to. Till then, he was going on. He wasn't going to let them think back to the 'good old days' of Jock Ritter. The whole damn responsibility horrified him but at least he had a chance to get his teeth into something, in big chunks.

He sat down. They clapped again, hard and sharp, waiting to get on with the business. Most of them were worried. They wanted to air their views and hear others.

Tim stood up again.

"The second and last item on the agenda in front of me," and here he held up the piece of paper handed to him by the vice chairman, "is infiltration. There have been consistent rumours of unwanted elements being planted into this area to stir up trouble. For many reasons, no one has been able to point a definite finger. The men won't talk, they're too frightened. If, however, we can pool what information we have, it may be possible to lay bare the pattern of their methods. Who will start the discussions?"

Three people moved to stand up. Tim selected the eldest, marking down the names of the two to follow.

"Mr Baker." He sat down and the elderly gentleman stood up.

"Gentlemen," he began, "I'm not even certain that in my case it's infiltration. For twelve months I haven't taken on a new labourer and I've made a close check of the compound to determine if anyone is permanently squatting. I have found no evidence of this. But for all that, in the last four months a definite aura of fear has fallen on the span. It's very marked, what is more. No longer do they laugh at the most unlikely things; no longer do they rib the comic of the span; no longer do they get blind drunk on a Saturday night. The trade in my native store has fallen twenty-five per cent. All this in four months and with no apparent reason. It's uncanny. From being normally high-spirited, all of my boys, together, have sunk low, looking damn miserable into the bargain. They're obviously paying dues to a party, but why, and who, and where, I have been unable to trace."

Eight farmers spoke and their experiences were similar:

discontented workers who refused to give the reason. In each case, extensive research had failed to show up any one African as the cause of the trouble. One farmer had called his span together and talked to them for half an hour. They had listened but gone away silent. In each case also, there was no outward malice towards the Europeans. This wasn't surprising: in six years, wages had increased to four pounds per week, with free housing, food and medical attention. The white government had legislated this as a minimum wage. A number of bad farmers had gone under but the majority had improved their methods to pay for the large increase in expenses. The result was a well-paid labourer who didn't want to lose his job.

A South African stood up. His farm was at the top of the block.

"I have listened with interest to what everyone has said. The pattern is the same on my farm with one exception. I am certain who is causing the trouble."

The seated farmers turned to give the South African their complete attention.

After a pause he went on.

"I have tried sacking the man but, when I do, the span refuse to work. I have tried picking him out, making his life difficult, but he merely jabbers to the others of his afflictions, makes them laugh at his troubles and leers back at me. If I disciplined him, he'd go straight to the law which would have to uphold him. If he did anything wrong I'd jump on him straight away, but he never does. I might add that it's extremely frustrating."

"Does he often leave the farm?" Tim's mind was working fast.

"It's difficult to say," replied the South African.

"Will you watch his movements?"

"Certainly," the man said as he sat down.

"Oh, one more thing," Tim said. "Could you get your wife to take a photograph of the span at work, making sure of getting this particular gentleman in the picture?"

He then addressed the meeting as a whole, especially Gary Fairburn who was feigning sleep.

"I'm wondering whether this one could be operating throughout the block. It wouldn't be impossible with a bicycle. However, if every time he tries to go onto another farm we kick him off, it may curtail his activities. We are well within the law removing him from our own farms. If we each have an enlarged photograph, it may be possible to pick him out on his travels, if in fact he travels."

The evening produced that single suggestion of significance. The rest appeared to have little value.

The meeting ended. Groups of friends congregated and moved out onto the veranda. It was still cool at night and after the close oppression of the room, the night air was sharp.

Gary Fairburn, having detached himself from the chair which prevented sleep, found himself between Tim and Lance Grant on his way to buy a round of drinks. At his rear, Steve Ritter was keeping him on the move, denouncing the victim's irresponsibility in a loud voice. Needless to say, the accusations were being hotly contended.

"Fancy sleeping through a meeting."

"My dear chap, I wasn't sleeping." And then in a self-righteous tone, "In fact I heard every word."

"Don't talk nonsense, you were fast asleep."

"I heard every word."

"What was the fifth speaker talking about?"

"Don't be ridiculous, old chap, I'm not a mathematician."

"And what has mathematics got to do with it?" enquired Lance Grant, taking him firmly by the elbow.

"Well, damn it all," the prisoner protested, "I wasn't giving each of them a numerical number as he sat down."

"Of course you weren't," interrupted Steve swiftly, "you were asleep."

"That's just it, old boy," explained a miserable Gary, "I couldn't sleep on that chair, it was too hard."

"Now we have the truth," pronounced Steve triumphantly, "he has admitted guilt from his own mouth. Trying to sleep in a Police

Reserve meeting. That, gentlemen, is a heinous crime, which may only be mitigated by purchasing doubles, not only for us, but for our wives as well."

"But I'm broke," Gary protested.

"You'll be broken as well if you don't keep quiet," interposed Tim.

They wheeled him round the corner into the main veranda, the two outflankers and the rear guard in perfect step.

"What are you doing to Gary?" exclaimed Marguerite, getting up from her chair as the three poker-faced guards propelled their prisoner to the bar.

"We haven't completely decided," explained her husband.

"I think he should ask to be shot," Lance Grant said, taking a firmer grip on the elbow.

A prod from the rear.

"What are you drinking?" Gary asked Marguerite pathetically.

"He's taking the coward's way out," Steve said.

"On the contrary," explained Gary, "I'm going into liquidation."

"I always hoped he'd liquidate himself," affirmed Tim. "It's always such a messy business for other people. You'll be a good chap, of course, and dig your own grave. We'd hate to stand back and see the vultures consume your remains."

"I'd think they'd turn their noses up at such polluted flesh," declared Lance.

"Yes, you're right," agreed Steve.

"So be a good chap and dig a grave," concluded Tim.

They ordered their drinks from Gary. Gary paid.

"Cheers. Oh and congratulations," Lance said, turning to Tim.

"Why?" asked Marguerite, puzzled.

"Tim's taken my father's place," explained Steve.

A cold hand seized her spine and ran up its length. She shivered at the words.

"Oh," was all she said.

Steve saw the agitator walking towards his compound three

weeks later. He studied the man's photograph in his wallet before making a final decision.

He spoke sharply in Fanagalo.

"What do you want?"

"I'm going to see my brother," replied the African in a supercilious tone and the same language.

"Oh no you're not," replied Steve. "You're getting off this farm."

"You can't tell me where I can go," replied the troublemaker.

"Oh can't I just? This is my farm and you don't work for me and if you'd like to study the law a little closer you'll find that I'm perfectly within my rights. If I find you on this farm again I'll run you in."

The troublemaker was trapped but he wasn't going to give up. He looked around for help.

"You won't find any men to help you around here. I was born on this farm, along with most of the men, and we trust each other, a trust you're not going to break. You make me sick. When it comes to a showdown and you're on your own, you're a bloody coward. Now get off my farm."

The African hesitated, twisted his head again to look for help. No one was there, or at least no one was willing to come forward. The African feinted and then turned back to Steve with a long knife in his right hand.

Steve surveyed it contemptuously, though secretly he hoped the African didn't know how to use it.

"That's just what we needed to put you inside for a couple of years – threatening behaviour."

"I'm not threatening," replied the African, "I'm going to kill you."

"We'll see about that."

The African moved. Steve braced himself for the attack. The man was tall and lithe. Hatred poured out of him.

"The white bwana is afraid," he leered.

"Come a little closer and find out,"

"I will, I will," answered the African, "but all in good time. I'm enjoying this and the Party will reward me later."

"So will the police," replied Steve, watching the knife, "with five years' hard labour."

"We shall see," said the African.

Civilisation had dropped from the man like scales from a rotten fish; he was pure animal, with animal instincts. He had slipped back seventy-five years, where there was no rule, no authority, except that of the witch doctor. He was cornered, and like an animal he was going to fight.

The African bowed his knees and crouched, knife glittering in the sun, eyes glazed with hatred. He shuffled in the dust to distract; then again; the knife flashed at the end of the arm. He came a step closer and gave an animal grunt, then a screech, howling at Steve in sheer frustration. Another screech, mingled with fear this time, for the white man didn't move, just waited. There was a taut gathering of sinews throughout the black man's body; he gave a final howl, and the knife flashed out at this hated bwana who spoiled his plans. Then again, closer. Then it came hard and straight at its target, all the coiled strength behind it unwinding with an endless howl of murderous rage.

Steve flung himself from the killing knife and hit at the man as he went by. The knife caught his other arm and ripped it open. The African fell forward onto the pathway. Steve recovered but the African sprang up again, knife in hand. The position was as before, except that the African was crouching lower, panting with his lust, and blood was oozing from Steve's left arm.

Steve watched, carefully, not feeling the cut in his arm. This time he was going to attack, with his bare hands. They circled around each other. Steve knew the very clumps of grass behind him: he had always studied the nature he loved, remembered its pattern, even down to the smallest details.

The troublemaker didn't know what was behind him. Steve saw him catch his foot. He moved his own up the six-inch ridge he knew to be there on the side of the path, up to its zenith. He watched the African circle to his own ridge, saw him feel his left foot into it, expecting it to give way as the other clumps of grass had done. It didn't. He stumbled, glanced at the obstacle, and as he did so Steve flung himself from the ridge and kicked hard at the knife. It spun away, the sun picking at the steel before it dropped into the dry African bush. Steve hit him with his right hand – the left was numb and he didn't have time to wonder why. At the end, he brought his knee up hard into the African's groin. It was all over.

The man cringed, crawled to Steve and clutched at his foot, letting out his fear in great gasping sobs. His shoulders were hunched and the blood from Steve's arm dripped onto his neck. He cringed closer, sought the ankle, not the boot – he wanted the white man's mercy, not a black man's execution. Steve held himself erect, gathering his strength to drag the snivelling wretch to the house.

Evalyn passed out when she saw the torn flesh of her husband's arm. With his right hand encumbered by the troublemaker, he was unable to help his wife. He left her on the veranda, slouched in the chair from which she had risen in her horror as he stumbled inside.

When he got to the telephone, he stared at it while a pool of blood formed just below the cord. How the hell was he going to wind the bloody handle? He couldn't let the stupid bastard realise he hadn't much strength left. He looked round. The door to the lavatory was opposite. He shoved it open with his foot, kicked the African inside, measured the farm-built window with his eye to make sure his prisoner couldn't get out, and took the key from the inside, slamming the door shut and locking him in.

He leant against the door.

'Hell,' he thought, 'I'd better do something about this arm,' and began a weaving blood trail towards their bedroom. He found a handkerchief, took the ends and, using one hand and his teeth, tied it around his arm just above the slash. He pulled hard and cut off the main flow of blood. It took him five minutes, by which time the carpet was a mess.

He made for the door and the telephone and met an ashen-faced Evalyn looking for him in horror as her terrified eyes followed the trail of blood.

"Oh my God, oh my God," was all she could say as her swaying husband appeared, framed in their bedroom doorway.

"Could you phone Tim?" he said quickly, trying to make his brain clear. "Tell him to get over here in a hurry as I've got his troublemaker locked in the lavatory." He wavered. "If you don't mind I think I'll go and lie down."

As he turned, he called back over his shoulder.

"Oh, and you'd better take my gun, the lavatory door isn't very strong."

She was torn between the telephone and her husband.

"The gun first, then the telephone, and then me," he called, without looking back.

He crawled up onto the double bed, lay himself down and passed out.

She hesitated, then dashed into the bedroom, grabbed the gun and ran back to the telephone. She called Tim, somehow made him understand, and then went to her husband.

She was hysterical.

Tim put down the receiver and called loudly.

"Marguerite!"

She was in the kitchen. "What is it?"

"Get Juliet into the car. There's trouble at Karilla and we're in a hurry." Lately, they never left the child alone on the farm.

"Juliet! Juliet!" called her mother. The child didn't answer.

"I don't know where she is," she called to a receding Tim.

"Well, find her," he shouted back in his frustration. His mind worked fast. Evalyn had sounded frantic on the phone and his questions had been left unanswered. Why had she phoned and not Steve, if the only trouble had been someone locked in the PK? Had she called him willingly? Hell. Could it be a trap? He had reached the car. He stopped and ran back up the veranda steps to get a gun.

"Have you found her?"

"No," Marguerite screamed back. "She must be out in the lands somewhere."

"We'll have to leave her," decided Tim, "Philip will still be here."

"I don't like it."

She had come into the lounge and was watching him take a pistol from the gun case and load it.

"Neither do I," he replied, "but we're in a hurry. I don't know what the hell's going on at Karilla but Evalyn could barely get three words out coherently."

He slapped the magazine into the gun. "Right, let's go."

He drove the distance fast, very fast. The car skidded sideways for a stretch of ten yards on loose sand and Marguerite held her breath. For a moment she was thankful that Juliet was not in the car.

"Sorry, darling," called Tim with a faint smile as he managed to turn the front part of the car to face down the road again.

She even smiled with him.

On a clean stretch of dirt track the needle reached eighty-five. 'We only need a flat tyre,' she thought, tensing herself against the burden of speed.

He took a hand from the wheel, without losing a fraction of his concentration, and squeezed the small hand, white with being clenched too hard, which lay on the dusty seat between them.

She felt better, and better still when he got both hands back on the wheel.

They slowed down for a bridge, a slab of concrete supported by boulders, cast into the stream. The water at the height of the dry season was still just flowing over the concrete – half an inch deep in the middle, where the concrete dipped in sympathy with the bed of the stream. Tim slowed to what he thought was a steady twenty miles per hour. The previous speed deceived him; they cut through the water at forty miles per hour, the splashes hurling themselves up six feet on either side.

"The car won't have to be washed tomorrow," was all he said.

Marguerite could only grimace fearing what lay ahead of them.

They drove close to the compound on their way to the house. Chickens squawked, flew, ran and scattered in many directions. Miraculously, none were hurt.

They reached the house and stopped the car outside.

"Stay here," said Tim shortly. "I'll go in first."

The house was quiet. No one had greeted them on arrival. He was certain something was wrong as he made his way through the lounge, one hand firmly holding the revolver in his right pocket. Still no one in sight. He passed down the corridor to the bedroom block. Tried two doors and then the door to the lavatory. It was locked.

Then he heard it. A faint sobbing coming from the main bedroom. He walked faster, taking the gun out of his pocket, and went through the open door into the bedroom.

Evalyn was crouched on the dressing table stool. Steve was either asleep, passed out or...and a fierce pain cut into him. He looked closer and relaxed a little; the prostrate figure on the bed was breathing. He caught sight of the arm, now roughly bandaged; looked at the blood saturating the counterpane. He turned his attention back to Evalyn who hadn't yet registered his presence.

"It's all right now, Evalyn," he said softly.

She looked up, hair bedraggled, eyes red, a ghost of fear still haunting the sockets. She stared at him. Tears welled again.

"It's all right."

The pent-up sobs burst and flooded out. She flung herself at Tim.

"Thank God you've come."

He let the tears flow for a while, and waited until they had subsided a little.

"What happened?" he asked eventually, holding her away from his shoulder.

"Steve's been knifed." She sobbed again loudly.

"And the agitator?"

"He's in the lavatory," and here the fear came back again.

"He's still there," Tim told her comfortingly. "I tried the door on the way in."

Once she'd started to regain possession of herself, he set her back down on the stool then bellowed down the corridor.

"Marguerite, can you come and help?"

He looked at Steve, and then at the quantity of blood on the carpet and floor. His breathing looked all right; the bandage on the arm seemed to have stopped leaking; probably lost a lot of blood but little else. He hoped so, anyway.

"What on earth has been going on?" asked Marguerite from the corridor as she followed the trail of blood into the bedroom."

"Steve's been knifed."

"Good God!" Marguerite stopped dead at the sight of Steve, prostrate and out cold in a carnage of congealed blood.

"Will you have a look at him?" asked Tim. "I hope it looks worse than it is."

She went over to the bed.

"Where's Mrs Ritter?" she asked, gently prising back the handkerchief's flaps.

"Evalyn?" Tim prompted.

"She had to go to Salisbury, to see the solicitors about probate," replied Evalyn, starting to pull herself together.

Marguerite spoke as she tried to appraise the extent of the knifing.

"We could certainly do with her to deal with this. It's ironic she chose this day to leave the farm when normally she doesn't leave for months. I shall need hot water," she continued, "and a mild disinfectant. Until I've cleared away the mess, I can't see how serious it is."

"You stay with him," directed her husband. "I'll put some water on and give Evalyn some brandy at the same time."

"Will you make some tea as well? Hot, sweet tea will be exactly what Steve wants when he comes around. I'll be surprised if he isn't suffering from shock."

There was nothing she could do without hot water. She

remained seated on the bed next to the still unconscious Steve and meditated on the vagaries of Africa. In Africa there was always the unexpected. Some people said it made the place exciting. She wasn't so sure that she wanted to be excited; not like this anyway.

Tim returned with a bowl of hot water, a kettle and a bottle of TCP. He mixed a small amount of disinfectant into the water, handed Marguerite a fresh roll of cotton wool and held the bowl ready for her to use.

She cleaned the wound, replaced the tourniquet and bandaged the arm.

She was feeling faint by the end. During the process Steve had fitfully come to. Tim went out to get the tea. She bathed Steve's forehead and slowly consciousness returned, together with pain.

"I'm afraid I'm being a nuisance," was all he said on recognising Marguerite.

"Don't be bloody silly," said Tim as he came back with the pot of tea.

After he had poured a cup and added five teaspoons of sugar, he handed it to Marguerite.

"Can you sit up?" she asked.

Together they propped Steve up enough to be able to take the tea.

"This tastes wonderful," he murmured halfway through. He finished the tea in four gulps. "I feel as weak as a kitten."

"I'm not surprised," said Tim. "You must have lost a good few pints of blood."

"Is he still in the lavatory?" Steve said, suddenly remembering his responsibility.

"Yes," replied Tim. "At least, the door's still locked."

Steve's mind began to clear.

"Where's Evalyn?" he said, trying to look around.

"She's all right now," explained Tim, "but she didn't take it too well."

"Poor girl." Steve subsided back into the pillows. "I'm afraid she's never seen anything like this before."

"The first time is always a shock," agreed Marguerite. "I had the same reaction when Tim tried to burn himself alive just before our wedding."

"We'll have to get you into Marandellas tonight," put in Tim. "Your arm will have to be stitched and a doctor ought to give you an antibiotic injection. Anything could have got in the wound. We'll take our friend in at the same time."

"What happened?" Marguerite asked.

Steve told the story in brief outline.

"You're lucky to have got away with it so easily. Fanatics can be dangerous."

"Thanks," replied Steve.

Evalyn came back, quickly sat herself on the bed close to her husband, took his good hand, and gently brushed back the hair which had fallen over his forehead.

"You frightened me, darling," was all she said.

"I won't do it again," he replied like a small child, and pulled her head down to be kissed.

After Steve's second cup of sweet tea they helped him into Tim's station wagon. Tim went back to unlock the lavatory while the others remained in the car. On the way he found some electrical flex to keep the African's hands out of mischief on the drive to the police station.

He listened at the door but could hear nothing inside. Frowning, he unlocked the door and gently let it swing open while he stood back a little, waiting for trouble.

Slowly the picture became apparent. As the door swung open, Tim saw a limp leg hanging halfway up the far wall. Then the toilet seat came into view, and finally, as the door swung fully open, another leg. Each looked as forlorn as the other. Rear-quarters can look particularly forlorn, especially when the front quarters are stuck in a lavatory window. The fellow had obviously thrashed himself to a standstill and now he hung exhausted from the sill, like a soggy piece of cod bent at the tail.

As the picture unfolded, so the mirth in Tim began to boil over and finally it burst out in great shrieks of laughter which only doubled in force when the bottom gave a twitch. He had to go and get his wife. Together they found it even funnier. The tension had been building up long enough, but now the valve had been turned, releasing the pressure.

After considerable trouble they managed to unhook him from the lavatory window and dump him in the back of the car, a totally spent force. Tim looked at the flex and left it in the glove compartment.

Steve took the journey well. The doctor prescribed seven stitches, an injection and a couple of days' rest. Being otherwise strong, Steve would quickly mend.

The African was taken to the police station and charged. Three months later he was sent for trial in Salisbury. They'd found the knife and when it came up in court, Evalyn had to look away to prevent herself from fainting. The blade was a foot long, an ugly weapon, worn in a specially made pocket in the man's trousers, against his thigh. On seeing the weapon, even Steve was surprised that he hadn't been killed.

The fanatic was sent down for five years on a count of attempted murder. The block quietened down but it was never the same again. The pattern of life had been broken. A gulf had opened up between black and white which would become more and more difficult to cross with the passing years.

The knifing was only the beginning. 1968 saw the rot set in, but in comparison with what was to follow, it was a gentle disagreement between two people who at the end were inclined to raise their voices. It was the thin edge of the wedge which was to be slowly, relentlessly driven home: by fanatics, black and white; by world opinion; by the sheer wilfulness of human nature; by the more repulsive instincts of the human race. In Africa, over the next five years, humanity was destined to sink low. True values, brave men and sanity, all were to be pushed aside.

When Africa boils, it explodes and southern Africa was about to explode, to provide history with yet another sickening tragedy.

Everyone saw it coming but the people who could do something about it turned their backs and refused to square up; they didn't believe it would come, yet it came.

The moderates, in their millions, were tossed about by the bloody gale and suffered most.

The apathy of the leaders, who could have stopped up the breach, was appalling. The Rhodesian Government fought with words, but what did the voices of a mere half million count against the self-righteous hypocrisy of the rest of the world?

In the 1970s, the English-speaking public throughout the world believed what the papers said: they didn't want to think for themselves. It was much easier to believe the written word and agree with their favourite TV announcer. The papers gave them only what they wanted to read and they wanted to be great liberators from their armchairs. They felt good about it; never mind about the facts. Africa for the African had become a fine phrase. It sounded good. Grand. Anyway, it was easy enough to be benevolent when you had nothing to lose.

The politicians liked it that way and did everything to further its encouragement. They didn't wish to offend a new, emergent country with a literate and illiterate population of ten thousand and five million respectively, especially when those ten thousand had a vote equal to their own one hundred and sixty thousand in the United Nations.

Rhodesia was a pawn on the chess table of world politics, and therefore expendable. 'Well I mean, old chap, the rest of the world wanted it that way. If a few thousand starved to death as a consequence who are we to judge? I mean, we couldn't very well have disagreed with our allies, could we? By the way, where is Rhodesia? Well I never knew that. Extraordinary! I must remember to tell my wife before we turn on the telly tonight.'

11

A STRAW IN THE WIND 1974 TO 1975

"Now to hell with politics," suggested Tim, "let's enjoy our Christmas. There's enough trouble in the world without dwelling on the subject. Have another glass of champagne, Gary? I don't think they're going to bring much more into the country; most of the dealers in Salisbury have got cold feet. Make the most of it!"

He was determined to brighten up their Christmas and fixed his red paper hat at a more jaunty angle.

"Come on, Evalyn, surely you'll have some? There's a good girl," and he topped up her glass. "Steve, there's still some in the bottle. It's all right, vicar," he called across the room, "I've still got one more in the fridge. Marguerite, could you fetch the other bottle?"

"Can I have some, Daddy?" asked his twelve-year-old daughter.

"We'll see, we'll see," replied her father, ruffling her hair; it didn't make much difference as the hair was cut short to the head, moulded with the face.

The younger generation was now the older generation in the block. The vicar, at sixty-three, was their last contact with the Jock Ritters, the Jack Carters. Age and six more years had taken its toll on Mrs Ritter and Van Campher. The pathetic relic that was once Colin Mandy had mercifully been taken away to join his wife.

At Urangwa, Shadrac, the boss boy, only supervised light work. He was old, very old. His curly white hair gave him great distinction, enhanced by the wrinkled, wise face, which lately seemed troubled. The old man feared for the future.

When Madazi had died, Juliet had cried and thrown a tantrum and told everyone they were telling fibs and that he was only sick and would be back in the house before the end of the week. Tim, too, was affected more than he showed by losing a lifelong friend. They had understood each other so well, had been able to weld their varied backgrounds together to form harmony. They had overcome so much in nearly forty years. They never spoke of it; they didn't fully appreciate what had happened. A great deal had died with Madazi.

The eldest of the Grant boys, the one who had been page boy at their wedding, now twenty-two, was offering cocktail snacks to his two sisters aged sixteen and nineteen respectively. The other brother was at university in England, having won a scholarship: you couldn't buy education anymore.

A five-year-old Cony Ritter was playing hell with her mother, insisting that nuts should join the champagne in her mother's glass. Her father was waiting, ready to pounce when the situation worsened.

"But my dear chap, being a bachelor is just the answer. Isn't it, vicar?" called Gary, halfway across the Urangwa lounge.

"I'm afraid I have to agree with you on that score," replied the vicar, coming across to them, holding a small champagne glass in his podgy hand.

"I'm in my mid-forties," continued Gary, "and as free as the day I was sent down from Oxford. Marvellous life, absolutely marvellous," and he meant every word of it. "Stay single," he concluded to Bruce Grant who was listening with great attention on his right.

Getting old had certain advantages, or so Gary had found. People listened to him seriously, the young even hung on his words. He enjoyed the whole thing as a huge joke and played up to the full.

Life was marvellous if you didn't take it seriously, or so said Gary, not once, but many times.

"Why were you sent down from Oxford?" asked the Grant boy.

"Yes, I've never reached the bottom of that one," put in the vicar.

"You really want to know?" asked Gary.

"My dear chap," began the vicar who wasn't allowed to finish his sentence.

"Over here then," said Gary, drawing them away from the others. "I don't want too many to hear my sins of a quarter century ago."

The Grant boy seemed a little embarrassed.

"Oh don't worry," said Gary, "it's quite fit for a vicar's ears."

"I don't think I like your invitation," replied the vicar stiffly.

"Do you know," said Gary, turning to Bruce Grant and ignoring the vicar's sally, "this is the only belligerent person I have had the fortune or misfortune to encounter in my forty-something years."

"The simple truth is that God-fearing men keep well away," explained the vicar. "You were saying about being sent down from Oxford?"

"It was really rather bad luck. At that time I had an insatiable appetite for playing practical jokes. They put up with my preliminary skirmishes but then I grew too big-headed and embarked on some rather larger enterprises."

"Which was the straw that broke the camel's back?" asked Bruce Grant enthusiastically.

"A haystack might be a better simile."

"I think we'd better hear the worst," said the vicar.

"I tried to model myself on a certain gentleman who practised the art of practical jokes at the turn of the century. He was reputed to have spent fifty thousand pounds in the process and, amongst other things, arranged a tour of the Royal Navy for the head of state of a Middle Eastern country, and then proceeded to impersonate the particular gentleman in question and received a twenty-one gun salute at Spithead. There was quite a stir when the Navy found out some two days later."

"I hope you didn't try and keep up with the times and inspect the RAF?" suggested the vicar.

"No, I didn't get that far," replied Gary in all seriousness. "I knew a chap who had just come back from what was then the Belgian Congo with twelve large, very much alive crocodiles, which he had been commissioned to bring back for a private reptile zoo for an exorbitant fee. I got him rather tight at a party of mine in the flat at Kensington and in his cups he promised to lend me four of the beasts. He was a little concerned the next day when sober but being a gentleman he held to his word. The two-day loan was put into operation and feeding instructions were given. In the end my friend was persuaded to assist in the job and drove his truck up to Oxford with me and the four beasts who made the most alarming noises in their pens at the rear. The idea was to place, in the early hours of the morning, the grotesque beasts in the fountain at the centre of the college quadrangle. To get to the quadrangle one had to pass from the driveway down a long, stone corridor. We were in the process of encouraging the first crocodiles down the corridor when we were surprised by a senior professor. What the hell he was doing there at such an hour I never discovered."

"How did you lead a croc down a corridor?" asked Bruce Grant in disbelief.

"My friend had drugged them before we started the walk, so there wasn't any danger. It was just the size of the brute that impressed the professor."

"After that, you didn't return?"

"Oh yes, I carried on my studies till the end of the term. These people never do anything in a hurry. Anyway, they eventually decided that that had been the culmination of enough practical jokes and they weren't prepared to chance their arm again. So I was asked to terminate my studies, which I did."

"How many terms did you have at Oxford?" asked Bruce Grant.

"Just that one," replied Gary.

"I would like to have seen the professor's face," said the vicar as the picture conjured itself before his eyes.

"Yes, it was rather amusing," agreed Gary. "My friend said after that he didn't mind whether he sold them or not."

"Did he?"

"Yes, he got the fee all right."

Steve, having admonished his only child, crossed to the window to survey the evening sky. Tim joined him.

"We're going to get a storm," Tim murmured after a while. The two men continued to look out, alone with their thoughts. Tim's false high spirits had been expended.

And then again, when his thought had completed its particular circle, Steve replied.

"Yes, I think you're right."

There was another long pause.

"How many barns have you reaped?" asked Tim.

"Five."

"How does it look?"

"Not bad," replied Steve. "Should get a good crop if the men aren't told to go on strike in the middle of the season."

"Yes, it's rather expensive. The men suffer most."

"They don't have any choice," Steve said, irritated. "If they work, they get knifed. Which would you do? Anyway, you fed yours while they didn't work last year."

"It wasn't their fault. How could I see Shadrac and his family go hungry? Or any of the others who've been on Urangwa all their lives?"

"You're right," agreed Steve. "I'd do the same."

"I couldn't do it again though. I haven't got any money. You can't get credit, so that's that. I've told Shadrac and it made the poor old boy cry. He said he'll bring even more pressure to bear on the rest to make them work if the Party tell them to stop."

"It won't do any good."

"I know," agreed Tim, "and so does he."

"They get at the wives and then threaten the children."

"It's impossible to compete with organised terrorism, however small the band of terrorists."

"The police have found that," agreed Steve, watching the storm clouds build up.

"Do you think they'll start on us?"

"I'm surprised they haven't already."

"They're basically extreme cowards and find their own people easier meat. They might get knifed back if they came up here and they wouldn't like that."

A sheet of lightning cut down to the ground.

"Here we go," pronounced Steve, happy that his storm prediction had come true so soon; fatalistically so.

Tim was unable to reply. The clap of thunder appeared to originate just above the veranda in front of them.

"I could do with some rain," replied Tim without conviction, when the noise had receded. And as they turned back to the party, "Funny, you know, the weather hasn't changed its old pattern."

"About the only thing that hasn't," agreed Steve, giving up his vigil of the sky.

They heard the rain coming a long way off and smelt it before it arrived in its torrents. The thatched roof softened the blow of hard falling water. They were all cheered by the rain. It relieved the oppressive heat and in Rhodesia it was always an exhilarating sound. Tim's automatic welcome of the rain was justified.

He sat on the arm of his wife's chair. She broke into his thoughts.

"Do you remember our first Christmas together?" she asked.

He cast his mind back, back into calmer times, away from the troubles which presently engulfed him.

He found himself in the small flat. He was young, not his present forty. The turkey, purchased in the turmoil of the Portobello Road, was providing delicious smells; the candles barely flickered.

"Yes, I remember," he said. "It was fifteen years ago."

"It is rather a long time," she laughed, looking at Juliet. "It's been a wonderful fifteen years," she said more seriously, taking his hand. "I wouldn't have missed it for anything."

"Not even a nice, safe bank clerk for a husband?"

"Certainly not." And then she saw he was teasing and they laughed together.

"I still love you just as much," he whispered into her ear and would have drawn away if she hadn't pulled him back again.

"I think I love you even more," she whispered.

They went into dinner just before seven, early because of the children. Afterwards the three families, the Grants, Ritters and Carters, together with the vicar and Gary, sat on the veranda enjoying the cool evening air, made fresh by the rains.

At first everything seemed silent and then the noises of the African night became apparent: frogs, croaking happily with water to play in; crickets, rejuvenated by the rain; night birds; and then away to the right, the drums started and were answered by more in Tim's compound: first softly, a rhythmic beat, then more, vying with each other, exciting, frightening, powerful. By the end, five compounds were playing to the night, dying, growing, growing more, a steady fevered beat, defying the night, defying anything that wasn't part of itself.

"They must have brewed plenty of beer for Christmas," suggested Lance Grant.

They had all been listening to the sound of Africa. Tim loved it, had been born amongst it, this was his; if he didn't understand their meaning, he understood their message. His heart strove in unison with the drums. Marguerite was frightened. She wouldn't admit it, but she was always frightened by the drums. Juliet, in her child's mind, loved it. She knew nothing else, having never set foot outside Africa. It was all part of the life she had been born to. There was, therefore, no reason for her to question it.

The servants brought in the coffee. At one end Marguerite poured, at the other Evalyn Ritter served the multitudes.

Sometime later, Tim announced that he must look at the barns. There were twenty-eight on the farm, used for curing the tobacco leaf.

"I'll come with you," said Steve from out of the darkness. They had turned off the lights to thwart the flying insects.

"We might as well walk," suggested Tim, having found his torch.

"I could do with some exercise after the meal," agreed Steve.

"What a wonderful night," he said a little further on, "it seems impossible that all this could blow up overnight."

They couldn't see each other's faces, each other's expressions. It made talking on unsavoury subjects so much easier.

"I think it will," said Steve.

"So do I," agreed Tim, "but when?"

"We may get a couple more years of this type of stability. But nothing's allowed to rest. When things look like getting better, someone outside starts to stir it up again."

The gum trees hung restfully above them in the still air as they passed down the avenue. The barn fires glowed red at the foot of the tall buildings, watchful eyes in the dark night, picked out as they came round the back of the grading shed.

The barn boy had gone to sleep; luckily the barn temperatures were correct.

"I ought to give him an earful," said Tim. "But after all it is Christmas. They've probably filled him up with beer."

He nudged the prostrate African, curled up close to the fire. It was one of his older boys who at last woke, sat up, blinked, saw who it was, jumped to his feet and broke into a lengthy explanation of how he couldn't possibly have been asleep. The Europeans smiled to themselves. They had been dealing with this for so long that both of them could have recited a similar dissertation before they had even woken the sleeping barn boy.

At the end of the discourse came a silence while the African maintained his appearance of indignity at anyone suggesting he might have been asleep on duty. In fact, no one had done so as yet. Neither of them could see his expression in the dark but both knew exactly what it portrayed.

Tim only spoke after the expected, respectful pause.

"Don't go to sleep again, Fourpence." The man liked his name and would never have considered changing it. He had given it to himself, amongst a collection of seven others, as it seemed to portray wealth.

"No, *baas*," agreed the offender. They couldn't see it in the dark, except for an increased expanse of white teeth, but they knew he was grinning and he knew that they knew he was grinning and the expanse of white teeth grew larger. They checked the temperatures of the other barns with Fourpence in attendance.

On their way back to the house, Steve asked, "Do you think we're well enough prepared for trouble?"

"I was glad when the police issued us with Sten guns; you could at least hold your own against a mob for a decent length of time. The shortwave radio sets were a good idea too; if they really meant trouble they'd be sure to cut the telephone wires beforehand. I have also got Marguerite fairly accurate with a revolver."

"I daren't ask Evalyn to use one," said Steve, "she'd be frightened to death."

"So was Marguerite, believe me," laughed Tim, seeing the funny side of an otherwise sickening question.

"You haven't changed your mind about getting out?"

"No. That would be doing exactly what the Nationalists want us to do. I have decided to deprive them of that bit of pleasure. If they want to get rid of me, they've got to do more than they've done up till now. If I have to, I'll close up the farm, grow enough food for the family with my own hands and wait for the trouble to die out. When the masses get hungry enough they'll soon sort out the people who caused the trouble and then I'll get my labour back and we can start again. At the moment, there is more reason for my span to keep in with the fanatics. When they're starving, there will be more reason not to. If they strike again, it will be out of my control to help anyone apart from my own family."

"The whole thing makes you sick," agreed Steve, as they reached the house.

"You can say that again."

The Christmas wasn't a success but it was more of one than they had expected. It was good to have all their old friends in the same house again; that part they certainly enjoyed. But the undercurrent was too much to make it hilarious.

The telephone rang. Marguerite was in the kitchen, supervising the cooking. She crossed the courtyard from the kitchen block into the main section of the house. The phone was still pumping out its incessant jangle and she was glad to stop the offensive noise by picking up the receiver.

"Hello?"

"Hello, is that Urangwa Estate?" The voice was distant, very clear, but as though it emanated from a long tunnel."

"Yes," answered Marguerite, puzzled as to who the caller might be.

"May I speak to Mrs Carter?"

"Speaking."

"This is Myles Featherstone," pronounced the voice at the other end.

She was jarred, as if a voice had spoken to her from beyond the grave. Incredulity spread through her mind and then she dismissed it; someone was playing a practical joke.

"Hello, hello," repeated the voice. "Are you there?"

"Would you say who is speaking again?" asked Marguerite, bringing herself back into the present.

"It's Myles Featherstone. Is that you, Marguerite?"

"Yes," she replied, still unconvinced and still waiting for the practical joker to announce his true identity. And then she thought again: no one in Rhodesia had even heard the name Myles Featherstone apart from Tim, and she could hear him moving around in the lounge, having come in from the lands for his lunch.

"Hello?" The voice was getting insistent again.

"Is that really you Myles?" she replied, still disbelieving.

"I wouldn't say it was if it wasn't."

And then he laughed and a peculiar, unnatural shiver came over Marguerite. She recognised the laughter from the past and as she did so she smelt the salt air, the air of the Isle of Purbeck.

"But this is fantastic," she burst out, at last excited. "Where are you?"

"In Salisbury," replied Myles. "I've been here for three weeks and have only just discovered your address. I met an amusing chap called Gary Fairburn at a cocktail party last night who told me all about you both. Before I met this chap I had almost decided to phone all the Carters in the telephone book. In fact I tried two of them but received such extraordinary answers that I forwent the other thirty-five."

"I can't believe it's really Myles Featherstone. Do you realise we haven't spoken to each other for eighteen years?"

"Yes, only too well," he replied and she was again puzzled, this time by the tone of his voice.

"You must come up to the farm," she suggested, remembering her sense of hospitality.

"I'd love to," he replied. "I'd hoped you would suggest it." His voice was back to normal.

"Bring your family with you," she added.

"What family?" he replied, the voice puzzled in its turn.

"Well, your wife and children."

"I haven't got a wife."

"You mean to say you haven't married? But you must be nearly forty."

"Thirty-nine to be exact."

"Well, come yourself."

"Fine."

"When are you free?"

"Any time."

"How do you work that?"

"Work what?"

"Well, doesn't your boss object when you run out to distant farms, just at the drop of a hat?"

"I haven't got a boss, not here anyway."

"What are you doing then?" she asked. "Are you on holiday?"

"Don't you read the papers?" he replied, laughing.

"Not very well," she conceded. "We only get the gossip twice a week. Why?"

"For the last three weeks I've been the High Commissioner in Salisbury."

"But that's fantastic!"

"Thanks."

"You'd better come out tonight and tell us all the news. You haven't met Tim, have you?"

"I'm looking forward to it," he replied.

"Six-thirty tonight. It's sixty-eight miles out on the Marandellas Road." And she gave him the directions.

"Bye," she said.

"See you tonight," he replied and she heard his receiver go down.

'Good lord,' she thought, a little shaken. She still felt peculiar when she went through to the lounge and told Tim. He was reading yesterday's paper.

"Darling," she said, "you could never guess who was on the phone."

He put down the paper and smiled at her. "Who?"

"Myles Featherstone."

"How extraordinary," he replied. "They were talking about the new High Commissioner on Thursday at the club. They said his name was Featherstone. Unusual to hear it twice in so short a time. Gary was going to some cocktail party in his honour."

"It's the same person," she replied.

"He must have done well," he said enthusiastically.

"Yes," she replied, "and what's more he's coming to dinner tonight so you'll have a chance to pick his brains."

"Why, that's great," he said. "We should hear the news at first hand. When did you last see him?"

"Eighteen years ago," she said quietly from the window.

"That's a long time," he replied without expression, having taken up his paper again.

He didn't see the mist in his wife's eyes.

Marguerite, forever a sentimentalist, was unsettled. All the old pictures came back in snatches. Boats with straining sails; a cricket match; a beach bathed in the early morning sun. If analysed, she was mourning her youth, mourning the part of her life without responsibilities, without these paramount worries. Her mind jumped forward from one forgotten scene to another and into the picture came Tim. She traced her life forward again, to Rhodesia. On, in fact, till her soft eyes came to rest on him: hair ruffled, boots filthy, face the colour of mahogany, home-cured tobacco pervading the room with the smell of burnt rubber as the smoke curled heavily from the furnace of his pipe, the quiet concentration on his face.

She crossed the room noiselessly and kissed him softly behind the ear. He put down the paper, took hold of the hand which rested on his shoulder and looked up at her.

"What was that for?" he asked playfully.

"Just to say that I love you."

Sitting where he was, he quietly drew her round by the hand from the back of the chair, pulled her over the high arms and into his lap. The paper fell to the ground.

"I could eat you," was all he said.

The car ground into the driveway at seven forty-five. It was nearly dark, the quick African twilight having all but run its course. Marguerite's nervousness had returned and she hesitated on the veranda, above the line of steps which ran down to where the car was pulling up. She took control of herself and thought how ridiculous it was for a woman of thirty-five to behave like a girl at school.

She walked down the steps and as he got out of the car she held out both her hands.

"Hello, Myles," she said.

"Marguerite." And he held her hands firmly.

They didn't speak for a moment but looked at each other in the dusk, seeing each other as they wished to, not as they were: the shadows hid the previous eighteen years.

"Come in," she said. "Come in and meet Tim." He closed the car door and made to follow her up the steps. They went through the veranda into the lounge where Tim was standing in front of the empty fireplace. He was dressed in a suit, an unusual accoutrement for a tobacco farmer.

He came forward and took the hand offered him by Myles.

"Hello," he said. "It's most extraordinary to meet someone for the first time who you know so much about."

"I've heard a lot about you also, from Marguerite's mother," replied the Englishman as he shook the other's hand firmly.

Marguerite looked at them both: both tall, strong men. Then she looked at Myles's face in the electric light and she was shocked. He was two years younger than Tim but looked ten years older.

"What are you going to have?" Tim was saying as the two men crossed to the cocktail cabinet. Suddenly eighteen years had to be filled in and a young cricketer was translated into a high Commonwealth Office official.

"Sorry, darling," Tim was saying over his shoulder, "what will you have?"

She didn't answer. She was still looking at the back of Myles Featherstone. As she did so the romantic past was replaced by the present and she became completely Mrs Tim Carter, thirty-five years old and mother of a thirteen-year-old daughter.

"Will gin and lime be all right?" asked her husband without looking round.

"That's fine," she said, and collected herself a cigarette to complete the return to normal.

"May I have a lime juice?" asked Juliet as she came into the room.

Myles turned to be introduced to the newcomer. For a moment his mind was numbed, numbed as though he'd been slapped in the face.

The picture fell: the nail which held it had been torn from the wall.

"You needn't tell me who this is," he said. "She's so

extraordinarily like her mother at that age that for a moment I thought it was."

He wanted to laugh. It wasn't the type of laughter brought by amusement, it was the type that came through relief. Over the last eighteen years he had built a mental picture of Marguerite standing paramount on a pedestal. It was the part of his mind that was sentimental. When he came down from Oxford with his honours degree and cricket blue, he had found there was something missing, something vital to his happiness and then he had found it was Marguerite. By the time he had made up his mind to do something about it, it was too late. She was engaged to this Tim Carter and that had been that, though the yearning remained. He met a lot of women, grew fond of a number, but never enough to want to marry them. There was always this barrier, this Marguerite. He compared them all to her and they never came up to the picture his mind had painted. Myles was comparing the love of youth with mature sophistication. Sometimes he met a young girl and thought he saw the spark and then he would find the immaturity intolerable. So he remained, fallen between the two stools. At one stage he was concerned that there was something wrong with him, that he was hard, that there was no love in him to give. He tried a series of affairs to see if he was peculiar in any way. He wasn't. But it didn't resolve the mental barrier. Every time he thought he might be falling in love, something would remind him of Marguerite. In fact, it was the sadistic side of his subconscious mind bringing her up because the conscious mind, if the truth were admitted, liked to be hurt. It liked to think of Marguerite, it liked to be miserable by itself, it liked to yearn for the impossible. It was the one thing in which he had failed. It was the only thing that could make him feel sorry for himself. Everything else had gone too well. This was his failure and up till now he had let it grow out of all proportion. The little girl with the lime juice had cut it down to size and he was thankful to her for it.

He had come to Urangwa hoping that the mother would destroy forever his painted picture of her. He had hoped that by seeing her he would see reality and not a fantasy. The picture had fallen, yes, but the cord had been cut by the child.

He came out from under the burden of his past and was once more the United Kingdom High Commissioner. He felt much better.

AFTER DINNER they were forced to stay in the lounge as the flying insects on the veranda were more than insistent, the rains being at their zenith. They had talked of their families and the past. Tim wanted to talk of the future.

His chance came and he turned the conversation.

"What, as an outsider, do you think is going to happen to this country?"

"What a wonderful leading question," Myles joked, and then went on more seriously. "I don't know the ultimate answer to that, Tim." He was picking his words carefully. He was always plagued by the likelihood of being repeated. He couldn't afford to say anything offhand, however informal the company.

"I think," he went on thoughtfully, "that before your problems are settled, there is going to be bloodshed. What I am most worried about is that I fear it is going to happen soon. There are so many conflicting parties, so many conflicting ideas in the pot that sooner or later they must be mixed into an explosive combination. For what it's worth, I would say be prepared in the next twelve months. Don't be alarmed but be prepared, don't let anyone catch you off balance. There is a lot going on behind the scenes which I, with the sources of information open to me, am able to fathom."

Tim was looking at him as the United Kingdom High Commissioner and not as Myles Featherstone. His expression was hard, disturbing, and full of contempt.

Myles Featherstone met his eyes and held them firmly.

"I know exactly what you're thinking, Tim, and I can see your point of view." Here he leant forward in his chair. "But can you see ours? You think that any troubles out here have been caused by the British Government?"

"Largely," agreed Tim, coldly, "we think that is the case."

His expression changed for a moment as he remembered his responsibilities as a host. "Anything we say on this subject must never be considered personal."

"Of course not," agreed Myles, "but thanks for mentioning it. Discussions, where so much is at stake, can often become heated unintentionally."

"Juliet, I think you'd better go to bed," said her mother, interrupting. "It's ten o'clock already."

"Must I, Mother?"

"Yes you must," replied Marguerite firmly.

"All right then," she said, though she wasn't any too happy with the whole development. "Goodnight, everyone."

"Goodnight, Juliet," called Myles, "sleep well."

She kissed her mother and father and solemnly shook hands with the High Commissioner.

When the child had gone, he resumed. "No Tim, it's not all the British Government. We've made some mistakes, everyone does, but though you may think collectively that we are a bunch of bloody fools, let me assure you that we are not."

Tim didn't reply, though he averted his eyes.

"We are forced to think on a global basis. We can't just isolate our thoughts to Southern Rhodesia as much as I, personally, would like to. If you can look at it from our point of view for a moment, you will see that we must include a number of additional ingredients which you feel are irrelevant. If the black continent wanted to swamp you they could do so in three months. It would cost a lot of lives on both sides but in addition, it may tear the so-called peace of the world in half. You may be prepared to chance your luck, go it alone, sink or swim, but we can't afford to look at it that way as a large proportion of the rest of the world might be sacrificed in the process. It could be the spark to set so much else aflame. We can't chance that, Tim, and what is more we are not going to chance it."

No one answered him and he moderated his tone as he went on.

"Tim, it will all come out in the wash. It may be very unpleasant for a while but eventually we'll look back on any trouble as just another incident in history."

"I suppose you're right," said Tim getting up, "but it's still not very nice having to go through this 'incident in history', especially when you have a wife and child. Will you have another drink?"

"A whisky will be fine," agreed Myles warmly, seeing that enough had been said.

"You realise one thing," said Tim firmly, looking at the other man as he handed him the whisky. "You'll never kick out the people born in this country. This is my country, I have no other, I want no other, and I intend to have no other. It's a strong tie we have with our land. Do you really love your country for the land, the very feel of the place, just to be there, to submit to the bond of your own soil? That's how I feel, Myles, that's how a lot of us feel, and we feel it very strongly."

"I feel the same way about Mirelton. If anyone wanted to take my family home on the Isle of Purbeck, I'd fight the same way."

"Good," said Tim, "I really believe you do understand what I mean."

The first trouble began near Bulawayo, many miles from them. Marguerite read of the brutal murders and felt the chill of fear. At first they were isolated, then slowly they took on a pattern, an organised pattern.

Tim had called in Steve, Gary and Lance Grant to discuss his responsibilities as head of the Police Reserve. He wanted their opinions, he wanted any damn thing he could get from them to help clarify his own mind.

"I think this is it," he said, when they had all congregated on his veranda. "Instead of further fruitless industrial disturbances, they've decided to go for the country's life blood, for the tobacco industry. Why they haven't done it before remains an enigma.

Probably the answer is organisation; before, they hadn't got any, now they're using it damned effectively. If they can stop us selling tobacco they'll make the Government go bankrupt."

He looked round at the three taut faces. Well might they be grim; there was trouble for them all just round the corner. He went on.

"They seem to single out a good farmer, the key man in each area, especially if he's liked by his labour force. If they can't kill him they burn down his barns and generally make a bloody mess of things. They strike quickly, without warning, and as soon as they've completed their task they merge with their brethren and you can't tell a murderer from the rest. It certainly seems that at least one in each gang has been trained for these activities outside this country. Their methods are those of modern warfare. They come in under cover, make a clean attack, without any hysterics, and then achieve an orderly withdrawal. They are extremely well armed. Each unit consists of as little as eight men. They are efficient and should in no way be underestimated. It's thought there are fifty units operating throughout the country – that's four hundred fanatics determined to get what they want, and prepared to destroy anything or anyone who gets in their way. To combat such activities decisively would require a garrison on each farm. That would just as effectively bankrupt the country.

"The army has been broken into combat units and spread throughout the country. They are, however, like drops in the ocean as they haven't the first idea where the gangs are going to strike – neither has anyone else for that matter. The only thing to do is for us to defend ourselves and our families. If a farm is attacked, the owner must send out a distress signal on the R/T – a central unit is being set up to take calls at any time of the day or night. Distress rockets can then be fired. Wherever you are it will be necessary to tune into the R/T, find out where the trouble is and get over there as fast as possible. This will mean carrying a radio and a Sten gun at all times...

"Has anyone got any further ideas?"

"Don't you think it would be wise to move all women and children into the club?" suggested Steve. "I don't like the idea of leaving my wife on the farm by herself when there's trouble in the area."

"I think you can see the impractical side of that," replied Tim, after some thought. "We'd never see our families, there wouldn't be enough accommodation at the club, and generally we'd be doing what they want us to do – panic. It might, however, be a good idea for all wives and children to go to the club once the trouble starts in the area and the men are called away to deal with it. I think most farmers in the block have two vehicles; if they haven't, something can be arranged. A detachment can then be sent to the club to look after them."

"That sounds reasonable," agreed Steve.

"Let's hope it works," said Gary, not too enthusiastically.

"There's one more thing," said Tim looking out at the thick rows of shrubs, of creepers, of bougainvillea, of gum trees, which circled the house, giving it its peaceful beauty. "Any cover such as that," and here he let his hand draw a line over so much that had become an innate part of his life, "must be destroyed. As wide an area as possible must be left bare round the houses. We can't afford a surprise attack."

"I can't believe it," said Steve quietly, going over to the veranda parapet and standing with his back to them. "It's taken forty years to grow those gums and blend the garden to look like that."

"I know," replied Tim. Then with a sudden rush of hatred he spat out, "But a bloody lot of good it will do if some bastard of a black savage creeps up under cover and empties a Sten gun into my wife and child."

"Take it easy," said Gary, putting a hand on his shoulder.

"You're right," agreed Tim, "take it easy and let's all vomit together."

They didn't talk, just looked at him. Goaded, he went on impulsively.

"Well, doesn't it make you want to be sick? You spend two

generations turning a waterless wilderness into something that resembles a farm and a bunch of fanatical creeps come along and tear it to pieces for an evening's entertainment. Oh yes," he went on, through clenched teeth, "I just hope they try this farm. It will give me the greatest pleasure to empty a magazine into their little black bellies."

"They've made you panic," observed Steve.

"Oh no, oh no, you're wrong there, very wrong," replied Tim, shaking his head. "I've just decided if they want a fight they can have one, but, what's more important, if anyone is going to win it's going to be us and anyone who wants to think otherwise is going to have to kill me. And let me assure them, I am not easy to kill."

"You really are bitter," said Gary.

"Yes, Gary, I am bitter, but it's the only way to be in a situation like this. We can't afford to be soft, to think that the fellow over there with the automatic doesn't mean any harm to us personally when he pulls the trigger."

He wanted them to say something but they didn't. They looked away from him, but said nothing, and after a length of silence his anger began to subside.

He took control of himself and then of his voice.

"Okay, okay," he said wearily, "that was the first and last time this thing gets the better of me. Sitting ducks or no sitting ducks, if we organise ourselves there is no reason to panic inwardly or outwardly. Certain things will have to be sacrificed, but if we get down to it, this whole trouble can be stamped out once and for all."

"I see the army caught up with one unit yesterday," volunteered Lance. "It was on the radio this morning."

"I heard," said Gary, "it wiped out the eight and an army corporal."

"That's how it will go," said Tim. "We'll get organised and they won't find it so easy; then slowly we'll whittle them down and thin them out. It will take time and we hope little else. We'll call a meeting in this house tonight," he concluded.

That was how peaceful men went to war in the Rhodesia of 1975, with Sten guns, R/T sets and rockets poised at strategic points throughout the farms. Fear gripped the country. Where an African wouldn't pay his respects in hard cash to the outlawed organisation he was shot. A whole compound, thirty-seven huts, was shot up in the next block, a little more than forty-five miles from Urangwa. They lost count of the women and children when they counted the dead bodies. Shadrac, being an elder in the area, took his bicycle and went to try to help. When he came back he was a sick man, sick of the agonies being inflicted on his people, on his country. He had seen in his lifetime the country rise from singular poverty to comparative wealth, and now he saw certain of his people trying to reverse the progression. He talked to Tim about the deep hurt in his heart and Tim tried to calm the old man, but he did no good and only managed to depress himself the more. 'You can shoulder your own problems,' he thought, 'but it's very difficult to take on someone else's as well.'

Marguerite, having given up all idea of persuading Tim to leave the country, had sunk happily into the false security of 'it can't happen to us'. She was still English at heart and, being so, had an inborn confidence: though things could look bad, they never actually reached your doorstep. She forgot that Rhodesia was not an island in the sea.

"I'm going to cut away the shrubbery around the house tomorrow," said Tim that night.

"Oh don't be silly, darling, they won't actually make an attack here at Urangwa."

"Of course they won't," he agreed, echoing the air of false optimism he had found built into his wife. "It's just a precaution that's all."

"Well, if you think we ought to, then we must," she agreed, returning to her sewing.

What a blessing it is, he thought as he watched her plying the needle, she just doesn't believe it can happen here.

In February more gangs were beaten off than got through to their targets. There was a lull for a while. Some said they had had enough, others suggested they were licking their wounds and trying to learn from their mistakes. The bulk of the tobacco crop was being reaped and it certainly didn't look as though the country was going bankrupt. In fact the prices at the tobacco auctions were better than they had been for years.

Juliet went off to boarding school in Marandellas. When they had left her, and were driving away from the school, he complained to Marguerite that he must be getting old with a child of his at boarding school.

Tim was in the grading shed, watching the span grade the leaves of tobacco into their respective categories. The pure yellow leaves without spot went into one box, those with a tint of green into another, a third took the sponged leaves and so on till the hands of twelve leaves each were of the same grade, in the right box and ready to be baled and sent to the auction floor.

The R/T set was in the corner, away from the work, though near enough for Tim to hear any response above the general noise of the shed, which consisted of the women chanting in unison, the men talking, and the deputy boss boy walking round and round 'bossing up' the grading, making sure the categories were kept within a strict margin. Tim was standing by the baling box, watching the hands of tobacco being expertly handled into the box which would shape them into a square bale, ready for the hessian to be drawn together and take up the tension previously held by the board, and forced down by the compressing arm. Occasionally he took a hand and felt it for its moisture content. If it was too moist the tobacco went mouldy, if it was too dry the leaves would split under the pressure of the compressing arm. It wasn't bad tobacco, he thought, not quite rich enough in texture but a good enough colour; it was 'on type', which was most important. With a bit of luck the buyers would like it and maybe pay 60d a pound. 'You can never tell with the bloody buyers,' he said to himself. They were certainly the most unpredictable race of people he had ever encountered. One day they'd like it and give you 50d a pound for the rubbish and when you offered them a good bale of tobacco they'd say the veins were too close together or something equally ridiculous and give you 40d instead of 70d. They came next on his list, after the Americans and the Colonial Office. If, however, they ever made a mistake in his favour, they'd become his best friends overnight.

He jumped, and so did Shadrac standing next to him, when the high-pitched warning signal belted out of the R/T set. Tim moved quickly to it, trying to concentrate through the beating of his heart. He picked up the earphones, clamped them over his head, and sat down hunched in the corner with Shadrac. He tuned the set and picked up from the central office that a farm in the next block was being attacked. He went onto transmission, got through to his own operations centre at the club and gave his instructions.

"Broadcast that all available Police Reserve are to rendezvous at Urangwa. We move off at twelve-thirty, fifteen minutes from now, along the main Marandellas Road. If they can't make it by then, move off to the trouble area alone."

He grabbed the loaded Sten gun and the R/T set, told Shadrac to look after the grading, and dashed for the house and his car.

He reached the house considerably out of breath.

"There's an attack in the next block," he called to Marguerite from the driveway. Luckily she was standing on the veranda. "You'll have to get over to the club when the truck comes back with Philip." He jumped into the car and held the other door open in readiness for his assistant who was 'bossing up' some ploughing on the other side of the farm.

Marguerite went inside, picked up her revolver, went into the kitchen, and put as much food into a basket as she could. She then went back to the veranda, down the steps and round to the other side of the cars where Tim was impatiently listening to his orders being regularly transmitted over the R/T.

"The truck will be here in a couple of minutes," he said, forcing a smile at his wife. "Philip's got the truck on the other side of the farm by the dam."

"Be careful, darling."

"It's you who must be careful," he replied, taking her hand

which was resting on the car door. "I'll have an escort of a dozen Sten guns, you'll only have yourself until you get to the club."

Philip arrived. Marguerite took the truck and was gone. Tim tried to get his mind back on the trouble and away from worrying about his wife.

The first to arrive were Lance Grant and his son Bruce.

"Another seven minutes," called Tim.

Philip got into the car with the spare Sten magazines. Two of the Bullmastiffs tried to follow him without success.

Steve arrived looking flushed. Tim waved as his friend circled the driveway and brought his car up behind Lance and his son.

Gary was on duty at the club; Steve's assistant was in Salisbury. Four more cars arrived, thirteen men in all. At twelve-thirty they moved off in three cars, eating each other's dust. It would take them thirty minutes to reach the trouble spot and they hadn't any more time to lose. Tim knew the farm well enough, having been to cocktail parties with the owners, an English family called Hamden. He remembered the house was thatched, set away from the barns on a mound; not an easy target if well defended. It would be difficult to get a firebrand on the house in daylight. He wondered bitterly where Andrew Hamden and his wife were when the fun started.

They drove onto the farm and Tim saw that the barns were burning well. They stopped the cars and formed up on the roadway. Automatic fire came from the house and then in concentrated form from the right of the barns.

"We'll move in on the house," said Tim. "Fan out and move in under cover. Be careful to look at what you're shooting. There are sure to be some of the local farmers in the area."

They had trained for such a job and moved off towards the house with even distance between each of their crouched figures. Tim was in the middle, at the centre of the arrowhead formation, with Steve on his right and Bruce Grant on his left. Somebody fired up ahead and they dropped on their faces and began to crawl forward.

'It wasn't at us,' thought Tim, 'so we haven't been seen.' They closed in on the house. Tim signalled the others to cover their advance and Steve and Bruce closed in with him to the edge of the spacious lawn, where the long, coarse, dry grass gave way to the well-kept lawn which rolled on up to the house, standing stark, a sitting target, with already one side of its thatch aflame. As he watched, Tim saw two Africans move forward under cover of a clump of trees, unseen by the people in the house but more than visible to Tim and the other two. He held his fire, wanting to know where any other attackers might be. The firing increased from the direction of the barns and he guessed that the main concentrations on both sides had been drawn to the conflagration of the barns. He saw one of the Africans behind the clump of trees rise, kneel and light a firebrand in preparation for tossing it onto the thatched roof of the house. Tim fired a long, accurate burst and the firebrand went out. The dead man's companion tried to run for it but was cut down by a shot from a window in the house before any of them could direct their fire. Silence. They waited. Nothing happened and Tim signalled the others forward. They came up and completed a tight wedge, ten yards apart, behind Tim who remained at the tip of the arrowhead.

Tim called to the house, "Are there any more in your area?"

"I think there's one more where the others came from," came back Andrew Hamden's voice from the window farthest from the burning thatch.

"Jammy bastard," said Steve in a low voice to Tim, "he must have been in the house when they attacked and had plenty of time to signal for help on the R/T."

"It isn't over yet," replied Tim and scanned his surroundings for signs of life.

Nothing moved, not even a bush or blade of grass with the wind; there wasn't any wind.

He detached four of his troop to circle to the left of the area where they thought there was trouble.

They waited again. Tim watched the ground behind them. Even the area around the burning barns was silent.

"He's dead," a voice reported.

"Make bloody sure," Tim shouted back.

"I'm not that bloody stupid."

Tim laughed uneasily with the others.

He signalled the remaining nine to circle the other way and search at the back of the house.

Bruce Grant looked scared stiff, looking how Tim felt. They moved on through the long grass, not seeing a thing. They'd stumble on anything before seeing it. Tim just hoped there weren't any more of the African gang. He would have preferred to sit and wait but the burning roof didn't give him much time to spare. They moved on as cautiously as possible. A lizard shot out in front of Tim and made his heart come into his mouth and his finger tighten on the trigger. He moved on and round the back of the house. There was no sound save the crackle of the burning roof some fifty yards away.

Steve moved up behind him and spoke in a whisper. "Like cat and mouse."

"Which is the cat?" replied Tim, without looking round.

They circled round to where the other four had been told to wait together. Both parties had searched the immediate area of the house without finding anything.

They waited another five minutes after Tim had posted them on the perimeter of the garden, intermittently facing the house and down the hill. They couldn't see much that way, there was too much long grass.

"You'd better make a dash for it," shouted Tim towards the house, seeing that the fire had spread three quarters the length of the roof. "We'll cover your exit."

"There's only my wife and I," called back Andrew.

They waited and at length the elderly farmer showed himself at the window. Nothing happened. He helped his wife up onto the sill and she dropped the two feet onto the flower bed below without any trouble. Andrew followed. He took his wife by the hand, holding his Sten in the other, and made a dash to where Tim was standing up. Nothing happened as they crossed the lawn.

"Thanks," said Andrew Hamden.

"Are you all right?" said Tim to his wife.

"Alive, which is all that matters," she replied.

Then she broke down and clung to her husband and began to cry in terrified bursts.

"You were wonderful," he said and stroked the greying hair.

"I'm going to have a look at the barns with six of the others," said Tim.

"Fine," said Andrew, over the top of his wife's bent head.

There hadn't been any firing for the last fifteen minutes, since Andrew had last fired, in fact. They moved down the hill quickly, using as much cover as possible, then circled the open space between the sheds and the still burning barns in open line. They were jumpy, ready to shoot at anything.

A cockney voice greeted them from the door of the grading shed and Tim caught sight of three stripes and an army uniform.

"Christ, mate, where did you blow in from?"

Three of the Stens swung towards the door. Their owners realized what it was and self-consciously lowered their weapons.

"Are there any left?" called Tim.

"Don't think so," answered the sergeant, "but it's difficult to tell."

"Are there any local farmers about?"

"No idea. You're the first civvies we've seen."

"Police Reserve," corrected Tim.

"Sorry, cock."

"Do they rely on the army in this block?"

"Must do. First real trouble the Europeans have had in this area."

"You must have got here fast," said Tim.

"We did. Can't afford to bugger about."

"Anybody get hurt?"

"Some bastard tried to shoot my corporal's hand off," said the sergeant coming out of the shed, having decided there couldn't be any more trouble in the area with these bright Charlies marching up and down, using the bloody place as a parade ground. "I think the rest are okay. You have any trouble?"

"Not much," replied Tim.

"Made a bloody mess of the place," said the sergeant, looking at the burning barns and the house aflame at the top of the hill.

"Is Mr Hamden okay?"

"Yes, so's his wife."

"Good. Didn't get a chance to reach the house, the bastards pinned us down before we got there. Glad you arrived."

"By ourselves, we'd have been too late."

By this time they were all standing round. A cigarette was lit by Bruce Grant and then others smoked. Seven army and six civvies.

"They just vanish," the sergeant was saying.

"When it gets too hot."

"We got one."

"There are three more up by the house."

"Should discourage them."

"I hope so."

"Stupid bastards. They don't make sense."

They tried to get the fires out without a lot of success. Three of the barns, three out of twelve, were saved. The house burnt itself out, the fire having got too good a hold. Even the seven of Tim's troop he'd left behind had only managed to save some of the furniture. The Government would give compensation but it could never expunge the experience.

"It's so useless," Tim said to Marguerite at dinner that night at Urangwa. Steve was there, with Lance and Bruce Grant. They'd got over the initial shock but the sight of Mr and Mrs Andrew Hamden sitting at the top of the table didn't make the party go with a swing. Marguerite was glad Juliet was at school. She would read about it in the papers but it would never be as real for her as it was for them at the moment. Tim smiled at her from the other end of the table and she felt better.

Things began to return to normal when the Hamdens went back to their farm two days later.

"You can't afford to leave a farm, whatever the circumstances," Andrew said, as Tim and his wife helped them into the car which had been stocked by Marguerite with camp beds, paraffin lamps, anything in fact which would make it possible for the couple to camp in Andrew's small office which was attached to the grading shed.

"I ought to be thankful that the army prevented them burning the bulked tobacco in the grading shed. I'll still be able to sell the crop."

"I hope you don't have any trouble with your boys."

"Doubt it. They loathe these people as much as I do."

"And thank you again," said Mrs Hamden to Marguerite.

"Thanks, Tim," was all the man said as he let the car into gear but his eyes said all he really meant.

"I wish they were all like that," said Tim as he put his arm around his wife's shoulders to lead her up the steps into the house. "You get shot up, your house and barns burnt, and two days later you're camping in your office and grading tobacco as though nothing had happened."

The first shot actually hit the R/T set standing on the table. Coffee had been served and they were both relaxing before going to bed.

For a moment it didn't register, but only for a short moment. The three Bullmastiffs set up a distorted howl on the veranda. The barking moved out onto the lawn. A long burst of automatic fire was followed by silence.

"You bastards," snarled Tim. "Get down under the window," he shouted to his wife and made a lunge for the Sten gun next to the useless R/T set. Hell, he'd left the bloody thing unloaded and the ammunition was in the gun cabinet on the other side of the room.

"Stay there," he called to Marguerite, now crouching under the windows, "I've got to get some ammunition. I'll get your pistol at the same time."

She was so petrified, watching him crawl across the room, that she was unable to breathe. She saw him stop halfway, change direction and then slide a hand up the wall by the door to try and turn out the light. A burst of fire shattered the windows in the front of the lounge.

Tim flattened himself with the crash of the bullets and then, bracing himself, lurched at the switch and had it out and himself on the floor again before a second burst of automatic fire crashed into the room. 'Blast, we're surrounded,' was all he thought as with the lights out and the useless Sten gun in his hand he ran for the gun cabinet.

He could have screamed, but of course it was locked. One of the main points he himself had been labouring with the Police Reserve – never leave your guns locked. Then he searched for the keys in his pocket, found them and, in the dark, started the thankless task of finding the right key and fitting it into the lock. He tried them feverishly, one by one. He couldn't get them in the hole and if he did he wasn't sure about it: was it the wrong key or had he put it in wrongly?

Crouching where he was, one hand groping for the keyhole, made him hope he couldn't be seen from the outside. A single shot shattered the glass just above him and a splinter cut into his hand. The stupidity of his actions was immediately apparent. All he had to do was break a bit more of the glass and he could get what he wanted from the gun cabinet. He fumbled inside, cut his arm again, began to panic as he thought of the gang methodically closing in and he with nothing to protect them both with. Then the initial surge of fear was over and a deadly calm came over him. He found a magazine, fitted it into the Sten, and put four spare magazines into his pockets. The pistol he knew was already loaded. With this and its spare ammunition he crossed the room on all fours to Marguerite, crouching below the window.

It was quiet outside, meaning one of two things: they were either closing in, or suspicious of the lack of reaction from the house.

"Don't worry," he said, handing her the small pistol. "We'll get out of this," and he kissed her quickly behind the ear before another burst of fire confirmed the presence of unwanted company outside.

"I'm not frightened," she replied and her voice was calm. She had too much to lose by panicking.

"That's my girl," he replied. "Keep your eyes on the window and doors. If you see anything move, shoot it. I'm going to try and let go the rocket on the veranda."

He moved to the window, brought his head up at the side and to the left of the curtain. It was lucky they had been drawn on this side, he thought. He prised open a gap between the wall and the heavy curtain. Looking out he could see the lawn, dark, patchworked by the shadow of the gaunt, bare gum trees, the ones he had been unable to force himself to cut down. The moon was bright and shone directly onto the veranda. He could see the rocket, poised, just to the right of the pillar.

He could also see the three dead Bullmastiffs, cast up on the lawn, sprawled in the pale moonlight, lying as though the sun were warming their flesh but it wasn't, it was the moon, and they were dead.

If he could reach the rocket they'd have help within ten minutes. But they needed it right now.

A shape, crouched, began to form behind the lump in the ground to the right of the gum trees. It was moving forward and blending well with the patchwork of shadows on the lawn.

With deliberate hate he nosed the Sten gun through the curtain and the open window and took aim and fired. The sound of automatic fire crushed the silence in the room and made Marguerite leap to her feet.

"Get down," he bellowed to her and himself ducked below the sill, behind the brick wall protection. As he expected, a hail of automatic fire followed his reprisal. He lay flat on the floor as bullets ricocheted round the lounge, whirring, crashing into the furniture.

A pause, and he dashed to the other side of the room and locked the door which separated them from the bedroom wing. Into the dining room, he thrust the Sten gun through the window and let rip at the shadows. Back again on all fours, while the bullets hissed around him, he locked the dining room door. Then back at the first window he looked out again at the lawn. The lump still remained where he had seen it before. 'If they're running to pattern we should only have seven more to deal with,' he thought.

"Darling," he whispered in the pregnant silence, "can you fire over the top of the sill at the same time as me? Don't take aim, just level the gun over the top and pull the trigger. Whatever you do don't show yourself. Are you ready?"

"Yes," she replied, but she looked as well. There was something moving. She took an unsteady aim at the figure crouched ready to crawl towards the house. At first sight she had been surprised, but then, she thought, they were surrounded. Steadying her aim and being completely astounded at her callous calmness, she realised with a warm rush that any fear seemed to have gone, leaving her with a simple determination to live.

"Now," he said, and she fired and the gun jumped back from the window sill on which she had been resting it.

At first she didn't duck but as the return fire came back she threw herself flat on her face on the floor, facing her husband who was now kneeling below the window opposite.

He turned and saw the white of her face looking towards him.

"Well done, darling," he called softly, and would have said more if his voice had not been drowned by further firing.

This was no bloody good, he thought, I must send up that rocket. He edged himself up to the window and again saw it poised, ready to be fired, but out of his reach. He decided to make a dash for it. If that rocket didn't go up, they would. He began to crawl towards the door which led to the veranda and the rocket. He felt for his matches. They were there. Good.

"Where are you going, darling?" Her voice behind him was frightened this time.

"To set off the rocket."

A moment later, he was gone, out into the dark.

She didn't fear for herself. It was for him she feared. She couldn't lose him. She just couldn't lose him. She trembled and bit her finger to suppress the panic which was trying to invade her heart. Everything swam. She caught flashes of her past life with him. She feared more now. In bursts, she wanted to run to him, to stop him going outside, she wanted to say it was too dangerous, to shout to him, but she did none of these things because her voice felt too weak. She wanted to go to him but she couldn't. She was in mental agony, a nightmare. Surely she'd wake up, Tim would bring in the tea and she'd wake up. She did wake up. But it was to the sound of gunfire.

"Oh my God," she choked out.

The fire had not been directed into the lounge. Why not? She didn't mind. She'd have it all. In here. All of it in here, so long as it didn't go anywhere near the veranda where Tim had gone. But it had been aimed at the veranda, every last bullet.

The door burst open. Tim fell into the lounge backwards, firing as he came. He slammed the heavy door shut and crossed to the window, fired again, then dropped below the sill.

"They saw me light the match," he explained, as he changed the magazine on his Sten for a fresh one. "There must have been three of them on the lawn having a go at me." He laughed. And then the firing raked the lounge and he ducked even lower.

Silence again. A dead silence, with only the sounds of Africa to break it. The crickets returned as a ghostly aftermath. Two new shapes lay outside on the lawn, unmoving among the shadows.

"Can you fire a couple of shots your side?" he said. "It'll keep them guessing as to how many there are of us."

She fired again, at nothing in particular, and then clung to the floor.

Behind the compound, a single shadow moved. It was old, bent, but determined in its gait. Shadrac knew there was a rocket outside number 26 barn and the matches clutched in his right hand were going to send it up. Why had they come to Urangwa, he wondered, but his tired old brain wouldn't tell him the answer and he couldn't force it. He came round the barns from the back, having picked his way through the stacks of firewood waiting to be burned. He didn't see them, but if he had looked and changed his purpose for a fleeting moment he would have seen the fires at the foot of each barn, the fires which cured the tobacco and gave them all their living. He didn't look, however. He was bent on lighting a smaller fire and feared that if he didn't light the smaller fire, the fires that he knew were there and didn't look at, would go out. So he didn't look and moved towards number 26.

He found it. He fumbled with the matches. I'm tired, he thought, very tired, and he summoned all his energy, comforted by the thought of how his wife would look after him when he got back to their hut. Yes he was tired, very tired; but he had the match out of the box, his old fingers finding it difficult to feel the small piece of wood. Everything would be all right now, everything would be all right. The first match went out. He fumbled for a second... At length he sparked a flame, and shakily held it towards the touch paper, but his unsteady hand shook out the flame and he must try again. The third match attracted a burst of automatic gun fire and Shadrac wasn't tired anymore – he was dead.

Tim fired again and thought he killed the shadow. There was only one source of return fire – tracer –directed at the thatched roof. "The bastards," he said again out loud. "They're trying to burn the roof."

"Someone must have heard this racket by now," she called back to reassure him.

"You're right," he agreed, "and they can't come and bail us out too soon."

He didn't see the face at the window over to one side and neither did Marguerite. The first he knew of it was the automatic being fired ten feet to his right. He sprang back, firing from the hip as he did so, and the black face which merged so well with the black background slid down quietly to the floor of the veranda.

"He won't give us any more trouble," called Tim to his wife, and then his attention was taken by the barns. They were burning, burning well and with the dry timber inside they wouldn't take long to burn out. The flames gave him a solid backcloth of light in which to see any movement across the lawn.

"They're torching the barns," he called over his shoulder. "It could save us, though. I can't see anything approaching the house with that furnace lighting the way."

He checked his magazines. With any luck, he should have enough to last before help arrived.

"Will you fire a shot out of your window?" he called again. "It may discourage them at the back."

He waited for the shots.

"Just a couple," he called again in the silence.

But he got no reply, from the gun or from Marguerite, as Marguerite was dead and had been for a while now. The burst of fire from the window had been directed at her and most of it had found its mark. She had known nothing about it...except for a fleeting moment, a name, on her lips, on her mind, in her soul, in her heart. Tim.

He turned, saw the heap hunched below the window.

"Marguerite," he called softly, his voice strained, not fully taking in what he was seeing. Again, softer, "Marguerite," willing her to answer him. Yes, she'd reply in a moment, of course she would. And when she didn't he shouted, "Marguerite!" But still no reply and he shouted her name again and again. At last it sank in and he ran to her, to what he found was her dead body. First he hugged her, tried to wake her with his kisses and when he couldn't he let her slip from his arms. He stood up in full sight of the windows and backed away from her.

"I will not become a Colin Mandy," he told himself. And he swung savagely to where he had dropped his Sten, picked it up, and put in a fresh magazine, hitting it home hard.

"Right, you bastards," he said, "now I'm coming for you."

He walked to the door, threw it open and began firing as he

walked out into the night which was burning with his barns, burning with the loss of his wife. Something got up from the lawn and tried to move towards him. Tim felt the pleasure of squeezing the trigger and feeling the bullets pump themselves into the man in front.

He moved out onto the lawn and stood silhouetted against the barns and the now burning roof of his house. A funeral pyre to his wife. A wife now dead. Why the hell did he want to live? Yes, a funeral pyre and in its light he saw a shadow move, a man. It fired at Tim. Tim fired back and it stopped firing at him. 'There must be more than eight,' he thought happily to himself. 'More to kill...more on whom to sate my revenge.' They fired at him from two directions. He killed the first one before being hit. Killed the second too, but killed him too late. The man had fired first and made a good enough job.

Tim sank onto the bare, fire-washed lawn of his home, sank onto the earth of his own country, and as he died he was thankful for all these things.

Steve saw the barns burning from Karilla and gave the alarm.

They all arrived, but they all arrived too late.

Steve stood in the middle of the lawn, crying like a baby.

"He took his revenge," said Gary at his side. "There are four dead on this lawn, one at the back, and what looks like another on the veranda."

"What the hell's the good of that," blurted Steve, "when he's dead himself, just lying there and never going to get up again? And Marguerite too. I'm sure we'll find her in the ruins of the house. Why else would he leave the house without her, unless she was already dead?" He turned his head away and addressed the dead form sprawled out on the grass. "I'm sorry I couldn't save you, Tim. Either of you. Now what the hell am I going to do?"

He could say no more, so they left him to cry, a lone figure, standing upright in the firelight, his shadow falling across the other whose burning house furnished the light.

The vicar tried to conduct the burial service but was unable; his mouth moved but no sound came. More tears dropped and glinted in the African sun because it was a time for tears. The vicar fell to his knees and prayed in his sorrow and around him the others did the same, knowing how he felt.

At last he was able to stand again and finish the service, so that Steve, Gary, Lance and one other, Myles Featherstone, could cover the two coffins, set side by side in a single grave, on the high ground at Urangwa, looking across at the spread of the Karilla.

If that was not enough, Steve went to another burial that afternoon. They were burying Shadrac and Steve wanted to be there to represent Tim. He stood back from their ritual but joined his grief with theirs. The wrinkled figure of Shadrac's wife, her face pocked with grief for her husband, the grief that poured out as she huddled over his grave, was the final thrust which broke Steve's heart.

They gathered together that night at Karilla, what was left of them. Myles Featherstone wanted to stay with these people who had known them. He felt the same as them.

Gary had dropped his frivolity and took control. He talked forcibly because he felt strongly.

"This is not the end," he said to Lance and Steve, "in fact it should make us more determined to keep our small part of this country together. We are not going under, we never will, because thank God there are thousands more like Tim who love this country so deeply that they will sacrifice their lives to maintain what we believe in. In twenty years' time we will raise monuments to such as Tim and both black and white will remember them with happiness. He could have run away but he didn't and Marguerite backed him in that decision and though they have paid the price, we must build our strength to ensure that their reason for staying was well founded. It was well founded," he emphasised, "and it's going to stay that way."

They were silent, even the vicar, and they remained like that till dinner was served and life began to go on. Evalyn, as hostess, tried to maintain a conversation. In bursts, they tried to back her up but with little success. And then Gary asked the one question they had all been dreading.

"Who is going to tell Juliet?"

"I think I ought to do that," volunteered the vicar wearily. He felt it his duty.

"As her godfather, maybe it ought to be me," suggested Steve in a hollow voice.

"Is her only relation Marguerite's mother?" asked Myles. He had made up his mind but he wanted them to agree.

"Yes," replied the vicar.

"Would you mind if I told Juliet?" asked the High Commissioner.

They didn't reply so he went on.

"Her grandmother looks after my uncle, and I wonder if the best thing may not be for me to persuade her to go to England, to live at Mirelton. I know her mother was happy living there," he added, as though that would help to clinch the decision. "I can take her across with me. I have to go to London shortly."

"I think the child should decide," interposed the vicar. "She is fourteen in the middle of next month, and old enough to decide for herself. A holiday, maybe," he continued, turning to Myles, "but she may want to come back to Africa. She is Rhodesian, not English."

"If she does, she can live with us, can't she, Evalyn?" said Steve, turning to his wife.

Lance and Mary Grant offered their home as well.

Myles drove his own car to the school on the following day, having first spoken to the headmistress on the telephone.

Alone, in the headmistress's study, Myles felt like a hangman. He just didn't know how to deal the blow and when the girl came in by herself, in ill-fitting school uniform that had become too small for her, he was unable to find any words.

The girl broke the silence.

"How nice of you to come and tell me," she said.

And bracing himself, he replied, "Tell you what?"

He was no damn good at this sort of thing, that was for sure.

"About Mummy and Daddy," she replied. Her chin moved and then the girl controlled herself. "They announced on the radio that a farm had been attacked in the Marandellas area and then a rumour went round the school that the farm was called Urangwa and that the people had been killed. The other girls didn't know I lived there as I have only been at the school four weeks. I cried a lot yesterday," she explained, "but I have cried enough for a while, I haven't got anything left to cry with."

'You poor, poor child,' thought Myles, but was unable to say it.

After a while, and a very uncomfortable silence, he said, "Would you like to go to England and stay with your grandmother?" he asked.

"I'm not sure," she replied and then he saw her smile. "Daddy always says it's too cold." And then he realised that she had forgotten for a moment that her daddy was dead and when she realised it he saw the tears well and the child ran and buried her head in his chest.

And when her tears had cleared a little she looked up at him.

"Please let me stay awhile here," she said. "I want to be close as possible to my Mummy and Daddy." Then she looked at him calmly. "Tell me, are they really dead?" she asked, in a deep, controlled voice.

"Yes," he replied and would have liked to join his tears with hers. When she had again buried her head in his chest, so that she couldn't see his face, he did.

∽

AFTERWORD

WE ARE SURE you would agree, if you have any knowledge about the history of Rhodesia before it became Zimbabwe, how insightful *All Our Yesterdays* is – a very sad and poignant story foretelling the future of a tragic country. If only it had been published at the time... but we are glad to be able to do so now. The letter you see from Argosy, is one of the many letters Peter received when he was pursuing a publisher.

Kamba Publishing
    March 2020

ARGOSY

FLEETWAY HOUSE
LONDON, E. C. 4.
Telephone Central 8080

12th September 1962

Dear Mr. Rimmer,

Thank you so much for submitting the typescript
of your novel, "All Our Yesterdays."

It is a fascinating account of life in Africa
today, but since it shows only one side of the picture,
of a most complex political situation, I am sure you
will appreciate the difficult position of a fiction
magazine with a wide circulation in Africa.

However, I am sure you will like to know that
our readers' panel commented on the sensitivity of
the novel, of the conviction of its characterisation,
and its very real interest.

Regretfully, I am returning the typescript to
you.

Yours sincerely,

Director.

P. Rimmer, Esq.,
P.O.Box 2280,
Salisbury,
Southern Rhodesia.

Enc.   .

DEAR READER

~

Reviews are the most powerful tools in our kitty when it comes to getting attention for Peter's books. This is where you can come in, as by providing an honest review you will help bring them to the attention of other readers.

If you enjoyed reading *All Our Yesterdays* and have five minutes to spare, we would really appreciate a review (it can be as short as you like). Your help in spreading the word and keeping Peter's work alive is gratefully received.

Please post your review on the retailer site where you purchased this book.

Thank you so much.
Heather Stretch (Peter's daughter)

PRINCIPAL CHARACTERS

～

Marguerite Stearle — Main character of *All Our Yesterdays*

Eric Stearle — Marguerite's father

Harriet Stearle — Marguerite's mother and Guy Featherstone's housekeeper

Guy Featherstone —Local squire in the county of Dorset, England

Myles Featherstone — Guy Featherstone's nephew

Mrs Fenton — Marguerite's London landlady

Andy Carly — A Conservative Party committee member

Tim Carter — A Rhodesian tobacco farmer

Clara Carter — Tim's mother

Madazi — Tim's African servant

Colin Mandy— The social club manager

Shadrac — The boss boy on Urangwa

Jock Ritter — Rhodesian tobacco farmer

Evalyn Ritter — Jock's wife

Steve Ritter — Jock's son and Tim's best friend

Jenny Ritter — Jock's daughter

Cony Ritter — Steve and Eve's daughter

Lance Grant — Rhodesian tobacco farmer

Mary Grant — Lance's wife
Bruce Grant — Lance and Mary's eldest son
Juliet Carter — Marguerite and Tim's daughter
Gary Fairburn — Rhodesian tobacco farmer
Philip — Tim's farm assistant
Van Campher — An Afrikaner tobacco farmer

GLOSSARY

Baas — Afrikaans word for boss
Hamba manji— Shona word meaning walk along the road
Huku — Shona word for chicken
Munt— Derogatory word for an African person
Le petit déjeuner— French word for breakfast
Piccanin — Small African child
Sadza — Maize meal
Simby — Instrument like a gong to summon the workforce
Vlei— Afrikaans word meaning low lying mashing ground
Voetsak — An offensive, forceful Afrikaans word meaning go away

Printed in Great Britain
by Amazon

20132747R00140